Jane BITES Back

Jane BITES Back

A Novel

Michael Thomas Ford

BALLANTINE BOOKS TRADE PAPERBACKS · NEW YORK

A Ballantine Books Trade Paperback Original

Copyright © 2010 by Michael Thomas Ford

Published in the United States by Ballantine Books,
an imprint of The Random House Publishing Group,
a division of Random House, Inc., New York.

BALLANTINE and colophon are registered
trademarks of Random House, Inc.

Library of Congress Cataloging-in-Publication Data

Ford, Michael Thomas.
Jane bites back: a novel / Michael Thomas Ford.
p.   cm.
ISBN 978-0-345-51365-6 (trade pbk.)
1. Austen, Jane, 1775–1817—Fiction.   2. Vampires—Fiction.
3. Women novelists—Fiction.   4. Women booksellers—Fiction.   I. Title.
PS3606.O7424J36 2010
813'.6—dc22   2009043773

Printed in the United States of America

www.ballantinebooks.com

2 4 6 8 9 7 5 3 1

Book design by Elizabeth A. D. Eno

For Liz Waters,
who gives very good advice

Jane BITES Back

Chapter 1

My dear Cassandra, I do wish you could have been
at the party last night. I was compelled to converse
with the most disagreeable woman. But then, as
I have said to you before, I do not want people to
be very agreeable, as it saves me the trouble of
liking them a great deal.

—JANE AUSTEN, in a letter to her sister, Cassandra,
24 December 1798

IT WAS NOT, OF COURSE, EXACTLY WHAT JANE HAD WRITTEN TO her sister that long-ago Christmas Eve, but the sentiment was the same. Besides, after more than two hundred years, she could hardly be expected to remember every little detail of her voluminous correspondence. Although she supposed she could check for herself—there was a collection of her letters sitting on a shelf not ten feet away. Instead, she remained where she was and imagined how she would describe the disagreeable woman standing before her in a letter to Cassie.

Melodie Gladstone was slight, her birdlike arms and pale skin giving her the appearance of fragility, as if she might at any moment collapse under the weight of her own head. Her hair, blond as summer wheat, was gathered at the nape of her neck and tied with a pink ribbon. When she spoke her voice was soft, and every head in the room was forced to lean toward her as she read.

Elizabeth's spirits soon rising to playfulness again, she wanted Mr. Darcy to account for his having ever fallen in love with her. "How could you begin?" said she. "I can comprehend your going on charmingly, when you had once made a beginning; but what could set you off in the first place?"

"I cannot fix on the hour, or the spot, or the look, or the words, which laid the foundation. It is too long ago. I was in the middle before I knew that I had begun."

"My beauty you had early withstood, and as for my manners—my behaviour to you was at least always bordering on the uncivil, and I never spoke to you without rather wishing to give you pain than not. Now be sincere; did you admire me for my impertinence?"

"For the liveliness of your mind, I did."

"You may as well call it impertinence at once. It was very little less. The fact is, that you were sick of civility, of deference, of officious attention. You were disgusted with the women who were always speaking, and look-ing, and thinking for your approbation alone. I roused, and interested you, because I was so unlike them. Had you not been really amiable, you would have hated me for it; but in spite of the pains you took to disguise yourself, your feelings were always noble and just; and in your heart, you thoroughly despised the persons who so assiduously courted you. There—I have saved you the trouble of accounting for it; and really, all things considered, I begin to think it perfectly reasonable. To be sure, you knew no actual good of me—but nobody thinks of that when they fall in love."

Melodie Gladstone closed the book in her hands and gazed intently at her audience. "You see," she said, "Mr. Darcy fell in love with Elizabeth because she wasn't afraid to be herself. This was her reward for not accepting the first proposal offered to her."

A murmur of agreement rippled through the crowd.

"I told you we'd have a packed house." Lucy had come to stand beside Jane at the back of the store. She was surveying with obvious satisfaction the crowd perched on folding chairs set up between the bookcases.

"We certainly do," Jane replied to her young assistant. "I can't believe they're actually buying this nonsense." It was bad enough, she thought, that so many of them had arrived in cos‑ tume. She counted two dozen Elizabeths, and perhaps a quarter that many Darcys. *Although I suppose some of the Elizabeths could be Emmas. Or Mariannes or Catherines or Annes.* Possibly some of them were even Fannys, although she doubted this. Very few readers seemed to like Fanny.

"We've already sold sixty-three copies of the book," Lucy informed her. "And I guarantee you we'll break a hundred once she's done talking."

Jane said nothing. Although she was grateful for the sales, she couldn't help wishing they were for some other book. *Any other book.*

"We're all here tonight because we believe—as Elizabeth Bennet believed, and as Jane believed—that true love is life's most precious gift."

Jane regarded Melodie Gladstone with a mixture of active dislike and reluctant awe. How had this book of hers become such a phenomenon? She remembered glancing through an advance copy of it six months earlier and thinking it was doomed to failure. Now she realized that not only were very many people foolish enough to embrace it, they were embracing it with an excitement that bordered on the hysterical.

"The message of *Waiting for Mr. Darcy* is this," Melodie said, holding up her book as if it were some kind of holy text. "If you really want to experience the beauty of love—true love—you won't give yourself to anyone until you've found it."

The audience applauded. Melodie beamed, then raised a hand, silencing them. "I know many of you have already committed yourselves to this ideal," she said. "I can tell by the number of lockets I see out there."

Laughter filled the air as people turned their heads to look at one another. Some raised their hands to their throats and clutched at the silver lockets that hung from chains around their necks. Melodie held up an identical locket, letting it dangle in the air like a hypnotist's charm. Her sky-blue eyes surveyed her listeners.

"For those of you who don't know," she said, "this locket is the symbol of those of us who have decided that we will indeed wait for our Mr. Darcy to come to us." She opened the locket to reveal a portrait inside. "Isn't he handsome?" Melodie asked. "His portrait was painted especially for us by none other than Paul Henry Mattheson, the same artist who created all of the beautiful covers for the collection of Jane Austen novels my publisher has reissued in conjunction with *Waiting for Mr. Darcy*. This locket is available only to those who sign the contract found at the back of my book and send it in along with receipts for the purchase of the book and the novels. So, if you have one, you're part of a very special club."

Jane saw heads nodding all over the room. The reading was starting to feel like a religious revival. She half expected Melodie Gladstone to call forward those wishing to be saved from sin while the devout fell out in the aisles weeping and shouting hallelujahs. Instead, the author put the locket down and clasped her hands together.

"It has been such a joy to meet you all tonight," she said. "I can't tell you how thankful I am to see you all and to know that perhaps, in some small way, I've encouraged you to embrace our beloved Jane's message of purity and self-respect."

As the room erupted in thunderous applause, Lucy called out, "Miss Gladstone will be signing books in just a moment. As she mentioned, those of you who purchase a copy of her book *as well as* the set of Jane Austen novels will be eligible to also purchase one of the lockets with Mr. Darcy's portrait inside. We have a limited number of—"

Before she could finish, the audience stood up and stampeded for the tables stacked high with books, shouting and pushing one another out of the way. Jane stepped back as two girls, both in Empire-waist dresses, elbowed past her in a mad dash to be the first ones to the table.

They may be interested in purity, Jane thought as she watched the girls grabbing for books, *but their manners are sorely in need of reinforcement.*

The next hour and a half was a whirlwind of ringing up sales, bagging purchases, and marveling at the seemingly endless line of people who wanted Melodie to sign their copies of her book.

Many of the women, and not a few of the young men, left the shop in tears, clutching books to their chests and lovingly stroking the lockets around their necks.

Finally the last autograph seeker was shown the door by Lucy, and Jane let out a sigh of relief. The table of books she and Lucy had set out for the event was completely empty. Behind the counter she called up the night's sales figures on the computer screen. When she saw them she gasped audibly.

"That's more than we made in the last three weeks combined," said Lucy, who was peering over Jane's shoulder.

"It's unbelievable," Jane agreed.

"It's like that every night," sighed Melodie Gladstone. "Everybody loves their Jane Austen."

Jane was surprised to hear the change in the author's tone. She looked up to find Melodie sprawled back in her chair, her feet stretched out beneath the table as she massaged her forehead.

"Do you have any aspirin?" she asked. "Better yet, do you have any vodka?"

Jane and Lucy exchanged glances, then Lucy went off in search of aspirin. Jane smiled politely and said, "This tour must be exhausting for you."

"It's a fucking nightmare," Melodie replied. Jane cringed. "Every night it's the same thing. 'Don't have sex until you've found the right one. Keep yourself pure. Wear this stupid locket and one day your prince will come.' What a load of crap. But they eat it up." She waved her hand in the air. "You've seen the numbers."

"They certainly are impressive," Jane said wryly.

"That's why I do the dog and pony show," Melodie replied. "Every time one of these idiots buys a copy I picture another five bucks piling up in my bank account."

Lucy returned with a glass of water and two aspirin, which she handed to Melodie.

Melodie popped the pills into her mouth and drained half the glass. "My head is killing me," she said. "I should have taken a Valium."

"So," Jane said carefully, "you don't really believe what you say in your book?"

Melodie shook her head. "Please," she said. "Do you really think there are any Mr. Darcys left in the world? No, there aren't. I don't think there ever were. But these girls want to think there are, so I give them what they want."

"And in return they make you quite wealthy," Jane commented.

"It's just my piece of the Austen pie," Melodie said. "Everyone's in on it now. You've seen the books. Austen is all the rage. You put her name on anything and it will sell. Hell, my publisher is coming out with a Jane Austen massage book in the spring. You know what it's called? *Sense and Sensuality.*" She laughed. "I bet it sells two million copies."

"We can only hope," Jane remarked dryly. If she'd disliked Melodie Gladstone before, she now loathed her. The woman was vile, an opportunist who was using *her* name to make her fortune. *Meanwhile, I haven't seen a royalty check in almost two hundred years,* she thought.

Melodie, oblivious to Jane's growing animosity, snorted rudely. "I don't get the big deal about Austen myself," she said. "I mean, have you read her novels? I could barely get through them. Most of what I know I got from watching the PBS specials. But the books? Talk about boring." She made a grotesque snoring sound that caused Jane to clench her jaw in irritation.

"I love Austen," Lucy said. "I think her books are wonderful.

And if you ask me, they're not about finding Mr. Darcy at all; they're about young women breaking convention and going after what they want."

Jane sent Lucy a silent thank-you. *She gets it*, thought Jane. *It never was about Darcy.*

"All I know is that the more people there are who love Mr. Darcy, the bigger my royalty checks are," Melodie said. "I could care less about the rest of it."

You mean you couldn't *care less*, Jane resisted the urge to say out loud. Not only was Melodie Gladstone without dignity, she had appalling grammar.

"We have a few books left in the storage room," said Lucy. "Would you mind signing them?"

Melodie rolled her eyes. "I suppose not," she said. "I wish you'd had them out here for the reading, but someone is sure to snatch them up. I hear I'm one of the top five holiday sellers this year. I'd be number one if it wasn't for that book about that stupid blind kid and her dog."

Lucy retreated to the stockroom and returned with half a dozen copies of *Waiting for Mr. Darcy*, which she set on the table in front of the author. "When you're done I'll drive you back to the hotel," she offered.

Jane, who had been counting the cash drawer, looked up. "Lucy, I can drive Miss Gladstone back to her hotel," she said. "Why don't you go home?"

Lucy glanced at Melodie, who was signing the last of the books. "You're sure?" she asked Jane.

"I don't care which one of you drives me," said Melodie, snapping the cap back on the pen she'd used to sign the books. "But let's get going. I've got to be on a plane for Columbus or Detroit or some other shit hole first thing in the morning."

"I'm quite sure," Jane told Lucy. "You go on. I'll see you in the morning. Thank you for all of your work on the event."

"No problem," said Lucy. She turned to Melodie. "Thank you for coming," she said. "It was nice to meet you."

The woman nodded but said nothing. After a short pause during which it became obvious that Melodie had no intention of returning Lucy's thanks, Lucy shot Jane a look. "See you tomorrow," she said as she turned and walked to the front door.

"I'm ready to go," said Melodie, standing and putting on her coat before Lucy had even shut the door behind her.

Jane looked at the woman and smiled. "Well then," she said. "Let's tarry no longer in the parlor of joy."

Melodie stared at her.

"My car is out back," said Jane. "I'll just get my coat."

A few minutes later they were sitting in Jane's beat-up Volvo wagon, waiting for the heat to kick in. Melodie rubbed her hands together. "How old is this thing, anyway?" she asked dismissively.

"You should never ask a lady her age," Jane said primly, earning a peculiar look from Melodie.

She put the car into gear and pulled out of the lot. As they drove through the snowy streets of downtown Brakeston, Melodie looked out the window. "This place is so boring," she said. "How can you stand living here?"

"I find its unassuming character charming," Jane answered.

"If I had to live in a place like this, I would absolutely *die*," Melodie continued. "When I saw my tour itinerary I was like, Brakeston? Where the hell is Brakeston?"

"Lucy went to a lot of trouble to get you here," Jane informed her. "And I think the turnout was quite impressive, don't you?"

Melodie shrugged. "It was nothing compared to the New York reading," she said. "We had to turn people away from that one."

"Oh, the horror," said Jane sympathetically.

"Right," Melodie agreed. "Anyway, I guess I'm probably the biggest thing to ever come through here, so at least I added a little excitement to those people's lives."

"We're ever so thankful you agreed to grace us," said Jane. "I'm sure we'll be talking about it for months."

"I just can't wait to get back to civilization," Melodie said, sighing.

That's it, Jane thought. She suddenly turned off the main street and headed down a quiet side lane.

"The hotel is that way," Melodie protested.

"This is a shortcut," said Jane curtly.

At the end of the street she pulled the car to the side and stopped in front of a house that blinked red and green with Christmas lights. On the lawn a life-size Mary and Joseph stared at the car. Behind them Santa, Frosty, and Rudolph gazed rapturously down at the baby Jesus asleep in his plastic manger. Giant candy canes provided a backdrop for three elves bearing gaily wrapped packages.

"Where are we?" Melodie asked. "What are we doing here?"

"I just need to take care of a little errand," said Jane. She unfastened her seat belt and leaned toward her passenger, who was too busy looking at the bizarre Nativity scene to notice. As Jane opened her mouth the two fangs secreted in her upper jaw slipped from their bony sheaths and clicked into place. When her lips connected with Melodie's neck, Melodie jumped and gave a little scream, which was cut short as Jane pushed the young woman's face against her own coat and held it there as the blood began to flow past her lips.

Chapter 2

*She sometimes woke from these dreams fevered and
disoriented, as if during the night some phantom
had come into her room, filling her lungs with
fiendish breath that poisoned her mind. In the first
moments of consciousness she pulled against the
sheets twined about her and called out for rescue.
But in the empty house her voice went unheard.*

—Jane Austen, *Constance*, manuscript page 293

A LONG HOT SHOWER HELPED REMOVE MELODIE'S SMELL FROM
Jane's body. Afterward she wrapped herself in a soft robe and
went downstairs. Walking into the kitchen, she stepped on something soft and wet. When she turned the lights on she saw a small,
dead bird lying on the floor in front of the refrigerator. Its light
brown feathers were speckled with blood.

Tom, the black-and-white cat she'd adopted several years before, appeared and wound himself around her feet, purring as
Jane bent to pick up the bird. She shuddered at the way the creature's head lolled limply in her palm.

"Must you bring them inside?" she asked Tom as she deposited the bird in the trash can and washed her hands in the sink. She poured some dry food into Tom's bowl and set it on the floor.

The cat trotted over and ate hungrily, crunching the bits between his teeth and watching Jane out of the corner of his eye.

"Horrid beast," said Jane, scratching him behind the ear. She then turned her attention to the mail, which she'd brought in from the hall. Mostly it was junk, but at the bottom of the pile was a letter. Reading the return address, Jane felt her heart speed up. She ran her finger beneath the flap and pulled out the enclosed sheet of paper.

> Dear Miss Fairfax:
>
> Thank you for submitting your manuscript for our consideration. We regret to say that it is not right for our list. We wish you the best of luck in placing it elsewhere.
>
> Sincerely,
>
> Jessica Abernathy
> Fourth Street Books

Jane crumpled the letter and tossed it to the floor. Tom eyed it, as if considering whether or not to bat it under the table, but did not stop eating. Jane opened a bottle of merlot, took a glass from the cabinet and a chocolate bar from one of the drawers, and left both the paper and the cat in the kitchen as she went back upstairs to her bedroom. She poured a glass of wine and set it on the bedside table. Then she pulled open a drawer in the nightstand and removed from it a small notebook. Turning to a page somewhere near the middle of the book, she added Jessica Abernathy's name to the first unoccupied line, which in this case was almost exactly one-third of the way down, just below the name of Barlow McInerney of Accordion Press.

Beside Jessica's name Jane wrote the number 116. "One hundred and sixteen rejection letters," she muttered. "I'd say that makes the opinion unanimous."

She flipped through the pages of the notebook until she came to the first one. She hadn't been able to submit the manuscript to her usual publisher, John Murray, of course—that would have rather inconveniently given things away. So she'd been forced to seek elsewhere. At the top of the list of editors who had rejected her manuscript was one Geoffrey Martin Pomerantz of Pomerantz & Joygulb Publishers, London. Jane had no recollection of Mr. Pomerantz (or, for that matter, Mr. Joygulb). This lack of recognition, however, could be excused in light of the fact that her submission to them had taken place nearly two centuries before. Had the manuscript really been kicking around for that long? she wondered. She supposed it had, although that was difficult to imagine.

Tom, licking his chops, padded into the room and leapt onto the bed, where he settled himself on Jane's lap and immediately went to sleep.

"Perhaps, Tom, it's time to consider the possibility that I can no longer write," said Jane.

Tom, opening one golden eye for only a second before closing it again, said nothing.

Jane closed the notebook and replaced it in the drawer. She told herself, as she had done many times before, that she should just throw the manuscript out. Having it around was depressing. But there was something masochistically satisfying about documenting her rejection. She didn't save the actual letters—they would take up too much space, and anyway they would eventually fall apart from age—but the names she kept. Most of the people whose rejections she'd logged were dead now, which gave Jane some small amount of satisfaction. Yet the sting of remaining unpublished never fully faded.

"I'm a writer," she announced to Tom. "That's what I *do.* I *write.*" She paused a moment, then sighed. "Well, I *used* to write," she corrected herself.

The truth was she hadn't written anything new since finishing the manuscript that had garnered 116 rejections. She had revised it slightly over the years, but for the most part it remained the novel she'd finished almost two centuries before. She'd had to abandon *The Brothers*—which her family had retitled *Sanditon;* she still wasn't sure she was entirely happy about that—when she left Chawton cottage for the last time, but this manuscript she had kept a secret. She'd attempted to write new things since, of course, but the weight of the unpublished book on her thoughts had proved to be too great a block.

She suddenly felt very tired.

How long had she had the bookstore? She counted back. It was, what, eight years? No, nine. She'd moved to Brakeston after two decades spent in Phoenix, a city she'd chosen precisely because it was blessed with the polar opposite of the weather of her English childhood. But twenty years of unrelenting heat and sunlight had finally gotten to her, not for the reasons one might expect (the sun was not nearly as devastating to vampires as popular mythology would have the public believe) but because she was naturally fair. She turned pink after less than an hour in the sun, and never had been able to obtain even the semblance of a tan. The best she could manage was a kind of boiled puffiness, like a lobster or a cabbage. It was not a particularly attractive look.

For years she had tried to mimic the effects of time, dyeing her hair and simulating lines and liver spots. But there was only so much she could do, and besides, it was tiresome, so somewhere along the line (she vaguely remembered the year 1881, although it may have been 1900, which, being the start of the new century—and the year in which she had abandoned Europe for America—would have been a logical time to decide such a thing) she had given up trying and instead simply moved whenever her lack of aging began to be remarked upon. And so after many moves she had come to this town in upstate New York, choosing it more or less at random because she liked the sound of it.

Nine years, she thought. *That gives me about ten or so more before I have to think about it.* It was possible she could get even more time out of Brakeston. After all, wasn't forty the new thirty? She'd heard that somewhere recently. Clearly, whoever had said it hadn't been forty-one for the past two centuries. "It's more like forty is the new one hundred and ninety-two," she informed the cat, who was curled up on her stomach asleep.

She drank the rest of the wine and polished off the chocolate while flipping through the channels on the television, watching bits and pieces of different shows until finally the only things on were infomercials for vegetable peelers and fat-burning pills. Then, her head dulled by the wine, she felt her eyes close.

Not asleep yet not quite awake, she traveled back to a night long ago. She was standing on a veranda, looking out at a lake. It was twilight, and it was raining. A thunderstorm shook the world around her, and the waves on the lake were violent and angry. Thunder rent the air and lightning split the sky. She was afraid but also exhilarated.

Nobody knew where she was. She had told them she was visiting a friend, but in truth she had never met the man in whose house she now stood. Not in person, anyway. But they had exchanged many long letters, and through those she had come to know him. When he'd suggested she visit his house on Lake Geneva she had hesitated only a moment before agreeing.

She felt free. Away from her home and her family she could do as she liked. That she had come to the house of one of the most scandalous figures of her time only added to her excitement. And he was just as beautiful and stimulating as she had imagined him to be.

"What are you doing out here?"

She turned to see him watching her. His dark hair was swept back, and his eyes seemed to stare directly into her soul. When he smiled her heart skipped a beat.

"Watching the storm," she answered.

He walked toward her, his limp only barely noticeable. From what she'd heard of him, she'd expected it to be more pronounced. But nothing about him was exactly as he was described. It was as if he appeared in different forms to everyone he met.

"It suits you," he said when he was standing beside her. "The storm, I mean." He put an arm around her waist. "They all think of you as a quiet afternoon," he said. "But inside you rage with passion, don't you?"

She said nothing. How was it he could know her so well? Already she felt as if she'd known him for years, but it had been only a day since her arrival.

"The night shows stars and women in a better light," he said as thunder rumbled overhead. "Come inside. You'll catch your death of cold out here."

She allowed him to lead her back into the drawing room. But he didn't stop there. Instead he led her down the hallway lined with portraits and landscapes and into a bedroom. His bedroom. She paused, looking at the enormous bed of carved mahogany, its sides hung with ruby red velvet draperies. The sheets were a tangled nest, as if he'd just risen from them. Throughout the room candles burned, warming the air and filling it with the faint scent of flowers.

"I can't," Jane told him, suddenly afraid.

"Of course you can," he said. "There's nothing to fear."

She trembled as he turned and began undressing her. She closed her eyes for fear that looking at him would make her flee from the room. His fingers moved deftly over her body, slipping her dress from her shoulders. It pooled at her feet. Then he was undoing the laces of her stays. She barely breathed as he took them from her. Finally, he removed her chemise and she stood before him naked.

When his hands cupped her breasts she gasped, and when his mouth touched her skin she felt her knees buckle. He caught her, sweeping her up in his arms and carrying her to the bed. He placed her atop the sheets and stepped back. She watched through half-closed eyes as he removed his clothes. His chest was lean, his skin pale as milk. When he stepped from his trousers she glanced briefly at his manhood before looking away.

Then he was beside her, his hand stroking her as he told her how beautiful she was. His kisses covered her face, her neck, her breasts and stomach. His hands drew from her such pleasure that her breath caught in her throat.

In seconds he was on top of her, looking down into her face.

His eyes bore into her, and she could not look away. Outside the storm raged, the wind blowing one of the windows open and letting in the rain. At that moment he leaned down and kissed her. His mouth moved to her neck.

As his teeth pierced her flesh her eyes flew open.

Chapter 3

*As the gardener turned away and walked in the
direction of the potting shed, something slipped
from his pocket. Constance stepped forward and
took it up, surprised to find that it was a copy of
Milton's* Paradise Regained *prettily bound in
green leather. It was clearly much read, and as she
turned the pages Constance found herself
wondering if perhaps Charles Barrowman's
thoughts encompassed more than just the removal
of hedgehogs and the planting of hydrangeas.*

—Jane Austen, *Constance*, manuscript page 78

JANE WALKED INTO FLYLEAF BOOKS CARRYING THE VERY LARGE,
very hot, and very black coffee she'd picked up to banish the
headache left behind by the wine. Worse than the headache was
the lingering memory of her dream. *I behaved so badly,* she
thought. *Not at all like a lady.*

"Nice of you to come in," Lucy teased. She pushed a lock of
long, curly black hair behind her ear.

In her early twenties, Lucy Sebring was sarcastic, funny, and fiercely intelligent. At her interview two years ago she'd told Jane that she'd left college to play in an all-girl punk rock band whose song titles were lifted from well-known feminist works. After six months on the road together the four of them had all started to get their periods at the same time. They'd broken up one night when, in front of an audience, the bass player deliberately launched into "The Female Eunuch" while the singer shouted the opening lyrics of "Ain't I a Woman?" The resulting name-calling soon escalated into accusations and tears and ended spectacularly when the drummer, a mousy former philosophy major who had long passages from Valerie Solanas's *SCUM Manifesto* tattooed on her body, stood up and screamed, "Betty Friedan can't write for shit!" Lucy had related the story with such skill that Jane had hired her on the spot.

"By the way," Lucy said as Jane took off her coat and hung it up, "you might want to take a look at today's paper." She nodded to the copy of the *Daily Inquirer,* which was open on the counter.

Jane picked it up and scanned the front page. "Meade College receives endowment from retired state senator?" she asked, reading the lead.

"Below that," said Lucy.

Jane looked. "Brakeston Lady Beavers advance to district playoffs," she read.

"Give me that," said Lucy, snatching the paper from her. She began to read. " 'Noted author Melodie Gladstone was found wandering down Main Street early this morning after police received calls from several concerned citizens. According to Officer Pete Bear, one of two officers who responded to the scene, Gladstone appeared to be intoxicated or perhaps under the influence of an unknown substance. Gladstone is the author of the best-selling *Waiting for Mr. Darcy* and was in town for a reading at Flyleaf Books.' "

Lucy flipped the page. "There's a picture," she said.

Jane looked at the shot of Melodie Gladstone. She was in the street, flanked by the two police officers, each of whom gripped one of her arms. Her hair was a rat's nest, and her eyes were ringed with mascara and eye shadow. Her face wore a lost expression, and her mouth was slightly open.

"Good heavens," said Jane. "It looks as if they've caught a rabid raccoon. I wouldn't be surprised to hear that they'd had her stuffed and mounted on the wall at the station."

"You drove her back to the hotel," Lucy said. "Did anything happen?"

Jane shook her head. "I dropped her off and went home," she replied. "Although now that I think of it, she did say something about wanting to get a drink."

"Well, I'd say she got more like six or seven drinks," Lucy commented. "Just wait until this story gets out. Little Miss Perfect is going to lose a lot of readers."

"The poor dear," said Jane.

"Yes," Lucy agreed. "I weep for her."

The two exchanged a glance, and Jane detected a hint of satisfaction in Lucy's eyes, but they said nothing more. Then Lucy went back to work. She was opening boxes of books that had arrived in the morning's UPS delivery. This was one of her great pleasures, seeing the new titles come in. Her enthusiasm for them almost always made Jane feel better. She herself had become somewhat resentful of newly published books—much as childless women sometimes regarded new mothers and their infants with a mixture of jealousy and despair—and it was nice to see that someone was still excited by them.

"Oh, look," Lucy exclaimed, reaching into the first box. "Jane Austen paper dolls. They're *adorable.* This will be perfect for the Austen section."

"Austen section?" Jane said, looking up from the bills she had picked up from the counter and was sorting through. "What Austen section?"

Lucy rolled her eyes. "I told you last week," she said. "I'm going to put together an Austen section. You saw how popular that Gladstone book is. Just look at all the other Austen stuff we have. Besides her own novels we have novels *about* her. Then there's *The Jane Austen Cookbook* and the bios and the collected letters. Oh, and I just read in *Publishers Weekly* that someone has written a Jane Austen self-help book."

"A what?" Jane asked sharply.

"Yeah," said Lucy. "It's about figuring out which Jane Austen character you're most like and then developing a life plan around that personality type. It's called *Will the Real Elizabeth Bennet Please Stand Up.* Deepak Chopra wrote the introduction. Anyway, it'll be huge."

Jane gritted her teeth. She'd hoped the ridiculous cookbook would be the end of the Austen mania. But her popularity had only continued to grow. Just the other day she'd seen in a magazine that dresses based on the fashions of her time were going to be all the rage for proms and summer weddings.

Really, it was all too much, particularly as Jane herself was enjoying none of the benefits associated with being one of the most popular authors of all time. No royalty checks came her way. No one asked her permission to make the book group reading guides or gardening books or knitting patterns that sold by the cartload. The fact that she was for all intents and purposes dead did little to ease her annoyance.

She began the odious task of counting the drawer. She had made her way through the twenties and tens and fives and was starting on the always irritating singles (when one wanted them to make change there were never enough of them, yet when one hoped for a substantial day's profit there were always too many) when the bell above the door tinkled.

Hoping for a customer, she was slightly disappointed to see Walter Fletcher walking toward her. Dressed in his customary uniform of tan chinos and checked flannel shirt beneath a brown twill jacket embroidered with his name and the name of his house restoration company, he was as cheerful as he always was. In five years Jane hadn't once seen him frown.

Walter set a paper bag on the counter and slid it toward her. Jane opened it, and the air filled with the scent of cinnamon.

"You didn't," said Jane.

"I did," Walter replied.

Jane reached into the bag and pulled out a cinnamon bun. Sticky with sugar, it was still warm. She bit into it and groaned. Of all the misconceptions about her kind, the one she'd been most relieved to find untrue was that they lost their ability to enjoy food. True, it nourished her not at all, but the upside was that it also did not increase her figure. She remained precisely the size she had been at her death.

"They came out of the oven not ten minutes ago," Walter told her.

Jane had tasted many wonderful things during her two centuries, but few compared to the cinnamon buns made by the bakery located a few doors down from her shop. Jane was addicted to them. The fact that Walter had brought her one made her suspicious.

"What do you want?" she asked him.

Walter's blue eyes sparkled merrily as he watched her lick the sugar glaze from her fingers. "Who says I want something?" he asked, feigning indignation. "Can't I just bring a friend a cinnamon bun?"

"Come on," said Jane, taking another bite. "Out with it."

Walter smiled. "All right," he said. "I confess. I do have a tiny favor to ask you."

Jane waited for him to continue. Walter paused, clearly thinking about how to proceed. Before he could speak Jane said, "Walter, we've been through this before. I can't go out with you. I mean—"

"I don't want to go out with you," Walter interrupted.

Jane looked at him, surprised.

"I mean, I *do* want to go out with you," Walter said, blushing. "But I know you won't—"

"Can't," Jane corrected him. "There's a difference."

"Can't," Walter agreed. "Anyway, that's not why I'm here. I'd like you to come to my New Year's Eve party."

Jane groaned. "I detest New Year's Eve," she said. "So much fuss and nonsense about another year, all of it cleverly designed to result in the deepest of disappointment."

"It's just a party," Walter said. "There will be champagne."

"How grand," said Jane. "And I suppose there will be charades and the Minister's Cat?"

Walter gave her a look that reminded her far too much of a wounded puppy. "Please?" he said.

Jane took another bite of cinnamon bun and chewed it before answering. "Possibly," she replied. "But only because you bribed me."

Walter smiled. "Excellent. We'll be pleased to have you."

"I didn't say—"

"I've got to go," said Walter, looking at his watch. "We're tearing out Maggie Beecher's kitchen this morning, and she throws a fit if we're not there by ten sharp."

He hurried out before Jane could make any further protests. When he was gone Lucy said, "I don't know why you won't go out with him. He's been asking you for over a year."

Jane sighed. "We're just not a good match," she said.

"Because he's a carpenter?" asked Lucy.

"No," Jane said sharply. "And he's not just a carpenter. He restores old houses, and beautifully. But that has nothing to do with it. It's just that he . . . that I . . . we don't . . ." She couldn't finish the sentence in any way that wouldn't make her sound like a snob.

"I don't get it," said Lucy. "He's smart. He's funny. He likes books and art and all the same things you do. Plus he's a hottie."

"I suppose he's attractive enough," Jane agreed, thinking about the pleasing arrangement of Walter's features. *And he has such strong hands,* she thought.

"Then remind me again why you can't go out with him," said Lucy.

Because I'm dead, Jane thought. *Because he'll age and I won't. Because men generally don't like women who need to drink blood to stay alive.* What she said was, "I'm perfectly happy with my life."

Lucy made a vague humming sound.

"What's that supposed to mean?" Jane demanded.

Lucy stacked some books on a table. "Nothing," she said. "I'm just humming."

"I know that hum," said Jane curtly. "That's your 'whatever' hum."

"Sure it is," Lucy said. "Okay."

"It is!" said Jane. "And you know it!"

Lucy glanced over at her. "Whatever," she said sweetly. "Maybe I should date him."

"You go right ahead," Jane said, trying to sound as if she didn't care in the least. "Just because he's old enough to be your father, don't let that stop you."

"Ah-ha!" Lucy crowed. "You *do* like him."

"I do *not*!" said Jane. "I'm just pointing out a fact."

"You like Walter," Lucy said in a singsong voice.

Jane dismissed Lucy with a shake of her head. "Whatever," she said.

Chapter 4

She looked at the box, not daring to hope that
inside of it were the pens and paper she had
requested as her Christmas gift. Constance knew
her parents thought her request fanciful, and she
feared that her mother and father—not out of
cruelty or disapproval, but simply because they
could not conceive of their daughter wanting
to commit herself to the life of an artist—might
have instead purchased for her hair ribbons, paper
dolls, or yet another china kitten.

—Jane Austen, *Constance*, manuscript page 25

THE NEXT FEW DAYS WERE A BLUR. TRAFFIC AT THE BOOKSTORE
was brisk as shoppers rushed to cross off all the names on their
Christmas lists. Lucy's prediction that all things Austen would be
strong sellers proved correct, and Jane watched as stacks of her
books and their assorted spin-offs disappeared out the door. This
was both gratifying and depressing, as the thought of all the un-
collectible royalties gave her a headache.

"I knew we should have ordered the Jane Austen action fig-ure," Lucy remarked during a rare lull in the hustle and bustle. "I've had six customers ask for it today alone."

"No dolls," Jane said shortly. "It's bad enough I let you talk me into those Austen ornaments."

"Just like Jane hung on her tree!" Lucy said brightly, quoting from the box that the ornaments came in.

"Indeed," said Jane. *Never mind that virtually no one in England had a Christmas tree until almost thirty years after I was dead.* However, they'd sold all three dozen boxes at $29.95 a pop, so she couldn't complain.

Finally the evening of the twenty-fourth arrived. Jane let Lucy go at two, and at six o'clock she rang up the last customer, a harried man who had rushed in fifteen minutes earlier and raced through the store grabbing books from the shelves seemingly at random. As Jane rang up his purchases he ran his finger down a piece of paper in his hand.

"Emily, Frank, Sandra, Will, Jack, Maggie, Lloyd, Peter, Sally, Deirdre, and the other Jack," he read aloud. "I don't suppose you have any books a dog would like?" he asked hopefully.

"What kind of dog?" said Jane as she scanned the bar code on the back of the latest Anne Rice novel.

"French bulldog," the man replied. "Name of Gregory."

"Perhaps he'd enjoy some Victor Hugo," Jane suggested. "Or," she continued, reaching under the counter and bringing out a large rawhide bone wrapped with a green ribbon—another of Lucy's ideas—"this might do the trick."

The man beamed. "Perfect!" he said. "Now I'm done."

"Wrapping paper?" Jane asked.

"Damn it!" the man muttered.

"Over there," Jane said, nodding in the direction of the well-picked-over rack. "I think there's still some left that isn't too hideously cheerful."

The man picked out two rolls of paper and added them to his pile. Minutes later he was walking out the door with three bulging bags and $438 added to his next American Express bill.

"Merry Christmas," he called out to Jane as he walked away.

"Merry Christmas," she echoed as she shut the door and turned the OPEN sign to CLOSED. As she walked to the office she realized that her feet hurt. Rather than stay and clean up the disheveled store, she opted to turn out the lights and go home. The shop was closed the next day anyway; she could always tidy up then.

At home Tom greeted her enthusiastically when she came in, purring loudly and twisting about her ankles like some kind of furry motorboat.

"You only love me when you're hungry," she accused him, but knelt and scooped him up anyway, carrying him into the kitchen and depositing him on the counter. He ran to the cupboard in which she kept the tinned food, and looked longingly at the door.

As she readied Tom's Christmas Eve dinner, Jane couldn't help thinking about Christmases past. The season had always been a happy one for her, filled with delightful smells and sounds and plenty of laughter. Since her death, however, Christmas had become at best just another day and at worst a reminder of what she'd once had.

Now she found that she missed it terribly. She thought of one Christmas in particular, that of 1786. She and Cassie, recently returned from boarding school to the rectory at Steventon, had been eleven and thirteen. Free of the restrictions of school, with its rules and the stern matrons who enforced them, they were reveling in being home again. Like caged birds suddenly released, they flitted about the house, always underfoot.

She recalled the smell of roasting goose, of Christmas pudding and spiced wine. She heard her father's voice as he spoke with pride to anyone who would listen about twelve-year-old Frank, already serving in the Royal Navy. And she recalled fondly the sound of Henry, her favorite brother, singing as he hung the holly and the ivy. Then there were the dances and parties, all of which she experienced with the excitement of a girl longing for the time when she could move in the adult world.

Pushing these thoughts aside, she went upstairs to the smaller bedroom she used as an office. She sat down at her computer and opened the file for her novel. It was time to be realistic—it was never going to sell.

She had avoided accepting this for long enough. But now she had to admit that perhaps Jane Austen had written her last book. Was it possible the novels she'd produced were all that were in her? After all, she hadn't expected to live forever, and maybe she had said everything she had to say. It occurred to her that all of the editors who had rejected her manuscript might simply have recognized what she herself hadn't.

She clicked on the file, revealing the Options box, and highlighted Move to Trash. She wondered what her fans would do if they saw her poised to delete an unread novel. Would they attempt to stop her? *Of course they would,* she told herself. After all, they eagerly bought up the sequels other authors had written to her books, and even novels written *about* people who liked her novels. They couldn't get enough of her. *But they'll never know.*

She began to make the final click that would send her manuscript to its death. But then her eye was distracted by a flash in the top left corner of her screen. She had a message in her in-box.

Granting her novel a temporary reprieve, she opened her email and looked at the latest arrival. The subject line read:

I hope it hasn't already been snatched up. The sender was someone whose name she didn't recognize: Kelly Littlejohn.

It's probably just spam, she thought as she prepared to delete
it. But something about the name tugged at her memory, and she
instead opened the message.

> Dear Jane:
>
> Kindly excuse the shortness of this email. I am cur-
> rently on a train from Paris to Vienna, and am not at
> all confident that my wireless connection will last.
>
> I have just finished reading the manuscript you sent
> in September. In short, I love it. I fear, though, that I
> am probably too late and that another, more efficient
> editor has already claimed it. If that's the case, I will
> be disappointed beyond words, but will have only
> myself to blame.
>
> If, however, the novel is still available, I would like to
> put a claim on it. I will be traveling for the next few
> days, but please reply if this reaches you and you
> are interested in further discussion. If I don't hear
> from you, I will contact you when I am once again in
> New York.
>
> All my best,
>
> Kelly Littlejohn
> Senior Editor
> Browder Publishing

Jane read the email through four times in disbelief. On the fifth read she allowed herself to be the tiniest bit excited. By the seventh she was genuinely thrilled.

"Someone likes my book!" she called out. "Did you hear that, Tom? Someone likes my book. No, someone *loves* my book," she corrected. "Kelly Littlejohn loves my book."

She couldn't remember sending the manuscript to anyone called Kelly Littlejohn, but that didn't surprise her. She'd sent it to so many editors that their names cluttered her mind like scraps of paper. But she had sent it, and Kelly—bless her heart—loved it. She wanted to publish it.

Jane considered playing it cool and not responding to the email. And for a full minute she succeeded. Then, fearful that the editor might take her silence for rejection, she typed a quick note.

> Dear Kelly:
>
> Thank you for your message. Yes, the book is still available, and yes, I would be interested in speaking with you when you return.
>
> Sincerely,
>
> Jane Fairfax

She hit send before she could change her mind. She wanted her response to be positive but not fawning, interested but not desperate. "It's a fine line," she reminded herself.

She read Kelly's email again. After so many rejections she felt as if she were reading a message about someone else's book. For a moment she even feared that the editor had mistaken her book for another and contacted the wrong author. She was tempted to write again and confirm that it was in fact *her* novel Kelly wanted, but she refrained.

Money didn't enter her mind. Neither did the possibility of fame. She was going to be published. For the first time in centuries she would be able to hold in her hands a new book she'd written.

She read Kelly's email one more time, feeling for the first time in two centuries like a little girl on Christmas morning.

Chapter 5

She told herself that she detested parties.
In particular she was weary of the exchange
of frivolous gossip that masqueraded as
sophisticated conversation. What did she care
about Emilia Rothman's new dress, and what of
interest could be found in the whispered debates
regarding the handsomeness of Arthur Potts's
recently-acquired moustache?

—Jane Austen, *Constance*, manuscript page 17

"SO YOU'LL BE OKAY LOOKING AFTER THE STORE FOR A FEW DAYS?"

"Of course I will," Lucy told Jane. "It's a bookstore, not a day care."

"All right, then," said Jane. "I don't imagine you can do too much damage in that amount of time."

"You might be surprised," Lucy teased.

It had been a week since Jane had received Kelly Littlejohn's email. She still hadn't spoken to her new editor, but they had corresponded by email several times. Twice now the editor had called the novel "Austenesque," which always made Jane giggle when she read it.

Kelly had emailed Jane the previous evening to say that she was returning from Europe earlier than expected and to suggest that Jane take the train down to New York on the second of January so that they could meet in person. The publisher would put her up in a hotel. Jane had agreed before asking Lucy if she would mind the store, knowing full well that her assistant would jump at the chance to have free rein.

"I'd better not come back to find you've replaced all the self-help books with graphic novels," Jane warned.

Lucy grinned. "I was thinking more of putting them where the religion books are," she said. "And installing a cappuccino machine."

Jane groaned. "Why do I think I'm going to regret this?"

Lucy rubbed Jane's shoulders. "Oh, relax," she said. "It's New Year's week. Nobody buys anything anyway—they just return the stuff they got for Christmas."

"That makes me feel *much* better," said Jane. "Thank you."

She hadn't told Lucy the reason for her trip, at least not the real reason. Lucy thought she was going to New York to meet a friend and see a show. Although Jane badly wanted to share her news, she felt it would be a mistake to talk about it until everything was in order.

"Some time away from here will be good for you," Lucy informed her. "You've been so . . . tense lately."

Jane shot her a look. "Meaning what?" she demanded.

Lucy rolled her eyes. "Meaning *that*," she said. "You've just been a little snippy."

"I have *not* been snippy," Jane objected.

"Okay, okay," said Lucy, holding her hands up in defeat. "You haven't been snippy. My bad."

"Go shelve something," Jane said, trying not to laugh. She could never get mad at Lucy.

Lucy walked away grinning. "I get to be in cha-aa-aa-rge," she said in a singsong voice.

The phone rang and Jane answered it. "Flyleaf Books."

"Yes, could you please tell Miss Jane Fairfax that there's a gentleman caller on the line for her?"

"Hello, Walter," Jane said. "What can I do for you today?"

"I'm just calling to confirm your presence at tonight's New Year's Eve gathering," he answered.

Jane groaned silently. She'd forgotten all about Walter's party. She'd said she would go, but now that it was upon her she dreaded it. She considered telling Walter that she couldn't make it, but she was suddenly unable to think of a believable excuse. "Of course I'll be there," she replied. "What shall I bring?"

"Nothing but your fine sense of humor and your smiling face," Walter told her. "That will be more than enough."

"You're satisfied with so little," Jane joked. "What time do the festivities begin?"

"Nine," said Walter.

Nine, Jane thought. *That means at least three hours with those people.* She shuddered. "I'll see you then."

"Got a date?" asked Lucy when Jane had hung up.

"It's very rude to listen to other people's conversations," Jane told her. "And no, it is not a date. It's that party."

"Don't you just love New Year's Eve?" Lucy asked. "I do," she added, not waiting for Jane's answer. "It's like you're getting another chance to get it right."

"Get what right?" said Jane.

"Everything," Lucy answered. "Your life. It's a new start. You can be anything you want, do anything you want."

"You don't need a new year for that," said Jane.

"Of course not," Lucy agreed. "But it's symbolic. A new year, a new you. What are your resolutions?"

"I learned long ago not to make any," said Jane. "They only set you up for failure."

This was true. As girls she and Cassie had always made New Year's resolutions. They wrote them on pieces of paper that were then folded and sealed with the wax from their father's study, and gave them to each other for safekeeping. They did not open them until the next New Year's Eve, when they looked at what they had written and debated whether or not they had achieved their goals. Too often Jane had failed, although admittedly this was generally because her resolutions were along the lines of "stop gossiping about the neighbors" and "try to pay more attention in church." Cassie, who was much more likely to have accomplished her goals, never made Jane feel small. Regardless, her lack of success chafed, and she had eventually stopped altogether.

"Well, I have some," Lucy continued, undeterred. "I'm going to go to yoga three times a week, learn French, run a marathon, and get at least two poems published—and not online, in real magazines. Oh, and I'm going to volunteer helping underprivileged kids learn to read."

"Very admirable," Jane told her. "I applaud your determination."

"Or maybe I should just lose five pounds, finally paint my bedroom, and stop smoking," said Lucy.

"You don't smoke," Jane said.

"I could start," Lucy replied. "Then it would be easy to stop and I would feel better about myself."

Jane laughed, then left Lucy to her work and went into the back storeroom to check the stock. As she counted books she considered the notion of resolutions. If she *were* going to make any, what would they be? Losing weight was out—she was dead, after all—as was smoking (although she admired Lucy's novel approach to giving up vices).

"I suppose I could stop eating so much," she concluded, "or at least so *many.*" But without Cassie to determine the extent of her success or failure, there'd be no fun in it. Sighing, she pushed the entire matter from her mind and rearranged the cookbooks.

Several hours later, having sent Lucy home and locked up the store, she was faced with another decision—what to wear to Walter's party. As she looked through her closet, what little enthusiasm she had for the evening disappeared completely. Everything seemed either too drab or completely unsuitable. "It's not as if I go to a lot of parties," Jane informed Tom, who sat on the bed watching her.

Dressing had been so much easier in her day. True, there had been a few more undergarments to contend with, but by and large the actual dresses themselves varied only a little. "One always knew exactly what one should wear to what," said Jane.

She considered, and rejected, a number of different possibilities. She was surprised to realize that it wasn't because she couldn't decide what to wear, or even that she had to attend a party about which she was not terribly excited. "It's because I care what Walter thinks," she admitted to Tom, who was now asleep.

She suddenly felt very foolish. She was, for the first time in a very long time, worrying about how she appeared to a man. "It's just Walter," she told herself. "He doesn't care how you look."

But it wasn't about him; it was about her. For reasons she

chose not to dwell upon, she wanted to be attractive for him. It was a worrying prospect, but it was there nonetheless and she had to acknowledge it. *Stupid girl,* she thought as she renewed her search for something suitable. *Even Catherine had more sense.*

Eventually she decided on a sleeveless velvet dress in deep green. The occasion for its purchase was long forgotten, but it was the nicest thing in her closet, and so she put it on. It was decidedly modern, a far cry from the confections of her time. The hem fell just above the knees, and there were no unnecessary frivolities like bows or rosettes to get in the way. She vaguely recalled having purchased it somewhere in the late fifties (perhaps a party at the Kennedy summer home?), and for a moment worried that it was out of date. *But retro is in,* she reminded herself. *For once you'll be fashion forward, even if it's purely a result of never throwing anything out.* She added earrings and a necklace, then checked her reflection in the mirror.

Staring at herself, she wondered what Walter would think. Again she wished that Cassie were there to tell her she was presentable. *Maybe I should just stay home,* she thought. But she'd promised Walter she would come. And it was only for a few hours. "How bad could it be?" she asked herself.

Chapter 6

That Jonathan Brut had a scandalous past she had
absolutely no doubt. His reputation as a scoundrel
was common knowledge not only in London, but
also in the sleepy towns and villages far beyond
that city's bustling streets. It was said that he had
been the ruin of a score of women—maidens and
married alike—one of whom reportedly killed
herself with poison when he ended their affair.
It was for precisely these reasons that
Constance had chosen him.

—Jane Austen, *Constance*, manuscript page 71

"YOU LOOK STUNNING," WALTER TOLD JANE WHEN HE SAW HER.

"As do you," Jane replied. And it was true. Gone were Walter's usual work clothes. Instead he was dressed in a pair of black pants and a deep blue cashmere sweater over a white shirt. His hair was freshly cut, and he radiated happiness. Jane found herself slightly tongue-tied.

"There are so many people here," she said quickly, looking around the room. Walter's house seemed to be overflowing with guests, all of whom were dressed in holiday finery. Suddenly, Jane's plain green dress seemed woefully inadequate, despite Walter's compliment.

Walter placed his arm around her waist. "You'll have to excuse me," he said. "There are some Historical Society members here, and I promised to bore them with the details of my plans for the restoration of the library. But don't disappear. I'll be looking for you later."

Jane watched him go, feeling her discomfort increase. She'd arrived late, hoping to limit the amount of time she had to endure the party. As a young lady at Steventon rectory, she had loved parties, had looked forward to dancing and playing the pianoforte, to the lively conversations and drawing-room intrigues. How many times she and Cassie had sat together on a sofa, holding hands and whispering scandalously about the goings-on both seen and unseen. Now she scanned the living room for a place of refuge and saw, seated alone on the couch, Sherman Applebaum. The editor of the smaller of the town's two newspapers, Sherman was into the latter half of his sixties. He had a fondness for waistcoats and bowler hats, which Jane found charming. He was also, she knew from past encounters, an inveterate gossip. Her favorite kind.

She crossed the room and took a seat beside Sherman.

"Finally, someone has come to my rescue," Sherman said dramatically. "I was starting to think I might spend the entire evening alone."

Jane laughed. "Somehow I think you'd be your own best company, Sherman."

Sherman smiled and patted Jane's knee. "You flatter me," he said. "Please do continue. At my advanced age I don't have many opportunities to be complimented by attractive young women."

If you only knew, Jane thought. *Even your great-great-great-grandfather couldn't accurately call me a young woman.*

"Where did you get that lovely drink?" she asked. "I need one desperately."

"I'll get one for you," Sherman said. "Don't go away."

"No, no," said Jane. "I'll go."

"Nonsense," Sherman replied, standing up. "A gentleman never allows a lady to get her own drink. Besides, I fear that if I don't move around from time to time, I'll wither and die."

He got up and meandered toward the kitchen. Jane settled into the sofa to await his return, scanning the room for any signs of intriguing topics of conversation. Then, as if out of nowhere, a woman materialized in front of her.

"Jane," she said. "What a surprise."

Jane nearly jumped out of her seat. "Miranda," she answered. "How nice to see you."

This was not true. Miranda Fleck was an assistant professor of English at nearby Meade College. She was impossibly young, impossibly skinny, and impossibly ambitious. She spoke almost exclusively in declarative sentences, which had the effect of unnerving most people. To Jane's irritation, Miranda assumed Sherman's place on the sofa.

"I was in your shop earlier this week," said Miranda.

Jane waited for Miranda to continue, allowing the silence to grow. She was unsure whether to thank Miranda or defend herself. Imbuing her words with absolutely no emotion whatsoever was another hallmark of Miranda's speech.

"You have a particularly conspicuous display of that book combining the text of *Pride and Prejudice* with—how do they describe it—ultraviolent zombie mayhem," Miranda continued.

"It's one of our bestsellers," Jane replied cautiously.

This was true. The book, which had come out earlier in the year, was a surprise hit. Part of her bristled at the notion of someone taking *her* novel and inserting new, decidedly unorthodox text into it, and she'd briefly considered visiting some unpleasantness upon the author, but ultimately amusement had won out over irritation and she'd even begun to recommend the book to customers. Although receiving royalties from it would be nice.

"I know it's only *Austen*," Miranda continued. "Even so, polluting a beloved novel with something so crass . . ." She shook her head as if bemoaning a great tragedy.

"Have you read the book?" asked Jane.

Miranda snorted. "Of course not," she said. "I wouldn't read such trash."

"Perhaps you should," Jane said. "It's quite funny."

"Funny," Miranda repeated. "I suspect Austen wouldn't agree with that assessment."

"Don't be so sure," Jane told her. "Austen was a great fan of the novels of Ann Radcliffe. She had a real fondness for the gothic."

"I would hardly call zombies gothic," Miranda argued. "Vampires, perhaps, but not zombies."

Jane, with great relief, saw Sherman approaching with a drink in each hand. When he noticed Miranda, his face visibly stiffened. Then, just as quickly, a smile returned.

"Ladies," he said, "I have arrived with refreshments."

He handed a glass of wine to each of them. Miranda, as if she'd assumed all along that Sherman had gone to get her a drink, accepted her glass without comment. Sherman, now without his own glass, sat beside her. Jane almost offered him her wine, but she knew he wouldn't accept it. *He's too much of a gentleman*, she thought. *And Miranda is too much of a boor.*

"Jane and I were just discussing whether or not Austen would appreciate her landscape being overrun by the undead," Miranda told Sherman.

"Ah, the zombie book," Sherman said. "A rollicking good read."

Jane stifled a laugh. Miranda frowned.

"Mind you, I prefer the original," Sherman continued. "But there's nothing at all wrong with giving the classics a bit of a tweaking. I gave that book to my nephew's youngest. What would that make her, my great-niece? No, grandniece. At any rate, she's twelve. She loved it. Now she's reading all of Austen. So there you are." He looked at Miranda as if this were the last word on the subject.

"Miranda fears that vampires will be next," Jane said, unable to resist. "*Sense and Sensibility and Dracula,* perhaps."

"I'm partial to werewolves, myself," Sherman said. "I think Emma would make a fine lycanthrope."

Miranda sipped her wine. "Well, if they're going to bastardize anyone, I'm not surprised that it's Austen," she said icily.

Jane bristled. Miranda was a Brontëite, and like most of them, she not-so-secretly resented the fact that Jane's books regularly outsold those of the beloved sisters.

"Austen *is* our most popular author," Jane parried.

Miranda reacted to Jane's maneuver without flinching. "I suppose keeping your doors open requires appealing to the public's tastes," she remarked.

She'd do very well in a drawing-room battle, Jane thought, admiring Miranda despite her personal distaste for the woman. *One would never quite know what she was saying, or on which side of her opinion one fell.*

All of a sudden a sharp twinge stabbed through her side. She almost cried out. She placed her hand on the site of the pain. Again the feeling came, this time more intensely. It was followed by a flash of cold fire behind her eyes.

No, no, no, she thought. *Not now. Not here.*

She needed to feed.

"Everybody having a good time?"

Jane looked up to see a smiling Walter standing before her. "Wonderful," she said as the cramps hit her again.

"That's what I like to hear," said Walter. "So, what were you all talking about?"

Jane winced as the pain returned and made it impossible to speak. She needed to get out of here before it got any worse. But how could she excuse herself without seeming rude or, worse, letting Miranda think she was giving up the battle?

Thinking quickly, she jostled Miranda's arm, causing Miranda's glass to tip precipitously. Wine poured onto her lap, staining her dress. Miranda let out a little shriek.

"I'm so sorry!" Jane exclaimed.

"It's going to stain," said Miranda angrily.

"Not if we blot it with seltzer," Jane said. "Come with me."

She stood and, gripping Miranda's wrist, pulled the woman to her feet. Miranda let out another surprised squeal, no doubt shocked by Jane's strength.

"You'll excuse us, gentlemen," Jane said to Walter and Sherman.

"Of course," Walter said. "But make sure you're back in time for the countdown."

"I'll do my best," Jane assured him.

She hurried through the crowd, pulling Miranda behind her. Seeing that the door to the hallway bathroom was closed, she detoured into Walter's bedroom. She bypassed the bed, covered in coats, and dragged Miranda into the en suite bathroom. Closing the door behind them, she turned to Miranda.

"Now then," she said. "Let's take care of you."

"But we didn't get any seltzer," Miranda objected. She turned the water on in the sink and started wetting a hand towel. "It's going to set."

"First things first," said Jane. She spoke in a low voice, concentrating on clouding Miranda's mind. Glamoring was one of the few vampiric tricks Jane had at her disposal. She very rarely used it, saving it for times such as this. Now she concentrated on manipulating Miranda's thoughts.

Miranda hesitated, the towel in the stream of water. Slowly she let it fall into the sink, then turned and looked at Jane. "First things first," she said softly.

Keeping her eyes on Miranda's, Jane put her hand on the back of the woman's neck. "Relax," she said. "This will take just a minute."

She bit into the soft skin beneath Miranda's left ear, where her long hair would cover the bite marks until they could heal. Miranda slumped against Jane as she lost consciousness. Blood slipped into Jane's mouth.

As she drank, the cramps subsided. Miranda's blood was bitter, which surprised Jane not at all given the woman's literary preferences. But it did the trick and, more important perhaps, prevented Jane from drinking more than she needed. When the pain in her had abated, she released Miranda, who slumped to the floor. Wiping her hand across her mouth, Jane giddily murmured, "Austen one, Brontë zero."

Opening the door a crack, Jane peered into the bedroom. It was empty. Lifting Miranda in her arms, she carried her to the bed and placed her on it. Then she arranged the coats around her, not covering her but obscuring her enough that anyone taking a casual glance into the room would not immediately notice her. *And if they do,* she thought, *they'll just assume she's sleeping off her wine.*

When she returned to the living room, she found Sherman on the sofa exactly where she had left him. Smiling broadly, she sat beside him. "Here I am," she said. "As promised."

"I trust Miss Fleck has been taken care of?" Sherman said.

Jane nodded. "Yes, but I'm afraid she's decided to abandon our company for more agreeable friends," she said.

"Pity," Sherman replied. Jane noticed that in her absence he had gotten himself a new drink. She also noticed that Walter was missing.

"Walter was called away by his duties as host," Sherman said, as if reading her mind. "I'm so glad you're back. It's been dreadfully dull."

"Well then, let's make up for lost time," Jane said. "Tell me everything you know about everyone here."

In short order Jane learned that both Mr. and Mrs. Primsley were having an affair with the high school debate coach; that Miranda Fleck's dissertation was late not because of her need to research more primary sources but because her original work had been found to be not at all original; and that a surprising number of the party guests had at one time or another been arrested for shoplifting, driving under the influence, indecent exposure, or a combination of all three.

"Next you'll tell me that Walter has a sordid past," Jane remarked.

Sherman waved one hand and laughed. "Walter has no past," he said. "I don't think he's had even one date since his wife died."

"His wife?" Jane coughed, choking on her wine. "I didn't know' he'd been married."

Sherman nodded. "Evelyn," he said. "She died, oh, it must be almost fifteen years ago now. It was quite a tragedy. They'd been married only a few years."

"How did she— What happened to her?" asked Jane.

Sherman sighed deeply. "She drowned," he said. "On the Fourth of July. There was a picnic at the lake. She went swimming. No one knows exactly what happened. One minute she was waving to us, and the next we couldn't see her. By the time anyone realized something was wrong she was dead."

"How terrible," said Jane. "Poor Walter."

"He was devastated," Sherman told her. "We worried about him for a long time."

"He's never mentioned it to me," Jane said.

"I'm not surprised," said Sherman. "He never speaks of her. I don't think there are even any pictures of her in the house. It's as if she never existed."

Jane searched the room for Walter and found him talking to the head of the Historical Society. He was smiling and laughing and waving his hands emphatically. *You would never know he'd suffered such a tragedy,* she thought. Her heart ached for him. She suddenly wanted to go to him and tell him that everything would be all right.

"Ten!" someone shouted, causing Jane to jump.

"Nine!"

Jane glanced at her watch. It was almost midnight.

"Eight!"

"Seven!"

All around her people stood up and began counting down the New Year. They donned hats and held up noisemakers in anticipation.

"Six!"

"Five!"

Jane was hauled to her feet by Sherman, who placed a pointy cardboard hat on her head and handed her a small plastic horn.

"Four!"

"Three!"

Suddenly Walter was in front of Jane. "You didn't think I'd let you ring the year in alone, did you?" he asked, grinning.

"Two!"

"One!"

Walter took Jane in his arms and kissed her lightly on the mouth. "I'm glad you made it back."

"Happy New Year!"

All around them people cheered and tooted on their horns and kissed one another. Walter released Jane and cheered along with them. "Happy New Year," Jane said, but the celebration drowned out the sound of her voice.

Chapter 7

*London was as unlike Glenheath as a peacock was
unlike a wren. It swelled with life, boastful and
proud. The colours were brighter, the smells richer,
the sounds more cacophonous. Even the dogs
seemed filled with purpose, trotting beside their
masters as if they too were on their way to conduct
important business or attend the opera.*

—Jane Austen, *Constance*, manuscript page 80

TAKING THE TRAIN WAS NOT NEARLY AS INTERESTING AS IT HAD
been a hundred years ago. But it was faster, and that was something. As Jane sat and watched the dreary winter landscape pass
by, her spirits were buoyed by the knowledge that she would be in
New York City in a matter of hours. She could have flown, but she
still wasn't entirely trusting of airplanes. No matter how many
times the principle was explained to her she just couldn't quite
believe that something as large as a plane could stay aloft.

It had been difficult to focus on running the bookstore the past
few days. The prospect of meeting her new editor in person was
thrilling. At the same time she was relieved to be leaving Brakes-

ton. It had begun to feel claustrophobic. Her chat with Sherman had reminded her that too many people knew too much about each other's business.

Then there was the small matter of Walter's dead wife. Jane didn't know why, but the fact that Walter had never mentioned Evelyn to her was upsetting. And it bothered her that it bothered her. Why should she care if he'd been married?

"I don't," she said firmly. "I don't care at all."

Across the aisle a boy of about eight turned and looked at her. He'd gotten on at Utica along with an older woman whom Jane assumed to be his grandmother. Ever since, he had been playing some kind of handheld video game that emitted a continuous stream of beeps and chirps that sounded to Jane like electronic crickets. Now the grandmother was asleep.

"Don't care," the boy said, mimicking Jane. "I don't care." He repeated the phrase over and over as he continued to play his game. Maddeningly, the sound of the game provided a musical background to his chanting. "I don't care." *Bleep-bleep-bleep.* "I don't care." *Bleep-bleep-bleep.* "I don't care." *Bleep-bleep-bleep.*

Jane glared at him. He turned his head and grinned at her. "I don't care," he chorused.

Jane bared her fangs at him and watched as the expression on his face changed from smugness to horror. He gasped, dropping his game. He fumbled beneath the seat for it, and when he came up Jane smiled at him. He turned his face away and sat very still, like a small bird in the presence of a cat.

Maybe she *should* give Walter a chance, Jane mused while looking out the window again. When she was honest with herself, she had to admit that she did like Walter very much. He was precisely the kind of man she allowed her heroines to fall in love with—strong-minded but willing to let her be herself, thoughtful and curious without being condescending, talented but without vanity. Yet if she allowed herself to be with him, she would risk wounding Walter deeply. She was especially wary now that she knew of his tragic past. A dead wife was no small thing. *How would he ever accept an undead one?* she thought.

It was all rather maddening, and no matter how she looked at it she could not come up with a satisfactory ending for the story. Walter would die and she would continue to live. Or he would ask her to make him a vampire, which she would refuse to do.

She thought for a long time, coming to no conclusions, and was relieved when a voice announced their imminent arrival at Pennsylvania Station. She busied herself with putting her coat on and gathering up her things. Then she sat and watched as the train crawled slowly through the long dark tunnels, until finally they came to a stop at a platform and the doors opened.

Jane stepped out and walked along the platform, the heels of her shoes clicking on the floor and her suitcase rolling behind her. Travel had become much easier since her day, but part of her missed the feeling of sophistication that had once accompanied it. Now people moved about so easily that some of the adventure seemed to have disappeared along with the inconveniences. Now it felt less like *traveling* and more like simply *going somewhere.*

As she ascended the escalator to the main concourse she noticed the boy from the train walking with his grandmother ahead of her. He turned back once and, seeing her following, pulled his grandmother quickly in a different direction. Jane cheerfully wondered how long he would have nightmares about the woman on the train, and at what point he would decide that she had never existed at all.

In the station's cavernous main hall she stood for a moment, feeling the sea of people moving around her. She sensed their excitement, their hurry, their anxiety and joy. It rippled through her like electricity. She'd forgotten what it felt like to be in a city, particularly one as glorious as New York. Now she shivered with anticipation. Despite the passing of two centuries, she still felt like the girl from the countryside coming to London for the first time.

She hurried outside, anxious to be on the streets and among the crowds. As she passed through the doors of the station she felt New York envelop her. Its cacophonous voice filled her ears and its breath blew cold on her skin. For a moment she stood absolutely still, her eyes and ears adjusting to the many different sensations that flooded her mind.

"Move it, lady."

A man brushed by her, his head bent toward the ground and his hands thrust into the pockets of his coat. Jane laughed at his rudeness. It too was part of New York's charm.

Settling into a taxicab, she could hardy believe she was in New York, on her way to a publisher's office. All of her previous books had been represented by her brother Henry. Not only had she never once visited a publisher, they hadn't even known it was her work they had published. But all that was about to change.

I wish Cassie were here, she thought. She imagined sharing the city with her sister, seeing Cassandra's face as she marveled at the buildings and people, hearing her voice as she chattered joyfully and reached for Jane's hand, as she always had when they'd visited Henry at his house in London. She would, Jane thought, give anything to be able to see her beloved Cassie again.

The cab swerved in and out of the stream of traffic, ten minutes later pulling to a stop in front of the Browder Publishing building. It towered into the winter sky, its gleaming black glass reflecting the snow that fell lazily from the clouds that crowned the city.

She crossed the sidewalk with her suitcase and pushed through the revolving doors, entering a lobby lined with the blown-up, framed covers of some of the most popular books of the past few years. As she walked to the elevators she gazed at them, imagining her own cover hanging among them. Then, just as she reached the elevator bank, she saw that she already was. On the wall the cover of *The Jane Austen Workout Book* hung between the latest novels from a popular romance writer and the biggest name in thrillers.

Horrified, she gazed at the cover image—a pen-and-ink drawing of a woman (she gathered it was supposed to be her) wearing an Empire-waist dress and holding a small barbell in each hand. It was ghastly, and she found herself feeling sick to her stomach.

The ding of an arriving elevator blessedly distracted her, and she tore herself from the poster and entered the car. Selecting the button for the seventeenth floor, she stood with her eyes closed as she was lifted into the air. *Don't think about it,* she told herself. But the image of the book's cover remained in her mind.

When the elevator stopped, Jane stepped out into a brightly lit reception area. Behind a raised copper and glass desk a lovely young woman sat speaking into a headset. "I'd be happy to connect you with publicity," she said. "One moment." She touched a button on a telephone, then smiled at Jane. "How can I help you?"

"I'm here to see Kelly Littlejohn," Jane said. "I have an appointment," she added, fearing the young woman might not believe her.

"And you are?" asked the girl.

"Jane," said Jane. "Jane Fairfax. I'm sorry."

The girl nodded as if forgiving Jane, then touched the phone panel once again. "Olivia, it's Chloe. Jane Fairfax is here to see Kelly."

Olivia, Jane thought. *Chloe.* They were such stylish names. She wondered if everyone in publishing was a stylish young woman with perfect hair and beautiful clothes and names that sounded like they belonged in her novels. *If the assistants are this lovely, I'm almost afraid to meet Kelly Littlejohn.*

"Kelly will be out in just a moment," Chloe said. "You can have a seat over there." With a nod of her head she indicated a smart leather couch against the wall.

Jane sat down, tucking her suitcase beside the couch. She was suddenly quite nervous, and didn't know what to do with her hands. She heard Chloe laugh, and for a moment feared the young woman was laughing at her, before realizing that she had simply taken another call. She looked at her shoes. *How dreadful they are,* she thought. *What was I thinking?*

She considered going to the restroom and changing (she had dressier shoes in her bag) but was interrupted by someone saying her name. She looked up and saw standing before her a handsome man of perhaps forty. He was dressed in a beautifully tailored suit of dark brown wool, and the knot in his red and gold patterned tie was perfectly dimpled. His hair, dark but silvering on the sides, was cut short, and Jane could smell the faint scent of violet, orange, and oak coming from him as he extended his hand.

"It's a pleasure to finally meet you," he said, his voice warm and deep. "I'm Kelly Littlejohn."

Chapter 8

She accepted the grape from Jonathan, parting her
lips and allowing him to place it gently in her
mouth. When she bit into it the flesh burst open and
her tongue was bathed in sweetness. She raised her
fingers to her mouth and covered it as she chewed
the fruit. She did not want Jonathan to see her
enjoyment so plainly, as if he had come into the
room at the very moment she had stepped
naked from the bath.

—Jane Austen, *Constance*, manuscript page 97

"KELLY," JANE REPEATED, TAKING THE PROFFERED HAND AND
feeling the strong fingers clasp hers. "Oh, no."

"Is everything all right?" Kelly asked.

"No," said Jane, blinking. "I mean yes. Everything's fine. It's
just that I thought you were a woman." Embarrassed, she spoke
more quickly. "I don't mean right *now* I thought you were a
woman. I mean before I saw you. Because of your name. We've
never spoken," she concluded, feeling like an idiot. "May I just go
out and come back in?" she asked.

Kelly laughed. "It's all right," he said. "It's not the first time someone has thought that. You should see how many query letters I get addressed to Ms. Littlejohn." He glanced at her suitcase. "Let me take that for you," he said.

"Oh, I can—" Jane began.

"I insist," Kelly said, flashing a smile that lit up his whole face.

"All right," Jane acquiesced, blushing as Kelly bent to take the case by the handle. *Stop behaving like a schoolgirl,* she scolded herself.

She followed Kelly as he held open the door. "After you," he said, and again she couldn't help thinking about how dashing he was. *A true gentleman.*

They walked down a hallway lined with offices. Inside each one an editor sat at a desk, peering at a computer screen. Jane glanced at their faces as she passed by. They all looked impossibly young, not at all like editors in her time, most of whom had been men well into the second half of their lives who peered out at the world from behind thick spectacles, their eyes ruined from years of reading in inadequate light, and their fingers perpetually ink-stained and chapped from constantly turning the pages of manuscripts.

"Here we are," Kelly said, entering a corner office. "Welcome to my castle."

The room was not terribly large. A desk, piled high with folders and what Jane assumed were manuscripts, sat in front of a bank of windows that looked out on the street. The floor too was covered with stacks of manuscripts, and one whole wall was taken up by shelves filled with books. Jane, relieved to see evidence of the publishing world she had always imagined, felt herself relax.

"It's not much, but it's all mine," Kelly said. "Please, have a seat."

Jane took one of the two chairs across from Kelly's desk. She looked around the room, trying very hard not to stare at him. "Do you have to read all of these?" she asked, indicating the mountains of manuscripts.

"My assistant reads most of them first," he answered. "But I try to look at everything. I like to make decisions for myself."

Jane wondered if her manuscript had languished among the paper, and how Kelly had come to rescue it from the crowd.

"It's something of a miracle that anything gets published at all," said Kelly, as if reading her thoughts. "Especially an unsolicited manuscript such as yours. May I ask why you don't use an agent?"

"It never occurred to me," Jane answered truthfully.

Kelly laughed, shaking his head. "I must tell you, it's refreshing to meet an author whose sole goal in life is to be published. Most authors come in here and I can tell that what they really want is to be famous. I don't get that from you, or from your book."

She wondered what Kelly would say if he knew that she was already one of the world's most famous authors, was in fact arguably the most popular writer of all time. And that she very badly wanted to be published again.

"Most of them want to be Stephen King or Danielle Steele," Kelly remarked. "I don't know when authors went from being storytellers to being celebrities, but more and more I think we cast writers rather than publish them."

Jane was nodding as she looked around the office. Then she noticed a book resting atop a pile on the corner of Kelly's desk. Her heart sank.

Kelly's eyes followed her gaze. "Oh, that," he said, sighing. "This is exactly what I mean," he added as he held up a copy of

The Jane Austen Workout Book. "Ridiculous, isn't it? But I guarantee you we'll sell a hundred thousand copies." He looked at the cover and snorted. "Austen would roll over in her grave," he said.

"Indeed," said Jane, chuckling with relief.

"You're British," Kelly said.

"Pardon?" said Jane. She was still staring at the image of herself on the book's cover.

"Your accent," Kelly said. "It's British."

"Oh," said Jane. "Yes, it is."

"How long have you lived in America?" Kelly asked.

Jane laughed lightly. "It seems like a hundred years. My parents moved here when I was quite young," she added quickly.

"I thought there was a British sensibility to your writing," said Kelly. "I think that's what attracted me to it. I'm a bit of an Anglophile." He smiled again. "Sometimes I think I was born in the wrong century."

"I know just what you mean," Jane said.

"You must be hungry after your trip," Kelly said. "Shall we have lunch?"

"That would be lovely," Jane replied.

Kelly stood and retrieved his coat from the back of the office door. "You can leave your suitcase here," he told Jane. "We'll come back before I send you off to the hotel."

They took the elevator down to the lobby, and as they walked outside Kelly said, "Is this your first time in New York?"

"I've been here once before," Jane said. "But it was a long time ago." *Before there were cars on the streets,* she thought. *And long before you were born.*

They walked several blocks until they arrived at a restaurant. Stepping inside, Jane found herself in a reasonable replica of a French bistro.

"Now then," Kelly said after a waiter had brought them two glasses of merlot, "let's talk about your book."

"I'm very glad you like it," said Jane.

"I don't just like it," Kelly replied. "I love it. In fact, I haven't been this excited about a book in a long time."

Jane felt herself blush with pride. "That's kind of you to say."

Kelly shook his head. "I mean it," he said. "There's something about it that's timeless. People don't write books like yours anymore. Especially for women. Now it's all about middle-aged women going to Bermuda and falling in love with twenty-two-year-old surfing instructors, or young women working at fashion magazines and whatnot. I wonder sometimes if people would even recognize a quality book if they were given one." He waved his hand around. "But your book is actually *about* something."

"Thank you," Jane said. She was slightly embarrassed by Kelly's effusive praise, although hearing it was not at all unpleasant after so many years of disappointment. "I feel it's important that a book make people think *and* feel."

Kelly lifted his glass and said, "To your novel. May it stay atop the bestseller lists for many weeks."

"Indeed," Jane agreed. "And to you for your most excellent taste in literature."

They both laughed. Jane took a sip of wine and set her glass down. "May I ask when you're thinking of publishing the book?"

"I'm glad you brought that up," Kelly said. "Normally we like a long lead time in order to pull together publicity. But I want your book out much sooner, preferably by summer."

"Summer," Jane repeated. *That's only five or six months from now,* she thought.

"I want to get it out in time for vacation season," Kelly explained. "I know it sounds crass, but it's a reality of the industry that books for women sell best in the summer."

Jane nodded, taking a long drink from her wineglass.

"And you'll be selling it in your own store," Kelly said. "When customers bring it to the register you can offer to sign it for them."

Jane smiled broadly. She wanted to tell Kelly how many times she'd been tempted to take a customer's copy of *Pride and Prejudice* and do exactly that. Now she could. *But what if Lucy—or anyone—notices the similarities?* she found herself thinking. *What if they discover who I am?* The thought dampened her joy.

"To get the book out so quickly, I need to get it to production immediately," Kelly said, drawing her back to the moment. "The good news is that it needs very little editing. I know we haven't even signed the contract, but I've taken the liberty of going through it and making a couple of suggestions. Nothing major. If you're okay with my edits, then we can go right into production. We'll do as much as we can while you're here, and I'll give you the manuscript to take back with you to finish up."

"I'm sure everything will be fine," Jane said, speaking more to herself than to Kelly. Her worries about being found out were fading as she reassured herself that no one would possibly think to connect her to the Austen of old.

Kelly cocked his head. "Are you sure this is your first book?" he asked.

For a moment Jane panicked. Had she said too much? Had Kelly somehow seen through her act? "No," she said hastily. "I mean yes, I'm sure. Why do you ask?"

"It's just that you're so calm about it all," said Kelly. "Usually first-time authors are nervous wrecks."

"If it helps, I'm a wreck on the inside," Jane assured him. "But I'm British. We have no visible emotions, you know. They were bred out of us centuries ago."

Kelly laughed. "I'll keep that in mind," he said. "So now that I've told you our big plans, I should probably tell you what our offer is."

Jane listened as Kelly explained the terms of the contract. In truth, she didn't really care about the advance or the royalty percentage or the subsidiary rights. But she pretended to listen intently, nodding at the appropriate points and even hesitating long enough at one point that Kelly increased the amount of her advance by 10 percent.

"Of course, you'll probably want to talk to your lawyer before agreeing," he concluded. "But I hope you'll say yes."

"Yes," Jane said.

Kelly seemed to be holding his breath. "You're sure?" he asked. "You don't want to discuss it with anyone first?"

"Are you saying I should be worried?" Jane said. "I took you for a most trustworthy man, but perhaps I should rethink my opinion." She was teasing him, but Kelly apparently mistook her remark for hesitation.

"I'll increase the royalty to fifteen percent," he said. "But that's as high as I can go. Honestly."

Jane reached out and patted his hand. His nervousness was charming, particularly as until then he'd seemed unflappable. "Relax," she said. "You sound like a first-time publisher."

Kelly chuckled and shook his head. "You had me worried for a second," he admitted.

"Just to be clear, I'll sign the contract," Jane said. "We have a deal."

"Good," said Kelly. "Now I can eat."

Jane scanned the menu. As usual, she wasn't hungry, but she knew she had to order something. She considered the chocolate mousse, but settled on French onion soup and a small salad. There was no sense in airing all her peculiarities to Kelly at once.

The waiter arrived, they placed their orders, and their conversation resumed. With the book talk out of the way, Kelly asked Jane questions about herself, all of which she answered with as little detail as possible. As soon as she was able to she turned the topic around to him. By the time their food arrived, she'd learned that he had grown up in Pennsylvania, attended school in Chicago, and moved to New York immediately upon graduating to work in publishing.

"My parents were very disappointed," he told Jane. "They were hoping I'd become an investment banker or, as my father once put it, something useful. I'm afraid books are not held in much esteem in the Littlejohn house."

Jane wanted to ask him more questions, but she felt it wasn't fair to pry too much when she was keeping so much of herself from him. It was a situation with which she was more than familiar after two hundred years of practicing the art of evasion. Instead, she asked about the other authors Kelly worked with. She recognized several of the names he mentioned, although she had read none of their books. She made a mental note to do so as soon as she was home.

When lunch was over she and Kelly returned to the office, where Kelly presented her with four copies of a contract. After once again reminding Jane that she was free to have someone look them over, he watched anxiously as she signed the final page of each copy. When she handed them back to him, he beamed.

"Do you want to go over the manuscript?" Jane asked.

Kelly nodded. "But first I have a little surprise." He picked up the phone and dialed. "Joanna, I have Jane Fairfax here. Could you come in, please?"

He hung up. "I think you'll love this," he told Jane. "At least I hope so."

A moment later a young woman walked into the office carrying a large piece of cardboard.

"Jane, this is Joanna Clarke. Joanna is the head of the design department."

Joanna and Jane exchanged greetings. Then Kelly said, "I was so excited about your book that I emailed Joanna from Paris so she could work on this."

He nodded at Joanna, who turned the piece of cardboard around, revealing a mock-up cover for Jane's book. It featured a photograph of a farmhouse at twilight. In one of the upstairs windows a light glowed, and through the open curtains a woman was visible, her back to the window. From the lower right-hand corner of the cover a man stood looking up at her, holding a bouquet of daisies in his hand.

"*Constance,*" Jane read the title. "Jane Fairfax."

"I wasn't sure what name you wanted to use, so I went with what you used on your letter," Kelly said. "Do you like it?"

Jane continued to stare at the cover. *That's my book,* she told herself. She was so used to the drab covers publishers put on her older novels—boring paintings of English cottages and girls in white dresses—that she'd expected the same thing. But this cover was different. It was modern yet timeless.

"I do like it," she said. "I think it's lovely."

Joanna smiled. "I'm pretty pleased with it myself. Of course there will be some tweaking once marketing puts their two cents in, but I think this is pretty much it."

"Would you like a copy to take home with you?" Kelly asked Jane. "We can have one printed out."

"Really?" Jane asked. "Of course I'd love one."

"I'll go get one for you," said Joanna.

"Thank you," Jane said as Joanna left the office. "I really do love it."

She looked at Kelly. "I can hardly believe this is happening," she said. "It's all a bit like a dream."

"We'll see if you think so once we've gone through my editing suggestions," Kelly said. "Shall we begin?"

Jane hesitated only a moment before nodding. "Yes, let's," she said as Kelly turned over the first page.

Chapter 9

She had promised herself that she would not fall in love with him. Experience—not love—was her objective. She reminded herself that a worldly woman should easily be able to distinguish between the two. Yet she could not pretend that Jonathan was not simultaneously everything she disliked and everything she desired in a man. Despite what she knew of him, she found herself wishing he would take her in his arms.

—Jane Austen, *Constance*, manuscript page 102

JANE STOOD AT THE WINDOW, LOOKING DOWN ON TIMES SQUARE. IT was one in the morning, and she was not the least bit tired. She still couldn't quite believe that her day had actually occurred. That morning she had been in Brakeston. Now she was in New York City, having signed a book contract and gone over the edits with her editor. Her handsome, funny, smart editor.

She brushed the thought from her mind. It was true that Kelly was all of those things. But thinking about him in that way was hardly professional. Still, over the dinner they'd shared following their work on the manuscript, she had found herself behaving more and more like a besotted schoolgirl and less like a woman of 234. It was during the performance of *Gypsy*, to which Kelly had taken her after dinner, that she had realized that he reminded her very much of Richard Mansfield, the enchanting nineteenth-century actor and star of the D'Oyly Carte opera company. She had attended seventeen consecutive performances of *The Mikado* just to see Mansfield, and her devotion to him had not faltered even during the nasty Jack the Ripper business, when he was one of the prime suspects. (She'd known the Ripper, and although charming, he was not nearly as handsome as Mansfield.)

Her crush on Mansfield had eventually faded, and she suspected this one would as well. It was just the excitement of once again being a published author. She turned and looked at the cover of her book, the poster of which she had taped to the mirror above the room's dresser. It hardly seemed possible that it was really *her* book. "*Constance*," she said aloud. "By Jane Fairfax." She giggled, embarrassed by how thrilling it was to say her name like that.

The title of the book, she had to admit, was not her best. She preferred something pithy. After all, could anything be better than *Pride and Prejudice* or *Sense and Sensibility*? True, *Mansfield Park* and *Northanger Abbey* were a bit drab, but that had been the fashion at the time. And at least they weren't as bad as Scott's *Tales of My Landlord*.

Anyway, she liked the cover. And she mostly liked being Jane Fairfax. She would have preferred to be Jane Austen, but that was of course impossible. Besides, she was used to being a Fairfax now.

Opening the minibar, she took out two Scharffen Berger dark chocolate bars and a half bottle of Shiraz. Then she lay down on the bed, sinking into the impossibly soft mattress with a contented sigh. Pulling the wrapper from the first bar, she nibbled the corner as she turned on the television and began flipping through the channels. She watched a minute or two of several different things, but none held her interest. She had consumed half of the chocolate bar before she recognized a familiar face on one of the channels and stopped.

It was Peter Cushing. And the film, she realized shortly thereafter, was *Brides of Dracula.* It was one of her favorites, and she had not seen it in a long time. Now she settled in to enjoy it, alternately sipping from the bottle of wine and taking bites of the chocolate.

One of the infamous Hammer horror films, *Brides of Dracula* was enormously fun, particularly, Jane thought, if you were a vampire yourself. Watching the young heroine fall under the spell of the gorgeous and tragic vampire Baron Meinster (the name made her cringe) amused her, as did the generally ridiculous plot and the fact that despite the title and one brief reference in the dialogue, not once did Dracula himself actually appear in the film.

Yet as she watched the story unfold, Jane found herself growing sad. For the first time, she identified with young Marianne Danielle, the innocent schoolteacher tricked into helping Meinster escape from the room in which he was being kept prisoner by his mother the baroness. Rather than seeing her as a stupid girl who overlooks the obvious, Jane saw her as a girl in love, a girl who sees a wounded man needing her comfort.

By the end of the film she had worked her way through the bottle and most of the second chocolate bar, and felt a bit sick. And although she was happy that Marianne had escaped the fate of the other vampire brides, the scenes in which the baron is first disfigured by holy water and then done in by a cross-shaped shadow added to her queasiness.

She couldn't help thinking back to the time when she'd been as innocent as Marianne. She too had trusted someone who had betrayed her. Unlike Marianne, however, she had not escaped.

"No," she said to the dark. "You're not going to think about that. You've let it go."

She felt foolish speaking the thoughts out loud. It was a trick she'd learned during an est seminar in 1972. That was the year she'd decided to become self-actualized. Along with a perm and bell-bottom jeans, it was one of many things she regretted. The technique of getting rid of unhealthy thoughts by speaking them aloud, though, was actually helpful. It had helped her release some of the anger she'd carried inside her for so long.

She turned on her side and focused her eyes on the window. Beyond the curtains the lights of Broadway blinked on and off and the sounds of car horns broke the stillness. "That was the past, this is now," Jane said. "That was the past, this is now." Another trick she'd picked up during that long-ago weekend.

She repeated the phrase over and over, until the sound of her own voice drowned out everything else. When she felt her eyes beginning to close, she rolled onto her back. Across from the bed the cover for her novel still hung on the mirror. "I am Jane Fairfax," she said. "I am Jane Fairfax."

Repeating this new mantra, she fell asleep.

When she awoke, the room was filled with dirty gray light. A quick glance out the window showed that it was snowing again. Jane was tempted to pull the covers over her head and sleep some more, but the numbers on the clock beside the bed showed that she was due to meet Kelly for breakfast in an hour to go over the rest of his editing suggestions. She was supposed to have looked through them, but the manuscript still sat untouched on the coffee table by the window.

She forced herself to get up and take a shower. Then, dressed in the fluffy white robe provided by the hotel, she raced through the manuscript, adding words here and there and occasionally muttering her disagreement with something Kelly had written. But mostly everything he'd done made sense, and she finished with just enough time left to get dressed and pack her suitcase for the trip home.

Kelly had arranged to meet her in the restaurant in her hotel, so she had only to go downstairs. Still, she was five minutes late, and found Kelly already seated at a table.

"I'm so sorry," she apologized as he stood and kissed her lightly on cheek. "I was up late going through the manuscript."

"I only just got here," he reassured her.

As she sat down and placed the manuscript on the table, Jane couldn't help noticing how put together Kelly looked. He wore a black suit with a white shirt and a blue striped tie. His hair was slicked back and he looked refreshed and impossibly handsome. *Meanwhile,* Jane thought, *I look and feel like the undead.*

"Did you sleep well?" Kelly asked as Jane accepted a cup of coffee from the waitress.

"Very well, thank you," said Jane.

"And is there anything in the manuscript you want to discuss?"

Jane shook her head as she poured cream into her coffee. "It all looks good," she said. "There were just a few little things. Nothing terribly important."

"I have to tell you, so far you're a dream author," Kelly told her. "I almost hope the book doesn't do well."

"Why?" Jane asked, startled by the statement.

"I'm kidding," Kelly said, noticing her reaction. "It's just that often when new authors have a bestseller they become, shall we say . . ." He waved his hands around as he searched for the right word.

"Self-important?" Jane suggested.

Kelly nodded. "Self-important," he agreed.

Jane raised her eyebrows and smiled. "I don't think you have to worry about that," she said.

She and Kelly went over the final edits on her manuscript. When they were done, Kelly tucked the pages into his briefcase.

"We should get you to Penn Station," he said. "Your train leaves in half an hour."

Jane went upstairs to retrieve her bag. Then Kelly flagged them a cab and they rode to the train station.

"Have a safe trip home," Kelly said, kissing Jane on the cheek again before she exited the cab in front of Penn Station. "I'll call you in a few days to discuss what happens next."

Jane waved goodbye and watched as the cab pulled away, her head filled with thoughts of Kelly, her book, and the new possibilities in her life. Had his lips lingered a bit longer than was strictly polite?

The train was not particularly crowded, and Jane had a row to herself. She settled into the window seat and opened the book she'd started on the journey down the day before. But she found herself unable to concentrate. She would have to tell people about her novel, of course. Lucy anyway. Perhaps Walter. Suddenly she thought of Walter. She saw his face, and imagined how excited he would be for her when she told him she was going to be published.

His congratulations would be genuine, not the insincere words of someone jealous of her success. Walter was incapable of insincerity.

Despite knowing it was foolish, Jane couldn't help comparing Walter to Kelly. They were so different. Where Kelly moved in a fast-paced world, Walter was content with small-town life. Where Kelly was worldly, Walter was simple. Yet both were kind men. Most important, Jane reminded herself, Walter had already expressed his feelings for her. Kelly was just her editor.

And yet she couldn't help wondering if Kelly might not become more. They were—at least as far as Kelly knew—roughly the same age. They shared many interests. And they would be working closely together. Wasn't it possible that romance could blossom?

Jane felt guilty for even thinking such a thing. But there it was. She couldn't deny that she found Kelly attractive. And part of her believed that he might accept the inevitable truth about her condition more easily than Walter would. *I imagine there are far more unbelievable things in New York than vampires,* she thought.

As the train left the station and began its steady crawl north, Jane continued to wrestle with the question of her romantic life like a dog worrying a bone. After two hundred years of romantic deprivation, it was time for a change.

"I won't do anything rash," she assured herself. "I'll just take things as they come."

It was a sensible decision, and she was pleased to have come to it. After all, she had made no promises to Walter. Until she did, she was free to do anything she liked. And at the moment she wasn't doing anything but speculating. If she found that Kelly was interested, then she would do the right thing and make a decision between them.

Having settled the matter, she returned to her book. She was trying, and failing, to make her way through Barbara Pym's *The Sweet Dove Died. She isn't a bit like me,* Jane thought as she finished a page. *I can't imagine why anyone thinks we're similar. She's all tea and garden parties and ladies' hats.*

Chapter 10

She had not expected him to be in attendance at the party. Yet when she entered the drawing room she saw him seated on a sofa in intimate proximity to Barbara Wexley. He whispered into her ear. The girl giggled and tapped him lightly on the knee, to which Jonathan reacted with feigned hurt, turning his gaze toward the doorway. Seeing Constance standing there, he smiled mockingly, and she felt her heart burn with hatred for him.

—Jane Austen, *Constance*, manuscript page 127

"SOMETHING'S DIFFERENT," JANE SAID, LOOKING AROUND THE store. "You moved something."

Lucy gave Jane a big hug. "Welcome home," she said.

"I was only gone for forty-eight hours," Jane said. "It wasn't as if I went off to war."

Lucy, who went to hang up her coat in the office, called back, "It's okay to say you missed me, you know." She emerged from the office and came to the front desk. "So, did you bring me a present?"

"As a matter of fact, I did," Jane said. She reached into her bag and brought out the little gift she'd picked up for Lucy at one of the numerous tourist traps surrounding Times Square. It was a snow globe containing a replica of the Empire State Building. A plastic King Kong was climbing up it, one arm outstretched as he roared in fury. Lucy shook the globe and the tiny pieces of plastic snow swirled around.

"It's beautiful," Lucy told Jane. "Thank you. I didn't have New York in my collection. Now I'm missing just South Dakota, Arkansas, and Maine. Oh, and I broke Florida, so I need to replace that one."

Jane's eyes suddenly locked onto an area to the left of the checkout counter. "What on earth is that?" she demanded, pointing to a spinning rack containing what looked like dozens of tiny bodies.

"Aren't they great?" Lucy said, smiling mischievously. "They're finger puppets of famous authors. I ordered them ages ago, but they came yesterday."

Jane walked over and picked up one of the tiny puppets. Its gray hair was done up in a bun, and the expression on its face was solemn.

"Virginia Woolf," Lucy said. She picked up another puppet and placed it on her finger. This one had wild black hair. "Dylan Thomas. We've got practically everybody. Well, everybody who's dead. I'm guessing they didn't want to pay anybody, so there's no J. K. Rowling or John Grisham. But we've got James Baldwin, Louisa May Alcott, Samuel Pepys, Poe. Of course there's Shakespeare, and this is the one I think will be our bestseller." She held up a puppet with brown hair and a white dress gathered at the chest.

"Jane Austen," Jane said, looking at her puppet self.

"I ordered fifty of her," said Lucy. "We've already sold five."

"Lovely," Jane said, trying to sound chipper. "I don't suppose we sold any actual *books* yesterday?"

"It was pretty good for January," Lucy answered. "But let's not talk work. Tell me about your trip. Was it fun seeing your friend?"

"It was," Jane said. She badly wanted to tell Lucy the real reason for her New York visit, but she didn't want to reveal her news too soon. Despite Kelly's enthusiasm for her book, part of her still feared that something might go wrong. "We saw *Gypsy*."

Lucy sighed. "I'd love to see that," she said. "I'd enjoy seeing anything in New York."

"Maybe we'll take a trip this spring," Jane said, surprising herself. "Just you and me."

"Really?" Lucy said, looking almost shocked. "I'd like that."

Jane took out the receipts for the previous day and started looking through them. She trusted Lucy completely, but she needed something to distract her. Now that she was once more surrounded by books, all she could think about was her own novel. She imagined piles of it sitting on one of the display tables. She pictured customers picking it up and recognizing her name. She thought about ringing up copies and putting them in bags. She was so preoccupied by her daydreams that she only barely noticed the sound of the bell as someone entered the shop. A few minutes later someone approached the counter and set a book down. Jane glanced at it and saw that it was a copy of *Emma.* Instantly the joy she'd felt while thinking about her new book disappeared as she was reminded of how long she'd been forced to keep her secret.

"It's my favorite of all your books," said a man's voice.

"It's a very good one," Jane said as she rang up the purchase.

Only as the scanner read the bar code and beeped its acceptance did she realize what the customer had said.

Her eyes jerked up. The man standing before her was striking, with pale skin and a face that could only be described as beautiful. His dark eyes were matched by the darkness of his hair, which was cut slightly long, so a lock of it curled over one eye. Jane's heart seemed to have stopped, and she found it difficult to breathe.

"You," she whispered.

The man smiled, and his eyes sparkled. "Me," he said.

Jane fumbled with the book in her hands and it fell to the floor. She bent to pick it up, hoping that when she stood up the man would be gone. But he wasn't. If anything, his smile had grown more intense.

"I see you've met." Walter's voice drew Jane back to the moment. He was standing beside the man.

"You know him?" Jane asked, looking at Walter.

"Brian is my client," Walter answered.

"Brian?" Jane repeated.

"Brian George," the man said.

"You know how I've been restoring the old Roberts place?" Walter said.

Jane nodded. Walter had done a wonderful job of bringing the neglected Victorian back to its former glory. He'd told Jane that he'd bought it for practically nothing and was going to sell it as soon as he was done with the work.

"Brian is the one who hired me to do the work," Walter said.

"I asked Mr. Fletcher to keep my purchase of the house a bit of a secret," said Brian.

Jane very much wanted to ask why Brian George wished to

keep his move to Brakeston a secret, but fortunately for her, Walter began speaking again.

"Brian is a writer," he said.

Jane looked at the man. "Is he?" she said.

"Well, I *try*," said Brian.

"Oh, yes," Jane said. "Now I remember. You wrote that book about the . . . um . . . those . . ."

Walter, watching her search for the answer, became clearly uncomfortable. Jane knew he was embarrassed for his client, although Brian himself seemed not the least bit ruffled.

Jane sighed. "I'm sorry. With eighteen billion books around here, I can't possibly remember them all," she said, ignoring the grin she could see forming on Brian's face.

"Brian is the author of *Winter Comes Slowly*," Walter said quickly.

"*Winter Comes Slowly*?" said Lucy, poking her head up from behind the shelves in the gardening section. "I love that book." She stepped into the aisle and walked to the counter.

"And who might this lovely young lady be?" Brian asked.

"This is Lucy," said Jane. "The manager of the shop."

Lucy turned her head toward Jane. "Manager?" she said. "When did—"

"Surprise!" Jane said, hoping to distract her. "I was going to tell you this afternoon."

"Wow," said Lucy. Then she looked back to Brian. "Wow," she said again, smiling, and Jane knew her tactic had failed. "I really loved your book. Your poetry is so beautiful. Spare and haunting."

Brian touched his hand to his chest. "I'm humbled," he said. "Thank you for saying that."

"Lucy," Jane said sharply.

Lucy turned her head, but slowly, as if she couldn't bring herself to stop looking at Brian.

"Hmm?" she said.

"I noticed that the display of new titles is a little untidy," said Jane. "Would you mind straightening it up?"

"Sure," Lucy replied.

"It was a pleasure meeting you," Brian said to her.

Lucy smiled. "For me too," she said.

Jane watched as Lucy walked away, turning her head and gazing with what appeared to be longing at Brian's back. Jane resisted the urge to yell at her to snap out of it.

"I came by yesterday looking for you," Walter said, interrupting her thoughts. "Lucy said you were in New York."

"Yes," Jane croaked, her throat suddenly dry. "I, um, went to meet an old friend."

"I love New York," Brian said. "It has such wonderful energy."

"Can't say I care much for it myself," said Walter. "Too loud. Too many people." Jane wondered if she detected a note of irritation in his voice, as if he was annoyed with her for going away without telling him.

Brian laughed gently. "There's nothing wrong with that," he said. Then he looked at Jane. "How about you, Jane? Are you a small-town girl?"

He was teasing her, and she knew it. *How dare you,* she thought. But she forced herself to smile and say, "I find that both have something to offer, if you know where to look."

She glanced at Walter as she spoke, and noted with some satisfaction that Brian's eyes had followed her gaze. "I see," he said. "I suppose that's true."

"Well then," said Walter, seemingly unaware of the tension in the air. "Brian's going to come to the Crandalls' house with me today," he told Jane.

"I'm thinking of working on a novel," Brian explained. "I'm considering adding a builder to my story, and I thought it would be good to have some firsthand experience with the trade before I attempt to write about it."

What are you up to? Jane wondered. *What possible reason could you have for coming here?* Whatever it was, she knew that nothing good could come of it.

"Jane," said Walter, "I'll give you a call later. Maybe we can all have dinner tonight at my place."

"Maybe," Jane said. "That might be nice."

Walter nodded. "Great," he said. "Now we'll get out of your hair."

Brian looked at Jane. "Until tonight, then," he said, bowing his head slightly. "I look forward to it."

Jane said nothing in reply. She watched as Walter and Brian left the store. Only when they were out of sight did she bring a hand to her forehead. *No,* she thought. *No, no, no, no, no.*

A moment later, Lucy had joined her at the counter. "I can't believe I just met Brian George!" she exclaimed. "I love his accent. It's British, right?"

"Scottish, actually," Jane corrected.

"Have you got a headache?" asked Lucy.

Jane took her hand away from her head. "Just a slight one," she said. "I'll be all right in a moment."

"I wonder what it would be like to date a writer," Lucy said thoughtfully.

"Hideous," said Jane. "It would be hideous. Especially that one."

Lucy turned to her. "What's wrong with him?" she asked. "And how do you know?"

"He's a poet," said Jane quickly. "Poets make dreadful partners. They're always mooning around and asking you what rhymes with what. It's so tedious."

"Okay," Lucy said slowly. "I'll keep that in mind. But he's still a hottie."

Jane wanted to say more, but she didn't dare. The last thing she wanted was Lucy getting near the man who called himself Brian George, but there was no way she could tell the young woman why without having to tell her many other things she wished to keep to herself. Most of all, she didn't want to sound like a bitter older woman.

Which of course is exactly what you are, she told herself.

Chapter 11

*She and Charles were returning from the picnic by
the river. She was wearing the crown he'd woven for
her out of daisies, and she carried her shoes in her
hand. Despite her hat the sun had pinked her
cheeks, but Charles, accustomed to hours spent in
the gardens, had simply grown even more brown.
He reached out and took her hand, and for a
moment she was perfectly happy. Then a shadow
fell across the path, and she looked up to see
Jonathan standing in their way.*

—Jane Austen, *Constance*, manuscript page 143

JANE PAUSED ON WALTER'S FRONT PORCH. *JUST RELAX*, SHE TOLD
herself. *There's no reason to worry.*

But there *was* reason to worry, and no amount of wishing it
away would calm her anxiety. She would simply have to get
through the evening as best she could.

Walter answered the door moments after she'd rung the bell.
He was wiping his hands on a dish towel, and an apron was tied

around his waist. It was spattered with what appeared to be some kind of sauce.

"Come in," Walter said, smiling and waving her inside. He appeared to be in a very good mood.

"Hello again." Brian George stood in the living room, a glass of wine in his hand. A second glass, nearly empty, stood on the table beside the couch.

"Hello," Jane said coolly as Walter helped her off with her coat and went to hang it in the hall closet.

"I'm so pleased you could join us," Brian said, as if he and not Walter were the host.

"Yes," said Jane vaguely, avoiding Brian's gaze. "Well."

Walter, oblivious to what was passing between them, returned with a glass and a bottle of wine. "Brian brought the most wonderful wine," he said as he poured a glass for Jane. "I've already had two glasses."

That explains the good mood, Jane thought as she accepted the glass. She hesitated a moment before taking a sip. Walter was right; it was delicious.

"Domaine de la Romanée-Conti," she said.

Brian nodded. "I brought a few bottles with me," he replied. "It's my favorite."

Yes, Jane thought, *I remember.* It was also one of the most coveted wines in the world, far too expensive for a poet to afford. She wondered if Walter realized what he was drinking.

"Have a seat," Walter suggested.

Jane waited until Brian took a seat on the couch, then seated herself in one of the armchairs on the side of the coffee table opposite him. Walter took the other chair.

"Tell me, Jane, how long have you lived in Brakeston?" Brian inquired.

"Nearly ten years," Jane said, her voice clipped.

"Ten years," Brian repeated. "Long enough to be considered a local, I think."

Walter chuckled. "Oh, she's definitely one of us," he said. "It's like she's lived here forever."

"So it seems," said Brian. He looked once more at Jane. "You're from the UK, though, if I've identified your accent correctly. Have you been long in the colonies?"

"Since I was a child," Jane answered.

A sly smile crossed Brian's face. "Then you don't miss your homeland?" he said.

Jane shook her head. "I was quite young when I moved here," she told him. "I don't remember very much about it."

"Have you been to the States before?" Walter asked Brian. He was pouring himself more wine. He offered the bottle to Brian, who accepted.

"No," said Brian. "This is my first time here. My family has lived in England for a very long time." He looked at Jane. "Have you any family left in England?"

"No," Jane said, meeting his gaze. "They're all dead, I'm afraid."

Brian took a sip of wine. "I'm sorry to hear that," he said.

A buzzer sounded in another room, and Walter jumped up. "That will be dinner," he said. "Everybody to the table!"

As he hurried to the kitchen, Jane and Brian stood. For a moment they faced each other. "What are you doing here?" Jane hissed.

"I thought Walter mentioned that," said Brian. "I've come to soak up the local flavor."

Jane gave a short, sharp laugh. "How fortunate for us," she said. "Are you certain that's all?"

Brian reached out a hand and stroked her cheek. Jane pulled away. "I had hoped to renew an old acquaintance," he said.

"Dinner's on!" Walter called from the dining room.

Jane turned and walked away, the sting of Brian's touch still burning on her cheek. In the dining room, Walter was placing a dish of peas on the table, which already held a roast on a platter, a bowl of mashed potatoes, and the usual assortment of cutlery and glassware.

"You sit here," Walter said to Jane, indicating a place on the left. "And Brian, you sit here," he continued, pointing to the head of the table.

They all sat, and Walter picked up the platter of beef. "I hope you like it rare," he said as he passed it to Brian. "I can't stand overcooked meat."

"This looks perfect," said Brian as he helped himself to several pieces before passing the dish to Jane. "I do like my beef on the bloody side."

Jane took a small piece of roast, then accepted the peas from Walter. As she in turn passed them to Brian, their fingers touched. The shock that passed between them startled her, and she dropped the bowl. Before it hit the table, Brian's hand shot out and caught it. Jane snatched her hand back and held it in her lap, rubbing it with her other one. Her skin still tingled.

"Jane, Brian is another Austen fan," Walter said. "I told him he should talk to you."

"Indeed," Brian remarked. "Tell me, Jane, what is your opinion of the Austen craze that seems to have possessed your country?" He paused. "My apologies. I mean, of course, this country."

Jane stabbed at the piece of meat on her plate. The juice from the beef was pink with blood, and she felt her mouth water. Before answering Brian, she took a bite and chewed it thoroughly, savoring the taste.

"I think the books appeal to readers of all times," she answered.

Brian nodded. "Women do like the romances," he said.

Jane flushed. "They're more than just romances," she said. "And their appeal is hardly limited to women."

Brian waved his fork in the air. "Of course," he said. "I myself thoroughly enjoy her work. But surely you agree that her subject matter is rather . . . lightweight, if you will." Instead of waiting for Jane to reply, he continued. "The critic G. H. Lewes once told Charlotte Brontë that she should study Austen's work in order to correct her own shortcomings as an author. Do you know what her response was?"

Jane snorted. "She said that Austen's work was like, and I quote, an 'accurate daguerreotyped portrait of a common-place face; a carefully-fenced, highly cultivated garden, with neat borders and delicate flowers—but no glance of a bright vivid physiognomy—no open country—no fresh air—no blue hill—no bonny beck,' " she said tartly.

"I see you've read the correspondence," Brian commented. "And that you disagree."

"I certainly do," said Jane. "What nonsense. Just because Austen's heroines aren't flinging themselves all over the moors and mooning over disfigured men and being tormented by madwomen and burning up in fires and who knows what other foolishness . . ." Her voice trailed off. She took up her wineglass and drank deeply. *Charlotte Brontë*, she thought. *Of all people.*

To her annoyance she saw that Walter and Brian were laughing. "What?" she said.

"You just sounded so irate," said Walter. "Almost as if Austen were a dear friend. Which I suppose she is, really."

Jane shifted uncomfortably in her seat. "I suppose *Jane Eyre* is a good novel," she said. "In its way. Personally, I find it devoid of warmth and overripe with melodrama."

"Perhaps it's a good thing Austen died before Miss Brontë passed judgment on her," Brian suggested. "The chill that would surely have pervaded the drawing room had they ever met would have been formidable."

"I'd very much like to see that," said Walter. Looking at Jane, he added, "Or perhaps we could get you to debate that Brontë scholar. What's her name?" He tapped his fingers on the table. "Violet Grey. She's not an Austen fan either."

"I've met Grey," Brian said. "And I agree, that would be interesting. Very interesting."

Jane refused to encourage further commentary on the subject. Instead, she inspected the peas on her plate with great curiosity. "Is this mint in the peas?" she asked Walter.

He nodded. "Do you like it?"

"Yes," said Jane. "How ever did you think of it?"

"Do you write?" interrupted Brian.

Jane looked at him. "I?" she said innocently.

Brian smiled. "You seem to have such passion for novels," he answered. "I thought perhaps you yourself might be a writer."

"When I was younger I wrote a bit," Jane said. "Nothing serious. Now I'm content to sell books."

"I should very much like to see the kind of thing you wrote," said Brian. "Perhaps I can convince you to show it to me."

"Don't bother," Walter told him. "I've been asking her for years. She won't do it."

"I'm afraid there isn't anything to read," said Jane. "It all was thrown away."

Brian frowned. "I'm disappointed to hear it," he said.

Jane said nothing, focusing on her plate and eating a few bites. Walter turned the conversation to something else, but Jane blocked it out. All she wanted was to finish dinner and go home. When a few minutes later she heard Walter speak her name, she looked up.

"Would you like coffee with your cake?" he asked.

Jane started to decline, thinking perhaps she could excuse herself early. But she felt that would be allowing Brian to win the little battle he was waging with her. Already he had landed several blows, and she was determined not to let him have the better of her.

"That would be very nice," she said. "Let me help."

She stood up before Walter could decline her offer, picking up her plate and the platter of beef and carrying them to the kitchen. Walter followed and began making coffee as Jane returned to the dining room for the rest of the dishes.

"He has no idea, does he?" Brian said as Jane picked up the bowl of peas.

"Of course not," said Jane.

"Do you love him?"

Jane, clutching the bowl, glared at Brian. "What business is that of yours?"

Brian laughed lightly, leaning back in his chair. "You haven't changed at all," he told her. "The same old Jane."

"You're one to talk," she replied. "I don't know what—"

"Here's the coffee," Walter announced, interrupting the moment. "And I'll be right back with the cake."

Jane started to follow him back to the kitchen, but Brian grabbed her arm. "Meet me tomorrow," he said.

"Why would I do that?" asked Jane, snorting.

"Because you want to," Brian said. "I can tell."

Jane hesitated.

"Tomorrow," said Brian. "You choose the place."

Jane sighed. "The bookstore," she said. "Nine o'clock, after closing."

Brian grinned. "I look forward to it," he said.

Dessert seemed to pass with agonizing slowness. Jane picked at the cake; despite its being chocolate, she couldn't bring herself to eat more than a few bites of it. She contributed little to the conversation, which had turned to American politics. When finally Brian announced that it was time for him to leave, she breathed a sigh of relief.

"Good night," Brian said to Walter after he'd collected his coat. "I'll see you tomorrow, I suspect." Then he took Jane's hand. "And I hope to see you again as well."

When he had gone, Jane offered to help Walter clean up. They were in the kitchen, Walter washing and Jane drying each dish as he handed it to her, when Walter said, "You've met him before, haven't you?"

Jane finished drying the plate in her hand. She was unsure how best to answer Walter's question. She decided to be honest. "Yes," she said. "I have."

"Why didn't you say anything?"

Jane took the bowl Walter held out. "I don't know, really," she said. "At first I was shocked to see him. Then . . . well, it's difficult to explain."

"He didn't say anything either," Walter noted.

Jane nodded. "I think he was just as surprised to see me," she said.

"Were the two of you lovers?" Walter asked unexpectedly.

"No," Jane said instantly. "Really, we only met briefly."

Walter finished rinsing the last dish. "I see," he said.

Jane could tell that he didn't quite believe her. And she didn't blame him. She was not telling him everything. Not nearly. But for the moment it was all she was willing to share.

"I should be going," she said. "Thank you for a lovely dinner."

"Thank you for coming," Walter said. He paused a moment, then leaned in and kissed her.

To her surprise, she kissed him back. *When did I decide to do that?* she asked herself. But apparently she had.

Walter pulled back. "I'll get your coat," he told her.

At the door he kissed her again. Then she was outside, walking home through the crisp, cold night. When she reached her house, she took her key from her pocket and began to insert it into the lock. But as she grasped the knob the door swung inward. She remembered having locked it as she left.

Stepping inside, she looked around. Everything seemed to be in place. If she'd been burgled, it had been by very neat thieves. Then she sensed someone behind her. The next moment a pair of warm lips grazed her neck just below her ear.

"You didn't really think I could wait until tomorrow, did you?" Brian whispered.

Chapter 12

"You knew what you wanted when you came here,"
Jonathan said. "We both knew what you wanted.
Yet now you hate me for giving it to you? That
strikes me as most ungrateful."

—Jane Austen, *Constance*, manuscript page 159

JANE SHOVED BRIAN AWAY, BUT HE WAS TOO STRONG FOR HER. HIS arms circled around her and he continued to kiss her neck. "It was all I could do not to take you there in his house," he said. "You're as lovely now as you were when we first met."

"That's because I'm *dead*," Jane said. She drove her elbow into his stomach. He let out a surprised grunt and his grip on her loosened. She took the opportunity to escape, whirling around to face him. "Get out," she ordered.

Brian, bent over as he tried to catch his breath, looked up and smiled seductively. "I don't think so," he replied.

Jane started to argue, but she knew better. He was stubborn. She could yell at him all she liked, but she knew he wouldn't leave. She briefly considered threatening him with calling the police, but that would achieve nothing.

"Oh, how I despise you," she said icily.

"You don't really," Brian said as Jane walked into the living room and turned on a light. "As I recall, you were once very fond of me."

"Not least because you led me to believe that you were fond of me as well," said Jane.

Brian laughed. "But I *was* fond of you, my dear. I still am. If I wasn't, why would I have come here?"

"Funny," said Jane. "That's exactly what I've been wondering ever since you appeared in my bookshop."

Brian sat down in one of the living room chairs. "I suppose it *has* been a long time," he admitted. "You probably thought I was dead. Well, more dead. Deader."

Jane suppressed a smile as she seated herself on the sofa. "The thought did cross my mind," she told him. "As you yourself said, 'I am not sure that long life is desirable for one of my temper and constitutional depression of spirits.' "

"I did say that, didn't I?" Brian laughed.

Jane glowered. "So, how did you find me?"

"Ah," said Brian, holding up one slender finger. "I'd like to say that it was difficult, but you must admit that you haven't exactly gone to great lengths to hide yourself. Elizabeth Jane Fairfax indeed."

Jane picked at the cloth of the couch. "Yes, well, I got rather tired of it all after a century or two, didn't I? Besides, you haven't exactly strayed too far from the path yourself in that regard, Lord *Byron*." She said his name with all the venom she could muster.

Byron laughed. "So we've both tired of being other people," he said.

Jane couldn't argue that point. She hesitated before asking, "Why now?"

Byron leaned back in the chair and sighed deeply. "Oh, I don't know," he said. "I suppose I've been feeling a bit nostalgic of late. Missing the good old days and all that."

"I don't remember there being a lot of good involved," said Jane. "At least not as far as you're concerned."

"Come now," Byron said. "Our time together wasn't all bad, was it?"

"No," Jane admitted. "Dinner the first night was quite nice, as I recall. It was everything after."

"Come now, Jane," said Byron. "Look what I did for you. Despite your age you were still a child. Why, you were practically *imprisoned* in that vicarage. I saved you from all that."

"Saved me?" Jane exclaimed. "I was perfectly happy in my little world."

Byron waved away her protest. "If you were happy, then why did you come to me?"

Jane started to speak, but found she couldn't. He had hit upon the weak spot in her argument. Sensing this, Byron smiled at her, his eyes bright. "You see?" he said. "You came because you wanted *experience.* You were determined to offer up your virginity to me."

"I came at your invitation!" Jane objected.

"Yes, yes," Byron agreed. "But it was you who wrote to me first. I simply did what I could tell you wanted. You didn't have to come. In fact, I believe you took great pains to make the journey."

Jane stood up. "You're impossible," she said. She turned away from him so he wouldn't see the frustration in her face.

He was beside her in a moment. "I'm sorry," he said gently.

"You're not," said Jane. "You never were."

Byron put his hands on her shoulders. She allowed them to stay there. "I am now," he said. "I've changed over time. I know now that what I did to you was wrong."

"It's a bit late for that realization," said Jane.

Byron kissed her hair. "I never meant to hurt you," he said. "I was careless."

"Careless," Jane repeated, shaking her head. "Is that what you call it?"

"What other word is there for it?"

Jane turned, facing him. She looked into his eyes. "Evil," she said. "I would call it evil."

She was surprised to see that Byron was genuinely hurt. He stepped back, his face twisted in confusion. She almost reached out to him, but forced her hands to stay at her sides.

"Do you really hate me so much?" Byron asked. His voice shook with emotion, and his eyes betrayed the sadness in his heart.

A long silence passed during which Jane wrestled with her emotions. *Don't let him in,* she warned herself. *Not even a little.* She knew she should listen. She should end things once and for all. But another part of her wept to see Byron in despair. *He says he's changed,* she argued.

"No," she said finally. "I don't hate you. Not anymore. Because of you I've seen and done wonderful things. Have I hated you sometimes in the past? I would be lying if I said I haven't. But what good does it do?"

Byron dropped to his knees before her and grasped her hands, laying his cheek on them. "I knew you couldn't," he said. "Jane, you don't know how often I've longed for you. But I couldn't face you, knowing how you must feel about me. About what I did."

Jane closed her eyes. She was remembering too much. Things she had buried deep within her mind were rising to the surface. Memories. Images. Feelings. None of them welcome.

"Stand up," she told Byron, pulling him to his feet. She continued to hold his hands as they faced each other. "I don't hate you," she said. "But I don't love you either."

Byron brought one of her hands to his mouth and kissed it. "No," he said. "Not now you don't. But perhaps you will again."

Before Jane could contradict him he kissed her. His mouth closed over hers, his lips full and warm. Jane struggled only a moment before giving in. She kissed him back, hating herself but unable to resist. His arms slipped around her, pulling her close so that their bodies were pressed tightly together. Almost immediately Jane was overcome with a tingling that flowed over her skin, causing her to shudder. She'd forgotten what it was like to kiss one of her own kind.

The sensation grew more intense the longer they kissed. Jane felt her thoughts begin to join with Byron's. She knew that soon she would lose all control as her connection with him intensified. She had only moments left.

Summoning what was left of her will, she pulled away from him. The separation was painful, and she gasped. It was as if she'd been torn away from a dream and plunged into reality. She was suddenly intensely cold, and put her arms around herself in what she already knew was a futile attempt at getting warm.

"I can't," she whispered as Byron reached for her.

"You can," he said. His voice was seductive, and for a moment she felt herself slipping back into the dream state.

"No," she said, shaking her head vigorously. "Please, just go."

She was surprised when Byron turned and walked to the door. He opened it and turned back to look at her. "Who listens once will listen twice," he said softly. "Her heart, be sure, is not of ice, and one refusal no rebuff." Then he was gone, and Jane was alone in her living room.

"Damn you," she said to the door.

She turned the lights off and went upstairs. In her bedroom Tom was curled up on her pillow. He opened one eye and gave her a brief look before returning to sleep. Jane sat on the bed and began to pet him, and he purred softly.

She still felt the effects of Byron's kiss. She knew it would last for some time, probably until she fed again. She resented the fact that she would have to feed earlier than usual. But she could go another day or so before the need became too great. Had she remained in his arms much longer the need would have been nearly impossible to resist.

As it was, her thoughts were all jumbled together. And some were Byron's. She saw faces she'd never seen, smelled scents foreign to her, felt longing and fear and lust that were not her own. It was as if she'd been drugged.

She undressed and lay down, slipping beneath the sheets and trying to sleep. But her body burned. She was unbearably hot. Kicking the quilt and sheets away, she tried to cool her overheated skin. Sweat beaded her forehead and dampened her nightgown. Tearing at the garment with trembling fingers, she drew it over her head and dropped it to the floor. The air around her was thick, and her breathing became labored.

Invisible hands caressed her, running over her arms and down her sides, cupping her exposed breasts. Lips teased at her neck, her fingertips, her nipples. To whom did they belong? There were two mouths, three, a dozen. She searched the darkness for faces but saw nothing.

These are his memories, Jane thought. She tried to banish them, to regain control over her mind, but it was like fighting off the effects of too much wine. Instead she became more confused. The bed seemed filled with bodies, with arms and legs intertwining. Hot breath licked at her while she tried to turn her head away.

"No!" she cried.

Cold descended. She was alone, standing on the shore of a wide, dark lake. Above her the sky was filled with glittering diamonds and the moon, impossibly full, was reflected in the water at her feet. She was naked. Then arms were around her and she felt the slow beat of another's heart against her back.

"It's time for your rebirth," Byron's voice said in her ear. "Come with me."

He took her hand and stepped into the water. His body, white in the moonlight, was like marble. His eyes burned like the stars. Jane looked into them as she allowed him to lead her into the lake. The water rose around her. Then Byron was lifting her, and she floated on the water, looking up into the eyes of the heavens.

Byron too was floating, his body beneath Jane's and her head resting on his chest. He held her in his arms like a child as he kicked his legs, pushing them into deeper water. As he swam he hummed a lullaby, the words of which Jane heard in her mind but which flitted away as soon as she tried to capture them.

They seemed to swim for hours, or maybe days. Then they came to a stop and floated on the still surface of the lake. Byron took Jane's wrists in his hands and crossed them over her chest, laying his arms atop hers.

"I feel as if I'm dreaming," Jane murmured.

Byron released her, his arms moving to her shoulders. He caressed her gently. "The great art of life is sensation," he said. "To feel that we exist, even in pain." His hands gripped her more tightly. "I'm sorry," he whispered, and Jane was pushed beneath the water.

She struggled for breath. Through the water she could see the stars. They broke apart, swarming like bees, as she thrashed around. Her ears rang with the sounds of her muffled screams. But Byron's hands, like iron weights, held her down.

Water poured into her mouth, filling her throat. She gasped and found no air. Her eyes grew cloudy, and overhead the stars winked out one by one, until all was black.

She woke up choking. She was in Byron's bedroom, cradled in his arms. He was stroking her hair and once again humming the tuneless lullaby. Jane turned and spat onto the floor, clearing her mouth.

"It's all right," Byron said. "It's all right now."

Outside, the storm was still raging. The stars were gone, and the moon was black. Although still naked, Jane was dry, as if she'd never been in the lake, never floated beneath the sky, never been pushed beneath the water.

"What did you do?" Jane asked. She felt her heart beating, but something was different. She was changed somehow.

"You've been reborn," said Byron. "I took your life, then gave it back to you." He showed her his wrist. Blood flowed from a fresh wound. Jane realized with horror that the liquid in her mouth was not water. She ran her tongue over her teeth and found them thick with the taste of meat and iron.

"No," she said, trying to push herself away from Byron. "Let me go!"

Byron pulled her back, holding her tightly against his chest. "It's too late," he said. "It's done."

"You drowned me!" Jane cried, beating at him with her fists.

"A dream," said Byron. "Of your rebirth. We all experience it differently. But you have never left this bed."

"What have you done?" Jane sobbed. "What have you done to me?"

The alarm woke her up. Tom was sitting beside her, staring down at her expectantly. He meowed once.

Jane sat up. Already the nightmare was fading. But she remembered enough of it. It hadn't come to her in a very long time. Now, she feared, it would return again and again. Byron's kiss had given new life to it.

"Damn him," she said to Tom. "Damn him for coming back."

Chapter 13

*To be a writer, she thought, must be the most
wonderful thing in the world, if for no other reason
than that one's characters would have to do exactly
as they were told. Unlike flesh-and-blood men, they
were not likely to behave in contrary ways, forever
leaving one perplexed and unsettled, never
knowing quite what they were thinking.*

—Jane Austen, *Constance*, manuscript page 167

"I'VE GOT GOOD NEWS."

It took a moment for Jane to recognize Kelly's voice. "Should I sit down?" she asked.

"You'll just jump back up again. We got a blurb from Margot Aldridge."

Jane couldn't suppress a squeal of joy. "*The Beauty of Lies* Margot Aldridge?" she said.

"Is there another one?" asked Kelly.

Jane laughed. "I certainly hope not," she said.

"She doesn't blurb *anything*," Kelly said. "But I know her editor, and I took a chance. Jennifer passed the manuscript on to Margot and she absolutely loved it. Do you want to hear it?"

"I don't know," said Jane. "Do I?"

Kelly ignored her remark and began to read. " '*Constance* is the rare novel that so deftly explores the lives of its characters that we forget they exist only on the page. Jane Fairfax's debut is absolutely magical.' "

Jane couldn't speak. "Are you there?" Kelly asked after twenty seconds of silence.

"Read it again," Jane said finally.

Kelly did. "And that's not all," he told Jane. "I think we'll be getting quotes from Fisher McTavish and Anne Gardot."

Jane gripped the phone tightly. "Keep naming my favorite authors and I'm going to have a heart attack," she said. "I can't believe it."

"I told you it was a great book," said Kelly. "Everyone here is excited about it. I haven't seen them push a book through so quickly since we did the tell-all by that woman who had the affair with the president. Bound galleys are already going out to reviewers, and sales is making a big push to the chains and Amazon to make sure they promote the hell out of this as soon as possible."

"Now I am sitting down," Jane said. "I can't believe this. It's only been two weeks since I was there."

"And it's just beginning," Kelly said. "You should be hearing from Nick Trilling later today. He's your publicity guy. We need to put together an author bio to send to the press."

Suddenly Jane's excitement waned. She hadn't even thought about a bio. Getting the book published at all was the only thing that had concerned her. Having to promote herself was the furthest thing from her mind.

"I suppose I can come up with something," she said. "But I'm not terribly interesting, you know."

"Are you kidding?" said Kelly. "A bookstore owner who writes her first novel when she's fortysomething? You're a publicist's dream. Every woman in America will be able to relate to you, Jane."

I doubt that, Jane thought. "Perhaps," she replied to Kelly. "Anyway, I'm happy to speak with—what did you say his name is, Nick?"

"Nick Trilling," Kelly repeated. "I've got a meeting to get to, but I wanted to tell you what's happening."

"Thank you," said Jane. "I must say it's all a bit surreal."

"Think of it as a dream come true," Kelly said. "I'll talk to you soon, Jane."

Jane hung up. *A dream come true,* she thought. *That's not always a good thing.*

She thought back to her dinner with Walter and Byron and to what had happened afterward. That night she'd remembered everything vividly. The secret visit to his house on the shore of Lake Geneva. The loss of her innocence. The pain that followed. It had all come back to her. Her death and resurrection. Her declaration of love for Byron once he'd explained what she now was. His callous dismissal of her affections, and her shameful return to England.

The worst of the memories was of having to leave Cassie. Staging her own illness and subsequent death over the course of a year was difficult, but she had managed it with the help of a sympathetic physician recommended to her by another of her kind, several of whom she had met seemingly by accident, though she now suspected that Byron had told them about her. Leaving

Cassie had been almost unbearable. For months she had done nothing but weep and wish herself truly dead.

It was this loss for which she couldn't forgive Byron. For now all she wanted was to tell Cassie about her book. Her earlier work had all been published anonymously, her identity known only to a small circle of friends. Fame had come after her death. She knew Cassie would be thrilled for her and would be more excited even than Jane was that she would finally get to hold a book with her name on it in her hands.

She had managed to avoid Byron for several days, and he had not called upon her. She assumed he was busy with his work, and was relieved to be free of him, if only temporarily. She had forced herself to feed so that she could be rid of the residual fogginess caused by their encounter, driving to a town an hour away and, assuming the identity of a weary housewife, asking a pimple-faced bag boy at the Price Chopper to help her to the car with her bags filled with corn chips, salsa, and lite beer. She had eaten quickly and left him to sleep it off beside a Dumpster in the parking lot, his head resting on a box of day-old donuts. Now she felt more or less herself.

"Hey. Whatchya doing?"

Lucy's voice startled Jane, who spun around in her chair.

"Sorry," Lucy said. "I didn't mean to scare you. I just wanted to let you know that we're officially out of Mark Twain finger puppets. Should I order some more?"

Jane rolled her eyes. "I think not," she said. "Don't we still have half a dozen Tennysons to get rid of?"

Lucy leaned against the desk. "Yeah," she answered. "But the Austens are almost gone. Mr. Hunky bought one yesterday."

"Who?" Jane asked.

"The new guy," said Lucy. "Brian George."

"He was in yesterday?" Jane inquired.

Lucy nodded. "When you went to the bank. I think he has a crush on you," she added.

"What?" Jane said, a little too loudly. Had Lucy really noticed something between the two of them? The thought horrified her.

"He said the puppet looked just like you," Lucy explained. She squinted at Jane. "Now that you mention it, you do kind of look like her," she said.

"Rubbish," said Jane. "All middle-aged Englishwomen look alike. Anyway, no more puppets. It was a fun idea, but I think we should stick to books."

"I guess that puts the kibosh on the *Little Women* action figures," Lucy joked. "Pity. I was looking forward to the Beth doll with real scarlet fever action."

"Out," Jane said, pointing to the door.

Lucy cackled evilly and scurried out, leaving a laughing Jane behind. Lucy reminded her a bit of Cassandra, always looking for the fun in things. It was no surprise that Jane was so fond of the young woman.

She was about to get up when the phone rang. Thinking it might be Nick Trilling, she picked it up.

"Good morning," Walter said.

Jane felt a twinge of guilt as she said, "Good morning yourself." Although technically nothing had happened between her and Byron, she still felt as if she were doing Walter a disservice.

"I was wondering if you might be free for lunch," said Walter. "I haven't seen you in a few days."

Jane hesitated. She really didn't want to see either Walter or

Byron at the moment. But she knew she couldn't put it off much longer. "I'd like that," she said. "Why don't you come by around one? We can get something at the Soup Kitchen."

"Wonderful," Walter said. "It's a date."

No sooner had she hung up than the phone rang again. "One o'clock," she said, assuming it was Walter, who almost always had to call back because he couldn't remember what they'd decided. "The Soup Kitchen."

"How did you know I was calling to ask you to lunch?"

Byron's voice practically purred through the line. Hearing it, Jane felt her pulse quicken. "I-I-I thought you were someone else," she stammered.

"I could pretend to be," Byron suggested. "I've been many different men since you last knew me."

"I'm sure you have," said Jane. "And I can't have lunch with any of you. I have an appointment."

Byron sighed as if he was deeply disappointed. "I see I've lost your heart to another man," he said.

"You never had it to lose," Jane snapped.

"We'll see," said Byron. "Perhaps dinner, then?"

"No," Jane told him.

"I'm just going to keep asking until you agree," said Byron. "Besides, I'm sure we can find something much nicer to eat than what you had the other night."

Jane bristled. "You followed me," she said.

"You weren't the only one out hunting," said Byron. "But really, being a blonde doesn't suit you. And that fellow you chose. What was his name? Paul? I bet he tasted of acne cream and too much sugar. I'm surprised you could stomach him."

"I feed to survive," Jane hissed, afraid that if she spoke any louder Lucy would hear her. "Not for pleasure."

"That's a difference between us," said Byron. "I find that I quite like American food."

"I'm hanging up now," Jane told him. "Please don't call me here again."

"Wait," Byron said, stopping her. "You haven't said when we can meet again."

Jane shut her eyes tightly and gritted her teeth. He'd already said that he wouldn't cease bothering her until she agreed to see him, and she knew he was serious about it. She was going to have to do it. But she couldn't give in so easily.

"I'll have to let you know," she said.

She could hear Byron laughing softly. "Very well," he said. "But remember, I'm not a patient man."

"Goodbye," Jane said curtly, and hung up.

She couldn't believe what a roller coaster the morning had been. First there'd been the high of Kelly's fantastic news, and now she felt deflated by the tiny matter of her life being turned upside down by Byron's arrival. Standing in the middle was Walter. Good, sweet Walter, who only wanted her to love him.

Men, she thought. *The downfall of women since Adam blamed Eve for that stupid apple.* She wondered briefly if it was too late to become a lesbian. "I'm sure they have just as difficult a time of it," she said to the empty room. "Love is dangerous for everyone."

For the rest of the morning she stayed in the office, catching up on the endless paperwork, poring over publishers' catalogs to see what books she might want to order, and generally trying to avoid interacting with anyone. She was feeling pulled in too many directions to think properly, and her thoughts raced from one thing to another as she attempted to sort out her thoughts about her book, Walter, Byron, and pretty much her entire life. She had half a mind to just disappear, run off to another town and start all over again. *But that would be only a temporary solution,* she reminded herself. *Also, it would be rude.*

Precisely at one Walter knocked on the office door. "Ready?" he asked.

"I just have to get my coat," said Jane, doing just that.

Five minutes later they were seated at a table in the Soup Kitchen, looking at the menu.

"I'm thinking clam chowder," Walter said. "How about you?"

Jane picked something at random, not really caring what she put in her stomach. "Perhaps the chicken and wild rice," she said.

They placed their orders and settled into what Jane felt was an uncomfortable silence.

"I want to apologize for the other night," Walter said after a few minutes.

"Whatever for?" asked Jane.

"For asking you about Brian," Walter explained. "It was none of my business."

Jane stirred a packet of sugar into the iced tea she'd requested. "Oh, it's all right," she said. "I'm sorry I was so mysterious about the whole thing. I hope you haven't been fretting over it."

"Maybe a little," Walter admitted, playing with his fork. "After all, he's a popular guy."

"Do you think so?" said Jane.

Walter nodded. "All the women in town are smitten with him," he said. "You should see them following him around."

To her surprise, Jane felt a pang of jealousy. She hid it by stirring another packet of sugar into her tea, rattling the spoon vigorously against the sides. "You don't say," she remarked.

"Personally, I think it's the accent," said Walter. "Women seem to love men with British accents."

"It's Scottish, actually," said Jane automatically. "But they're practically the same," she added hastily.

"Anyway, he's quite a hit," Walter told her.

Their soups arrived at that moment, saving Jane from having to reply.

"There's something else I want to apologize for," said Walter. He didn't wait for Jane to respond before continuing. "I'm sorry for not telling you about Evelyn."

Jane looked at him, her spoon halfway to her mouth.

"Sherman told me that you and he talked about her at the New Year's party," Walter said. "I should have told you about her a long time ago."

Jane returned her spoon to the bowl. "Walter, you don't have to—"

"Yes, I do," he interrupted.

Jane concentrated on her soup. Secrets were one thing she was not ready to share with Walter. But she let him talk, not only because it prevented her from having to, but also because she genuinely wanted to hear what he had to say.

"For a long time I blamed myself for her death," he said. "I know that it wasn't my fault, but I couldn't help it. I asked myself over and over why I didn't go into the water with her, why I wasn't there. Why I couldn't save her. Eventually I got tired of asking myself those questions. And I didn't want to talk about it anymore. It's not that I forgot about Evelyn; it's more that in my mind that loss happened to someone else. Not to me, to some other man. Does that make any sense?"

Jane was trying hard not to cry. What Walter had just said was very much how she felt about the loss of her own family. She reached across the table and took Walter's hand. At that moment she felt as if they shared something that went beyond simple friendship, or even love.

"It does makes sense," she said as a tear slid down her cheek. "It makes all the sense in the world."

Chapter 14

Her cheeks burned with fury as she fled the room.
What Jonathan had proposed was unthinkable. She
could never accept such an arrangement, not even
to protect Charles from harm. She cursed her
vanity. She cursed herself, too, for allowing Charles
into her heart. By doing so, she had perhaps
doomed them both.

—Jane Austen, *Constance*, manuscript page 181

LUCY YAWNED AND SHOOK HER HEAD. "I DON'T KNOW WHAT'S wrong with me," she said to Jane the next morning. "I feel as if I haven't slept at all."

"It's all that coffee you drink," Jane teased. Lucy was on her third cup and it was only a little past ten.

"Maybe," said Lucy, taking a sip from the mug in her hand. "But I didn't have any last night." She set the mug down. "Plus, I had the strangest dreams."

"What about?" Jane asked as she arranged a display of new paperback releases. She was in a particularly pleasant mood. Not only was she feeling good about the talk she and Walter had had a few days before, Byron hadn't once bothered her. Although his presence in Brakeston was still unsettling, and she was certain that he would cause more worry for her before long, for the moment she was determined to enjoy the relative calm in her life.

"I was in a house," said Lucy. "By a lake. I don't know where it was or how I got there. There was a thunderstorm. Then this man appeared. He was wearing a mask, some kind of bird face. A crow, I think."

A violent shiver ran down Jane's spine as Lucy continued. "Anyway, he took me by the hand and led me into a bedroom." She looked at Jane and smiled shyly. "It's kind of embarrassing," she admitted. "It's not like I go around having dreams about men making love to me or anything."

Jane cleared her throat. "Go on," she said.

"Well," Lucy replied, "while we were in bed I reached up to take the mask from his face. I remember touching the feathers, and I remember pulling the mask away. I caught just a glimpse of his face before I woke up."

Jane's heart pounded in her chest. "Do you remember what he looked like?" she asked.

Lucy shook her head. "That's the funny thing," she said. "Sometimes I think I remember it perfectly clearly. I can even picture it in my head. But then it changes to something else and I forget what the first face looked like. It's as if I'm seeing him in a mirror but the mirror keeps reflecting other men who are passing by behind me."

"I see," Jane said. A terrible thought was forming in her mind, one she didn't want to entertain even for a moment.

Lucy scratched at her neck. Jane, noticing it, had to force down the panic rising in her.

"Stupid spider bites," said Lucy. "They itch like crazy. Hey, maybe that's what caused the dreams. Spider venom." She laughed. "Wouldn't that be freaky?"

Jane walked over to her, the display forgotten. "Let me see," she said, attempting to keep her voice steady. She pulled back Lucy's long hair and inspected her neck. As she'd feared, two tiny red marks lay a few inches below Lucy's left ear. They had healed quickly. No wonder Lucy was dismissing them as insect bites.

"I think you're right," said Jane. Her hand had begun to tremble, and she pulled it away quickly. "Don't scratch them or you'll make them worse."

Lucy responded with a yawn, which she covered with one hand. "I'm just so tired," she said.

"You should probably take the afternoon off," Jane suggested. "You might be having a little reaction to the spider bites. I have to run a couple of errands, but I should be back in an hour or so. I can handle things for the rest of the day."

Lucy rubbed her eyes. "Maybe," she said. "I might feel better after some more coffee."

No, you won't, Jane thought. The effects of a bite didn't wear off quite so quickly. Nor would the effects of the dream Byron had apparently planted into Lucy's thoughts. He'd done it on purpose, of course, knowing that Lucy would likely tell Jane about it. He also knew that she would do what she was about to do.

"I'll be back soon," she assured Lucy. "Remember—no scratching."

Jane left the store and got into her car. As she drove to Byron's house, she promised herself that she wouldn't let him toy with her. "None of his nonsense," she said.

She parked at the curb and walked to the front door of the

house. Only as she knocked did it occur to her that Byron might not be there. But then she heard him call, "A moment, please."

When he saw Jane standing on his doorstep he smiled broadly. "This is an unexpected surprise," he said. "Come in."

Jane entered. She started to speak, but stopped when she saw the interior of the house. It had been meticulously restored. She could hardly believe how beautiful it was. The walnut woodwork had all been stripped of years of paint and refinished, the stained-glass window at the top of the stairs had been repaired, and the lights and other fixtures had been replaced with vintage pieces. Even the wallpaper—a handsome William Morris design of pink poppies on a black background—looked as if it could be original to the house.

Walter did an amazing job, she thought. She was so dazzled by the house that she almost forgot why she was there. Then she remembered. Without waiting for Byron she went into the living room and stood behind a leather wingback chair. She wanted something between her and Byron while she confronted him. "I know what you did to Lucy," she informed him as he walked into the room. "How dare you?"

Byron paused. "I didn't realize she was off-limits to me," he said innocently. "Besides, I didn't drain her. I only took a sip or two." He smiled wickedly.

Jane's face flushed and her jaw trembled. "Stop these games!" she said. "Leave her be!"

Byron cocked his head. "You're very fond of her, aren't you?" he said. "Perhaps she's almost like a daughter?" He paused a moment, then pointed one finger at Jane. "No," he said. "Not a daughter. A sister."

Jane understood his meaning perfectly. She placed her hands

on the back of the chair in front of her, gripping it so tightly that her nails left scratches in the leather.

"You. Will. Not. Touch. Her." She spat each word at Byron as if it were a weapon.

Byron frowned. "I don't see why I shouldn't," he replied. "After all, she's just a girl."

He swept across the room, leaning so close to Jane that for a moment she thought he was going to kiss her.

"It isn't Lucy I want," he said. His breath was warm on her face. "It's you. But until you give yourself to me I must make do with what I have."

"You won't have me," said Jane.

Byron leaned closer still. "Then I will have Lucy," he said. "Perhaps I will even make her immortal. Do you think she would like that?"

"No," Jane said, barely able to get the word out of her mouth. "You can't."

Byron stepped away, laughing. "Of course I *can*," he said. "What's to stop me?" He snapped his fingers. "Or perhaps it isn't female companionship I need," he said. "Perhaps it's time for a gentleman friend. Someone with whom I can discuss literature."

Walter, Jane thought. *He means Walter.*

"Yes," said Byron, as if reading her thoughts. "That might be nice. Then again, there's no reason why I can't have both."

"Enough," Jane said. "What do you want?"

Byron smiled at her. "You know what I want, Jane. I want you."

"And just how would that work?" Jane asked. Her anger was returning, and it gave a mocking edge to her voice. "Would we marry and settle here? Would we become respected members of the community? Is that how you see it playing out?"

Byron's expression was stony as he replied. "I expect you to leave with me," he said. "Return to England, where we belong."

"Ah," said Jane. "Perhaps we could set up house on the shore of Lake Geneva. I believe one of the movie stars summers in your old house now. George Clooney, I think, or perhaps it's the Jolie-Pitts. But I'm sure they would let us lease it the rest of the year."

She stared at Byron, awaiting one of his famous bursts of temper. She had pushed him, perhaps too far, but her anger had turned into a bright fire she could no longer contain.

She was surprised when he laughed loudly. "You've changed some since our last meeting," he said. "I like it."

He became suddenly thoughtful. "You know this life of yours has to end someday," he said. "What do you have, another five years? Perhaps ten? Then what? Are you going to tell your Walter what you are? Are you going to turn him?"

"I would never do that," Jane snapped.

"Turn him?" asked Byron. "Or tell him?"

Jane looked away.

"I thought as much," Byron said. "You see, you've already decided. Which leaves only my proposal."

Jane was shaking her head as he spoke. Now she steeled herself and lifted her head. "I don't love you," she said firmly.

Once more Byron laughed at her. "Who said anything about love?" he replied. "We're both far too old to believe in happily ever after, Jane."

"Perhaps you don't," said Jane.

Byron smiled. "Man's love is of man's life a thing apart. 'Tis woman's whole existence."

"Stop quoting yourself," Jane said. "It's vain even for you."

"Yet you know it to be true," Byron said.

Jane sniffed. "I've yet to become so cynical."

"Give it time," Byron told her. "At any rate, my offer remains the same. Come with me or sacrifice Lucy and Walter. Is that a price you're willing to pay?"

Jane fought off the urge to turn and run. That would be useless. Byron would find her. And she knew as well that if she refused him, he would do exactly what he was threatening to do.

"Walter would never understand what you are," said Byron, interrupting her thoughts. "And you would watch him grow old and die. With me you would not suffer that."

"Yes," Jane agreed. "It would be easier."

"Then you've decided," said Byron. "Good."

"I have decided," Jane answered, her voice gaining strength as she spoke. She took a deep breath. "I've decided to tell them the truth."

Chapter 15

She closed her eyes. His arms went around her,
pulling her close. His fingers stroked her hair. She
resisted only a moment. Then she opened her eyes
and looked into his face. As he kissed her, she
imagined it was Charles's mouth covering hers.

—Jane Austen, *Constance*, manuscript page 203

"DO YOU BELIEVE IN GHOSTS?"

Walter, who was dicing carrots, stopped chopping for a moment. "I don't know," he answered. "Do you?"

He resumed his knife work. The *nick-nick-nick* of the knife against the wood was annoying. Jane's nerves were already frayed, and the sound grated on her ears as if someone were rapping ceaselessly on a door. *Who can it be (cried I) who chops these unoffending vegetables?* she found herself thinking. She wished he would stop.

"I used to see them," she said, speaking more loudly than usual to be heard above the noise. "When I was a child."

Walter finished the carrots, swept them into a pan, and picked up an onion. "Really?" he said. He didn't sound incredulous or mocking, and Jane wondered if he'd even heard her. "My grand-mother believed she could see ghosts."

Jane was making the salad to go with dinner. She'd been told to tear the lettuce into smaller pieces. She'd done such a thorough job that she now had a pile of what resembled wet green confetti. It was useless, and she quickly deposited it in the trash can before Walter could see it. The conversation was not going as well as she'd hoped, mainly because she had no idea how to begin.

"Yes," she said. "Several times. Once it was a man who stood on the stairs of a church, and another time it was a little girl who appeared in our garden. She said she was looking for her cat. She said its name was Mogger."

"She spoke to you?" Walter said as he cut the onion in half. Although she was several feet away, Jane's eyes began to water almost immediately.

She nodded. "Isn't that odd?"

Walter shrugged. "Who can say?" he answered. "There are more things in heaven and earth, Horatio, than are dreamt of in your philosophy."

"Hamlet was mad, of course," Jane replied. "But the sentiment is appreciated."

"Why are you asking?" said Walter. "Have you been seeing ghosts?"

Jane shook her head and tore violently at a fresh piece of lettuce. *I wish that were all it was,* she thought. To Walter she said, "No. It's just that today Lucy was talking about something to do with them and it made me realize that I don't know much about what you believe about . . . things," she concluded inadequately.

Having finished with the onion, Walter rinsed his hands and dried them on a dish towel. "Things," he repeated.

"Yes," said Jane. "Things."

"Like ghosts," Walter said.

"Ghosts," Jane agreed. "And . . . I don't know. God, I suppose. Heaven. Hell. What happens when we die."

Walter raised one eyebrow. "Those are big questions," he said. "I think I'm going to need a drink if we're going to tackle them. Would you like one?"

"Please," Jane answered.

Walter took two glasses from a cupboard and selected a bottle from the half dozen cradled in the wine rack. He uncorked it and poured some into the glasses. He handed one to Jane.

"This has about another thirty minutes," he said, nodding at the lamb stew that was bubbling on the stove. "Why don't we go sit down?"

Jane gratefully abandoned the disastrous salad and joined Walter in the living room. He'd lit a fire, and the room was warm and smelled faintly of pine smoke. Under other circumstances she would have felt relaxed, but considering what she was about to do, she could enjoy none of it.

"Do you want to start with ghosts and work our way up to God, or start with him and work our way down?" Walter asked as he sank into the cushions of the couch. Jane began to seat herself in one of the chairs, but Walter patted the place beside him. "Sit here," he said.

Although she'd been hoping to keep some distance between them, Jane did as Walter asked. However, she sat as far away from him as she could without appearing to be rejecting him. He turned sideways, his arm along the back of the couch, and looked at her. "God or ghosts?" he asked.

"God," Jane said. "Might as well get the biggest thing out of the way first."

Walter rested his glass of wine on his knee as he spoke. "I was raised Episcopalian," he began. "Mostly we were Christmas and Easter Christians, but I did like all of the ceremony." He chuckled. "At one point in college I actually considered the seminary, until I realized it was only because I didn't think I could afford grad school. If it weren't for a scholarship, I might very well be delivering sermons instead of refinishing wood floors and restoring Victorian façades."

"So you don't believe in God, then?" Jane asked.

Walter drank some wine before answering. "There's no way of really knowing, is there?" he said. "It's not as if it can be proved one way or another."

"A bit like ghosts," said Jane cautiously.

"Except you say you've seen and spoken to them," Walter reminded her. "Some people believe they talk to God on a regular basis, and that he talks back. Just because you or I don't doesn't mean they're lying."

"Very true," Jane said. "So then do you think that things—creatures—might exist that to most people seem completely impossible?"

"Give me an example," said Walter.

Jane thought for a moment. "Unicorns," she blurted. "Angels. Werewolves. Vampires." She clamped her lips shut on the last word, so that it came out almost as a whisper.

"Now I know what brought this on," Walter said. "You and Lucy were reading those Posey Frost novels to each other, weren't you? I know you said you think they're trashy, but I had a feeling you couldn't resist."

It took a moment for Jane to realize that he was making reference to a wildly popular series about a woman who was a celebrated designer of lingerie by day and a monster hunter by night. They were terrible novels, but they sold out as quickly as they came in. Jane had tried to read one but had given up after the first fifteen pages when the heroine, the sultry Vivienne Minx, had dispatched a demon with a corset stay.

"You caught me," said Jane, making a face that was supposed to look comically guilty.

Walter thought for a moment. "People certainly love to pretend that those things exist," he said. "But whether they do or not, who's to say?"

"Arrgh," Jane growled. "You're impossible."

"What do you want me to say?" asked Walter, holding his hands up. "Do I think it's possible that there's a God, or ghosts, or . . . werewolves? Sure. Anything is possible. But have I seen one? Do I *know* that they exist? No."

"Fine," Jane said. She could tell that that was as much as she was going to get out of him.

"Don't be mad," said Walter.

"I'm not mad," Jane said in a voice that contradicted her words. "I just think that if we're going to continue seeing each other, we should be able to talk about anything."

"We are talking," Walter said. "Are you sure there's not something else you want to say? Do you really want to know what I think about God?"

"No," Jane said. "I mean yes. Not about God. I don't really care what you think about God."

"Then what is it?" Walter asked.

Jane turned and looked at him. It was now or never. "There's something you need to know about me," she began. "Something important. It's about who I am. It's about *what* I am."

"What you are?" Walter said. "I don't get it. What are we talking about here?" His eyes widened. "You're a Scientologist!" he said. "That's it. Or Wiccan! Hey, that's fine with me."

Jane held up her hands. "No," she said, stopping him. "I'm not any of those things. I'm . . ."

Walter was looking at her questioningly. Jane looked into his honest, kind eyes and saw that he believed with all his heart that whatever she told him he would be able to handle. *That's how much he cares for me,* she thought.

"I'm going to be published," she heard herself say.

Walter blinked. "Published?" he said.

Jane nodded crazily. "Published," she said, wondering where in the world that had come from. "A novel."

"You wrote a novel?" Walter asked. "Why didn't you say anything?"

"I don't know," said Jane. "I guess I was afraid I would look foolish if it didn't sell."

"A novel," Walter said again. He was beaming. "Well, congratulations! I'm so proud of you."

He scooted over on the couch and gave Jane a hug. "What's it called?" he asked her.

For a moment Jane couldn't remember. "*Constance,*" she recalled finally.

"*Constance,*" Walter repeated. "When does it come out?"

"May, I think," Jane answered.

Walter clapped his hand on her knee and gave it a squeeze. "I can't believe it," he said. "Here you had me thinking we were going to have some big talk about how we're incompatible because of our religious views. Unicorns. Werewolves." He laughed. "You really had me going there."

"I did, didn't I?" Jane said. "Well, now the secret's out."

"How long have you known?" Walter asked.

"Not long," she told him. "A few weeks, really."

"Is that why you went to New York?"

"Mmm-hmm," Jane murmured.

Walter shook his head. "You're certainly a sly one," he said. "Wow. A novel. That's amazing, Jane. Really amazing. I can't wait to read it." Then he gave her a serious look. "Are there any other secrets you're keeping from me?"

"I don't think so," Jane said. She took a sip of wine and choked as it went down the wrong way. "No, I think that's it," she added when she could speak again.

"Does anyone else know?" Walter said.

"Just you," said Jane. "And I'd like to keep it that way for now. I don't want people making a big fuss about it. It's just a book."

"It's not just a book," Walter said. "It's *your* book. And that *is* a big deal." He grinned. "You're a published novelist," he said.

And an immortal blood-drinking monster, Jane thought as she flashed what she hoped passed for a smile. "That's me!" she said cheerfully.

Over dinner Walter grilled her about the book. She fed him details as if they were morsels of food, enough to keep him satisfied but not so much that he knew everything. Now that she'd revealed her impending publication, she found that it was actually a welcome distraction from her real problem. That still lingered in the back of her mind. She had not told Walter her most important secret, the one that would likely result in his death if she withheld it for much longer.

"We'll have a big launch party at the store," Walter said. "Oh, and you'll have to do a reading."

By the end of the evening, Jane was exhausted from listening to Walter talk about her novel. At half past eight she thanked him for dinner, kissed him good night, and left with an enormous sense of relief coupled with a growing burden of guilt. She'd done nothing to improve his situation as far as Byron's threat was concerned.

The house was quiet when she entered. She'd half expected to find Byron seated in her living room again. She would almost have preferred it if he were. At least then she would know that Walter and Lucy were safe for the moment.

"I don't think he'll do anything for the present," she said aloud as she walked upstairs to the bedroom.

"I won't, will I?"

Jane, startled, gave a small scream. On her bed Byron was stretched out, his hands behind his head, completely naked. Tom was perched on his stomach, looking at Jane without interest.

"What are you doing here?" Jane demanded.

"Waiting for you," said Byron. "I assume your talk with your boyfriend went well. He seemed to take the news surprisingly well."

"I don't know if I'd go quite that far," Jane replied. Then a thought occurred to her. "You were watching us," she said.

"Guilty," said Byron. "To be honest, I was expecting more of a scene. It was really rather disappointing."

He saw us, Jane thought to herself. *But did he hear us?* If so, then he would know that she hadn't really told Walter about herself. But if that was true, why wasn't he mocking her for failing to do it? Did he know she was bluffing?

"Walter is surprisingly open-minded," she said.

Byron rolled onto his side, pushing Tom off the bed. The cat padded from the room, leaving them alone. Jane tried to avoid looking any lower than Byron's face, but he was making it difficult.

"And have you told young Lucy?" he asked.

"Not yet," said Jane.

Byron rubbed his fingers over his chest. "Then I can still pay her a visit," he said. "That's certainly an . . . *appetizing* possibility."

"Don't you dare!" Jane exclaimed. "I'm going to tell her."

"Ah, but you haven't," said Byron. He sat up and reached for his pants, which were on the floor.

Jane grabbed his arm. "No," she said. "Please."

Byron stroked her face with his free hand. "Sweet Jane," he said. "My beautiful, sweet Jane. For you I would do most anything."

"Then leave Lucy alone," Jane pleaded.

"Very well," said Byron. "But if I'm not to share her bed, then I require a substitute."

Jane, understanding all too well his meaning, started to pull away. Then Byron's lips parted to reveal two sharp fangs.

"I'm hungry, Jane," he said, his voice low and seductive. "Oh, so hungry."

Jane imagined Lucy asleep in her bed, Byron looking down at her. He had already fed from her once. Another bite and she was likely to turn. Unless he killed her. And the thing that would decide the matter was whatever words Jane next spoke. She closed her eyes and pictured Lucy laughing and smiling.

"All right," she said. "Stay with me."

Chapter 16

She wondered if there really was such a thing as
atonement. Would Charles, if he knew who she
really was, forgive her?

—Jane Austen, *Constance*, manuscript page 207

BYRON WAS GONE IN THE MORNING, THE ONLY PROOF OF HIS HAVING been there the pounding in Jane's head like the clanging of church bells. Her whole body ached, and she could barely stand the light. She'd forgotten what it was like when two of her kind joined together. All of their senses became heightened, but the drawback was that their frailties did as well. Jane was ravenously hungry. She hated searching for food in the morning, but she would have to if she wanted to get through the day.

First, though, she had to make sure that Byron had kept his end of their bargain. She reached for the phone and dialed Lucy's home number. As she listened to it ring, she scratched idly at the tiny bite marks on her thigh.

"Hello?"

"Lucy?" Jane said. "It's me." She realized then that she had no excuse prepared for why she was calling Lucy at—she glanced at the clock—8:22 in the morning.

"Hey, Jane," said Lucy. "What's up?"

"Well," Jane replied, trying to get her foggy brain to work, "I, um, just wanted to see if you'd like me to pick you up a bagel on my way to the store."

"Oh," said Lucy. "Sure, I guess."

"Great," Jane enthused. "What kind?"

"How about raisin?" said Lucy. "With plain cream cheese."

"You got it," Jane said, much too enthusiastically. "I'll see you in about an hour. Oh, say, how are those spider bites?"

"Gone," Lucy said. "No more itching."

"And you slept well?"

"Like a baby," said Lucy. "Anything else, Mom?"

"Very funny," Jane said. "I'll see you in an hour."

She hung up, feeling like a complete fool. What must Lucy think of her? " 'And you slept well?' " she said, mimicking her own voice. "Honestly, sometimes you're a right fool, Jane Austen. Jane Fairfax," she corrected herself. Her head resumed pounding.

After a hurried shower she drove to the deli and picked up some bagels and cream cheese. The smell of the food made her queasy, and she knew she couldn't hold out much longer. She had to feed, and soon.

The problem was that there wasn't enough time for her to drive to any of her usual places. She would have to hunt locally. That was a huge problem under the best of circumstances. In the daylight, with only twenty minutes before she had to be at the shop, it was almost impossible. But she had no choice.

She drove around for a few minutes, hoping against hope that breakfast would fall into her lap. She considered and rejected a jogger, a drunk asleep at a bus stop, and a man delivering fruit to a grocery store. She was just about to go back to the drunk when she found herself in front of Our Lady of Perpetual Peace. A sign outside said: GOD IS ALWAYS READY TO LISTEN. CONFESSION ALL DAY.

No, she told herself as she stared at the sign. *You can't. That's just not right.*

Despite this, she found herself driving around the corner and parking the car in a spot reserved for patrons of the hair salon that had yet to open for the day. Reaching into the backseat, she retrieved her bag of hunting clothes and selected from it a short blond wig, which she pulled on and arranged as best she could. She was already wearing sunglasses to shield her increasingly sensitive eyes, and she added a scarf so that her face was almost entirely concealed.

Getting out, she walked quickly to the church and up the steps. Inside, she scanned the sanctuary. It was empty. The confessional was to the right. The curtains on the penitents' chambers on either side were pulled back, but the one covering the central priest's chamber was closed.

Jane went to the left-hand chamber and pulled the curtain shut behind her. Kneeling on the narrow padded rail, she waited until the small window in the wall separating her from the priest slid back. She could just make out the outline of his face as he said, "What have you to confess, child?"

Focusing her mind, Jane spoke in a voice very unlike her own. "Forgive me, Father," she said, the words sounding more like an incantation than a confession. "I have sinned."

She seldom used her glamoring ability. Usually the men she chose were already otherwise incapacitated. But occasionally she had to use more esoteric means. She did so now. She knew that as she spoke, her words were fogging the priest's mind.

"Yes?" the priest said. He sounded confused.

"I have lied," Jane said. "Forgive me."

"You are forgiven," said the priest, although he did not sound at all sure about this. "You must . . ." His voice trailed off.

Jane exited the confessional and slid soundlessly into the priest's compartment. He sat on an ordinary folding chair, looking straight ahead with a peaceful smile on his face. Jane bent and removed the collar from around his neck. Then, holding his head gently in her hands, she fed.

Almost immediately she felt better. Within a minute her head ceased to ache and her eyes no longer burned. She took only a little more blood from the priest before releasing him. Taking a tissue from her coat pocket, she held it to the two small punctures on his throat. When she was satisfied that there was no more bleeding, she replaced his collar and fastened it.

"Forgive me, Father," she said as she turned and fled from the church.

She made it to the bookstore just as Lucy was unlocking the front door. Lucy waited for Jane to get out of the car. "What's with the cut-and-dye?" Lucy asked.

Jane, not understanding, said, "I didn't get my hair cut."

"It sure looks like it," Lucy replied.

Then Jane remembered the wig. She'd forgotten to remove it. "Oh, that," she said. "Right. I was just trying it out. What do you think? You know what they say about blondes having more fun."

Lucy looked at the wig, biting her lip. "Honestly?" she said. "It makes you look like a soccer mom."

"I think you're right," Jane said as she opened the door and went inside. "It was a bad idea." She set the deli bag on the counter and pulled the wig off. Her real hair was a rat's nest, but she could deal with it easily enough.

Lucy opened the bag and took out a bagel. As she unwrapped it she said, "Is everything okay?"

"Of course," Jane said. "Why?"

Lucy shrugged. "You just seem a little bit . . . I don't know. Edgy," she said. "You've never called me at home before. Not in the morning, anyway. And the wig. That's not you at all."

Jane busied herself with removing her coat and fixing her hair. She wasn't sure how to respond to Lucy's question. She couldn't exactly tell her that she'd spent the night with Lord Byron in order to save Lucy from joining the ranks of the living dead, then seduced a priest in order to drink a bit of his blood. But she had to say *something*. For all she knew, Byron was watching them as he'd watched her and Walter the night before.

"You're right," she said. "Everything isn't okay."

Lucy chewed the bite of bagel that was in her mouth and swallowed. "So what is it?" she said. "Problems with Walter? The store isn't doing well? Did I do something wrong?"

"No," Jane said quickly. "No. You haven't done anything. And Walter and the store are both fine. It's something else entirely."

"Is your Aunt Flo visiting?" asked Lucy, sounding sympathetic.

"I don't have an Aunt—" Jane began, then realized that Lucy was using her favorite euphemism for getting her period. "No," she said. "There are no houseguests at the moment."

"Well, I'm all out of guesses," Lucy told her. "Oh, unless you're pregnant. I forgot about that one."

"I am most definitely not pregnant," said Jane.

Lucy wadded up the wrapper from her bagel. "Then I give up," she said.

Jane started to say something, paused, then looked Lucy in the eye and said, "Brian George is a vampire. And as it happens, so am I. He's threatened to harm you and Walter if I don't run away with him, and frankly, I don't know what to do about it. Oh, and he paid you a visit the other night and bit your neck. It wasn't spiders."

She and Lucy stood staring at each other for what seemed an eternity. Now that she'd actually told the truth, Jane felt much better. Of course Lucy was going to think she was mad, but there was nothing she could do about that. *Unless you tell her you're playing a joke,* she reminded herself.

She was actually on the verge of saying just that, if only to break the quiet, when Lucy said, "That still doesn't explain the wig."

"The wig," Jane said. "Right. Well—"

"It's okay," said Lucy, interrupting. "I don't need to know. Anyway, I already knew about the vampire thing."

Jane wasn't sure she'd heard correctly. "What? You knew? But how?"

"Brian told me," Lucy replied. "Yesterday. Well, actually, last night. He took me to dinner."

"And he told you that he and I are vampires?" said Jane.

Lucy nodded. "He didn't mention coming into my room the other night, though. I'm a little pissed about that."

"Wait," Jane said, holding her hands up. "You believe him?"

"You just said yourself—" Lucy began.

"I know what I said," Jane broke in. "That's not the point. The point is that you don't seem at all upset about any of this."

"I wouldn't say that," said Lucy. "There's that whole breaking-into-my-room thing."

"Let's set that aside for a moment, shall we?" Jane said. "Let's start with the part where you actually believe that he and I are vampires. Vampires," she repeated. "As in the undead. Drinking blood. All of that unpleasantness."

"I have a general idea of what it means," said Lucy.

"Yes, but you're telling me that you actually *believe* that they—we—exist," Jane said.

"Why not?" said Lucy. "A whole bunch of people believe that some invisible dude in the sky created the world. My Uncle Todd believes he was abducted by aliens and has a tracking device implanted in his head. Besides, they're always finding new stuff we've never seen before. Last week some scientist in the Amazon discovered a frog that kills its prey using sound. If you ask me, that's way weirder than vampires."

"You're being awfully rational about this," Jane said. "You're not at all afraid of what it means?"

"Maybe a little," Lucy admitted. "But it's kind of romantic too, you know. Like Vivienne Minx." As soon as she'd said the words she clapped her hand to her mouth.

"You read Posey Frost!" Jane exclaimed.

"Just the first one!" Lucy said. "I swear. Okay, maybe the first two. Or three. But that's it. I couldn't help myself."

Jane shook her head. "How could you?" she asked.

"Me?" said Lucy. "Who's the one who forgot to mention something about being a vampire?"

"You're right," Jane said. "You're right. I apologize."

"Besides, they're not *that* bad," Lucy added. "I mean, I'm sure there's stuff she gets wrong, but I wouldn't be able to tell." She hesitated a moment, then asked, "So, are werewolves real too?"

"We'll talk more about that later," said Jane. "The important thing is that you need to stay away from Brian." She didn't know if Byron had revealed his true identity to Lucy. More important, she didn't know if he had revealed *her* identity to her assistant. She suspected not, as Lucy would hardly be able to keep quiet about it.

"It's okay," Lucy said. "We're good. All I had to do was say I'd let him make me a vampire."

"What?" Jane practically yelled the words. "You agreed to let him do what?"

"Make me a vampire," Lucy repeated. "He said it was no big deal."

"Oh, I'm so going to kill him," said Jane. "First he lied to me to get me to let him stay over last night, and now you're telling me he's talked you into letting him turn you?"

"He stayed at your place last night?" Lucy asked. She sounded hurt. "He told me he had to work on his novel."

"I'm not surprised," said Jane. "Lesson one—don't trust vampires. Male ones, anyway. Especially that one."

Lucy's eyes were beginning to tear up. Jane went to her and hugged her close. "Oh, sweetie," she said. "Don't let him hurt you. He's not worth it. Believe me."

"But he said such nice things," said Lucy. "He quoted poetry."

Jane rolled her eyes. "Yes, he's very good at that," she told Lucy.

"What are we going to do?" Lucy asked, sniffling.

"I don't know yet," Jane answered. "But whatever it is, he's going to wish he'd never been dead."

Chapter 17

Seeing Jonathan talking to young Minerva
Jones-Lipton, Constance felt herself inclined
to rush to the girl and snatch her out of harm's
way. As the girl prattled on, Jonathan regarded
her intently, his dark eyes sparkling. It called
to mind a hawk watching an oblivious field
mouse, waiting for the perfect moment to swoop
down and snatch it up in its talons.

—Jane Austen, *Constance*, manuscript page 227

"HOW OLD ARE YOU EXACTLY?" LUCY ASKED JANE.

"Old enough not to answer that question," Jane said. She was making room in the hallway closet and was discovering that she had far too many coats and scarves.

"Okay," said Lucy. "But are we talking old enough to have partied with the Beatles, or old enough to have partied with Mozart?"

"We can discuss that another time," Jane said.

She still had not given Lucy the details about her identity, and hadn't decided if she ever would. It was bad enough that she'd said anything at all. Despite Lucy's surprising willingness to believe Jane's story, Jane was regretting having said anything. *Whatever was I thinking?* she asked herself as she removed three umbrellas from the closet.

She blamed Byron. If he hadn't seduced her, she would have had a clear head. Worse, she had given in to him based on his lies. He'd already revealed himself to Lucy. *In more ways than one, I'm sure,* Jane thought. *What a horrid man.*

But what was done was done. Now the only thing to do about it was to try to undo Byron's plans. And Jane had come up with something she thought just might do the trick.

"He should be here any minute," she told Lucy. "Are you ready?"

Lucy nodded. "I think so," she replied.

Jane breathed deeply. "Good," she said. "You stay in here until it's time to come out."

"How will I know?" Lucy asked.

"Trust me," said Jane. "You'll know."

The doorbell rang, and Jane put her finger to her lips. "Inside," she whispered, pushing Lucy into the closet and arranging the coats as best she could to conceal the girl. "Oh, and don't forget these." She pressed something into Lucy's hand.

Lucy nodded as Jane shut the door. Jane checked her appearance in the hallway mirror, then went to greet Byron. When she opened the door, he gave her his most charming smile.

"Good evening," he said in a voice that came straight out of a Bela Lugosi movie.

"Stop it," said Jane. "That joke hasn't been funny for decades."

Byron stepped inside. "Personally, I find it's quite a hit with the ladies," he said.

"Calling the women you associate with ladies is stretching the definition a bit, don't you think?" said Jane.

Byron laughed. "You're in a mood tonight," he said. "What's brought this on?"

"What do you think?" said Jane. "I've had a headache all day."

"Ah," Byron replied. "Yes. I'm sorry about that. Has it really been that long since you've been with one of our kind?"

"You were the last," Jane told him. "Not that it's any of your business."

"Really?" said Byron. "How extraordinary. Have you really not associated with any of our people in all these years?"

"Not in that way," Jane said. "And in general, no. I did for the first fifty years or so, but I'm afraid I find most of them rather tiring."

"And humans aren't?"

"We *are* human," said Jane. "Or at least we were."

"True," Byron agreed. "But not anymore. I am not now that which I have been."

"You really do think a great deal of your own work, don't you?" said Jane.

"I think in this instance the critics would agree with me," he replied. "As I recall, *Childe Harold* was a favorite of yours as well."

Jane took a seat on the couch. "Yes," she said. "Well, at any rate, now we're very *old* humans. Please, sit down."

Byron sat on the other end of the couch. He was regarding Jane warily. "Why did you ask me here?"

Jane placed her hands in her lap. "I've been thinking," she said carefully. "About your . . . offer."

Byron lifted an eyebrow. "And?"

"And I think I've come up with a solution," she said.

Byron said nothing for a minute. He kept his eyes on Jane.

She forced herself to meet his gaze, not blinking. "Have you?" Byron said finally.

"As you know, I've told Walter about myself."

Byron nodded. "So it appears," he said.

Jane hesitated. Much of her plan hinged on whether or not Byron believed the lie she was about to tell. "He's agreed to share me with you," she said.

"Has he?" Byron said, sounding genuinely surprised. "And why would he agree to such a thing?"

"Because he loves me," said Jane. "He would rather share me than lose me completely."

Byron shifted in his seat. *He's buying it,* Jane thought. A fire of hope sparked in her.

"I must say I'm slightly disappointed," said Byron. "I'd expected a bit more of a fight from him. Trying to put a stake through my heart or whatnot. This is . . . unexpected."

"I was surprised as well," said Jane. "But it was his idea, not mine."

Byron's nose twitched. "And just how would this arrangement work?" he asked.

"I suppose there are several options," said Jane. "Alternate nights. Every other weekend. Or the three of us could share a bed."

Byron looked shocked. "Share a bed?" he said.

"Yes," said Jane. "Walter appears willing, and after all, you've been known to take a man or two into yours."

Byron looked away. "I knew I should have burned those letters," he said.

"It's too late now," Jane said gently. "They even mention them in your Wikipedia entry. Besides, no one cares about that anymore."

"I don't know," Byron said, sounding like a petulant child. "I don't think I want to share. I want you all to myself." Then, surprisingly, he smiled. "You looked me up on Wikipedia?" he asked.

Jane ignored him. "Then I'm afraid we have a problem," she said. "I won't leave Walter."

"I'll kill him!" Byron declared.

"Then you'll never have me," Jane said firmly. "Besides, I can always turn him if it comes to that."

Byron's eyes darted from side to side. Jane could see he was desperate. He hated to lose. She prayed he would play the card she expected him to.

"The girl!" he said, as if he'd just now remembered her. "I'll kill her. Her blood will be on your hands."

"You still wouldn't have me," said Jane.

Byron's face grew angry. He jumped to his feet, his hands clenched.

"Then I'll turn her!" he shouted. "I'll make her one of us!"

Jane said nothing. She was counting on her silence to infuriate Byron further. Predictably, it did. He rushed to her, dropping beside her on the couch and grasping her shoulders.

"I'll do it, Jane!" he said. "You know I will. Unless you agree to be mine and mine only."

"Please," Jane said. "Don't do that. She's done nothing to deserve it." She forced a tear from her eye.

"She reminds you of your sister," said Byron. "I can see that." His voice was gleeful. He thought he'd found her tender spot.

"She deserves a normal life," Jane said. "Not this." She hoped Byron wouldn't reveal that Lucy had already agreed to become a vampire if he wished her to. What happened next depended upon it.

Byron sat up. "Then make your choice," he demanded. "Come with me or I turn the girl."

At that moment the closet door flew open and Lucy emerged. "You're too late!" she cried.

Byron stared at her, his mouth open. Then he looked at Jane. His face was a mask of confusion.

"I already turned her," Jane told him.

"No," said Byron. "You wouldn't."

"You were right," Jane told him. "She does remind me of my sister. So much so that I decided I can't live without her. This way we can be together forever."

Lucy approached the couch. "You said you loved me," she hissed at Byron. "But you were only using me to get to Jane."

She knelt on the floor at Jane's feet. Jane placed her hand protectively on Lucy's head, stroking her hair. In response, Lucy opened her mouth, revealing two shiny white fangs.

"You see?" Jane said to Byron. "You have nothing left to threaten me with."

"I could still kill them," said Byron.

Jane laughed. "And risk being branded a traitor?" she said. "You know the rules as well as I do. You'd be hunted to the ends of the earth."

She actually didn't know if this was true, but she had heard as much, and hoped Byron had as well. She waited for him to respond, and was surprised when all he did was stand up and go to the door. He didn't look back as he left the house.

"What was that?" Lucy asked after a minute had gone by with no sign of his return.

Jane shook her head. "I don't know," she said. "I think it means he believed it."

Lucy reached up and removed the set of plastic vampire teeth she'd been wearing. "Thank God they still had some of these at the drugstore," she said, rubbing her gums. "I thought with Halloween over they'd be out."

"You played the part very well," said Jane. "Thank you."

"Don't thank me," Lucy said. "You did all the work. Frankly, I can't believe he fell for it."

"We took away his options," Jane said. "Without you or Walter he had nothing to threaten me with."

"Except that Walter doesn't know about you and I'm not a vampire," Lucy reminded her.

"But Brian doesn't know that," Jane reminded her. "And there's really no way for him to find out."

"He must have been a real jerk when he was alive," Lucy commented.

Jane considered telling her that she'd just escaped being made a vampire by one of the most famous romantic figures of all time. Lucy would probably love that. But the less the girl knew about Byron, the less she would know about Jane. Jane still wasn't ready to tell her everything.

"Do I really remind you of your sister?" Lucy asked.

Jane nodded. "Yes," she said. "You do."

"What was her name?"

Jane hesitated. Should she invent a sister to keep her life a mystery? Lucy would believe whatever she was told. *She deserves a bit of truth,* Jane told herself.

"Cassandra," she said. "Cassie."

"Cassie," Lucy repeated. "It's a pretty name."

"She would have liked you," said Jane.

They sat together, looking into the fire. Jane thought about Cassie. Lucy really was quite like her. Both had a fine sense of humor. Both took life as it came to them. Both made her feel as though she had someone in the world whom she could trust.

"What do we do now?" Lucy said.

"We wait and see," said Jane. "Mr. George is going to do whatever it is he's going to do. We'll deal with it when it happens."

"I can't believe I thought he liked me," said Lucy. "What an idiot."

"No more than I was once," Jane told her. "I believed him as well."

"But he does love you," said Lucy.

Jane shook her head. "He doesn't," she said. "He just wants to believe he does. He's starting to realize how lonely it is spending eternity alone."

"Eternity," said Lucy. "That's a long time." She laughed at her own joke. Jane, despite the silliness of it, did too. Then Lucy grew serious. "Will you really live forever?" she asked.

"I don't know," Jane answered. "Legends certainly say so, but I've found that legends are often just that. Still, it's already been quite a while."

"The Great Depression quite a while or the fall of Rome quite a while?" Lucy asked.

Jane rapped her on top of her head. "Enough questions," she said. "All in good time."

Lucy groaned. "You've got to tell me *something*," she protested. "After all, I almost gave up my soul for you."

"Another legend," Jane said. "The devil has nothing to do with it. My soul is still intact, thank you very much. But you're right; I do owe you something. So here's a clue—I once sat around a table while Madame Blavatsky attempted to summon my ghost for a group of curiosity seekers. She had no idea I was sitting across from her, and you can imagine my surprise when my spirit began to speak to the assembled guests. What a fraud she was, that one."

"Gee, that narrows it down," Lucy said. "Thanks."

"I'm afraid it's all you're getting for tonight," said Jane. "Now it's up to the guest room with you. I think it's best if you stay here tonight. It's difficult to say what Byron—Brian—will do."

Lucy looked at her and started to say something. Then she turned and walked to the stairs. "Good night," she said. "I'll see you in the morning."

"Good night," Jane called back. "I'll be up in a bit myself. I just want to lock up down here."

Lucy continued upstairs while Jane busied herself locking the door. She wondered if Lucy had heard her slip of the tongue and, if so, had understood what it meant. *Probably she'll grill me about it in the morning,* she thought.

She checked the kitchen door and the windows, although it was rather pointless. Byron would be able to get into the house if he really wanted to. But it made her feel better to do it. Afterward she sat down in a chair by the fire. Although she enjoyed it, she didn't have to sleep, and she thought she might as well stay up and make sure Lucy was safe. A moment later Tom jumped into her lap and curled up.

Jane opened up a book and started to read, but her thoughts kept returning to Byron. Would he really leave them alone? As much as she wanted to believe that the ruse had convinced him that he had no options left for blackmailing her, she wasn't satisfied that this was the case. Lucy couldn't play at being a vampire forever, and eventually he would see through her disguise. As for Walter, it would take only one pointed conversation with him for Byron to see that he had no idea what was going on.

Jane was relying on Byron's pride to be his undoing. He hated losing, particularly in matters of the heart, and she hoped that what he believed to be his defeat in that arena would force him to leave. If he didn't, she was going to *have* to tell Walter, and despite what she'd said to Byron, she wasn't at all sure that Walter would be as understanding as she'd made him out to be.

"Did I make a mistake?" she asked Tom. He looked at her for a moment, yawned, and went back to sleep.

"I thought you'd say that," said Jane.

She returned to the book. The beginning was slow, and she hoped it would get better. It was going to be a long night.

Chapter 18

She longed to show the poems to Charles. She
wanted to hear him read them aloud, and ached
to know his opinion of them. Yet the thought of
disclosing her passion to him and risking the
possibility that he might laugh at her was worse
even than having him turn away in disgust at
learning of her involvement with Jonathan Brut.

—Jane Austen, *Constance*, manuscript page 139

"WHAT DO YOU MEAN, HE'S GONE?"

Jane and Lucy exchanged a glance as they waited for Walter to answer Jane's question.

"He's gone," Walter repeated. "He left last night. Apparently there was some kind of family emergency back home. I went over this morning to do some final touch-up work on the veranda railing, and I found this taped to the door." He waved a crumpled piece of paper at them.

Jane stifled a smile. "It was a bit rude to just leave you a note," she said.

Walter sniffed. "Writers," he said. He looked at Jane. "Sorry."

Lucy, busy unpacking a box of books, said, "That's too bad. He seemed like an interesting man."

"That's not the word I'd use," said Walter. "I mean, I understand if there's an emergency, but to just take off like that?"

Jane was having difficulty containing her excitement. If Byron really had gone (and she wasn't completely convinced that he had), then her plan had worked more beautifully than she'd hoped. But she couldn't appear too pleased in front of Walter, who had no idea what Byron had wanted to do to him.

"I have to get back to work," Walter said testily. "I just had to tell somebody."

Jane affected a look of pity. "It's all right, Walter," she said. "These things happen."

Walter mumbled something unintelligible in reply. "I'll see you later," he said.

When he was gone, Lucy turned to Jane. "We did it!" she squealed, jumping up and giving Jane a big hug.

"Possibly," Jane agreed. "We still need to keep our eyes open. I wouldn't put anything past him."

"Too bad we didn't have him autograph a few of these before he left," Lucy said. She dropped a copy of *The Complete Poems of Lord Byron* on the counter. Jane looked at it for a moment.

"So you did hear me," she said. "I wondered."

"You know, I thought he seemed a little familiar," said Lucy. "But I figured he just looked like some actor I'd seen or some guy who'd come into the store before. Then when you called him Byron it occurred to me where I'd seen him before. On this book jacket."

Jane studied the portrait on the cover. "He's awfully handsome, isn't he?" she said.

"Mmm," said Lucy. "He's a hottie all right. A lying, cheating, blood-sucking hottie." She leaned against the counter. "So, who does that make you?"

"Why do I have to be somebody?" Jane asked. "Perhaps I'm just some ordinary woman who got involved with the wrong kind of man. Is that so unusual?"

"You could be," Lucy admitted. "But I don't think so."

Jane squinted her eyes. "And why not?" she asked.

"Because," Lucy replied, squinting back, "I found this on your dresser." She held up a locket. It was open, and inside was a small watercolor portrait of Cassie.

"You spied!" Jane yelped.

Lucy shook her head. "Actually, I didn't. I went into your room to see if you had a hairbrush I could borrow. This was open on the dresser."

"But you stole it," Jane said. "That's even worse."

Lucy rolled her eyes. "I didn't steal it," she said. "I *borrowed* it. To compare it to the portrait in this." She held up one of the several Jane Austen biographies the store carried. It was opened to a portrait of Cassandra. "They're practically the same," Lucy said.

"So I have a picture in a locket that resembles that one," Jane said. "What of it?"

Lucy snapped the book shut. "The jig is up," she said. "Out with it."

Jane shuffled some papers on the counter. "Oh, all right," she said. "Yes, that's Cassie. And yes, I'm . . ." She couldn't bring herself to say it.

"Jane Austen," Lucy said in a gloating tone. "You. Are. Jane. Austen." She enunciated each word separately. Then she stood with her mouth open, staring at Jane. "You're Jane Austen," she said again, this time in a voice filled with awe. "Jane Austen. You're Jane Austen."

"I know," Jane said. "You don't have to remind me quite so many times."

Lucy shook her head as if trying to wake herself up. "This is too weird," she said. "I was okay with the vampire thing. I mean, that's freaky, but I was okay with it. And I was even okay with the Byron thing. But this—this is just too much." She stared at Jane. "You're Jane freaking Austen!"

"Oh, for Pete's sake," Jane said. "Yes, I'm Jane Austen. And I'm a vampire. And it is, as you say, too freaking much. But that's how it is." She was talking loudly. She took a moment to calm herself before speaking again. "I'm sorry," she told Lucy. "I forgot that you haven't had as much time as I have to process this."

"It's all right," said Lucy. "I think I'm over it."

Jane looked up. "What? A moment ago you were acting as if you'd just seen Father Christmas."

"Yeah, well, now I'm over it," Lucy said. "I'm funny like that."

"Are you sure you're feeling well?" asked Jane. "Do you need to lie down or something?"

"You look different from your portrait," Lucy said. "Prettier."

Jane blushed. "Thank you," she said. "Cassandra had some talent as an artist, but I've always thought that portrait makes me look a bit mousy. Also, I've changed my hair, you know."

A smiled flashed across Lucy's face. "Does Walter know he's dating Jane Austen?" she asked.

"No," Jane said quickly. "And he's not going to. Lucy, promise me you won't say anything. If you do, I'll tell him you've gone mad or have a terrible addiction to painkillers or something."

"Relax," said Lucy. "I'm not telling anyone. For one thing, I wouldn't do something like that. For another, I owe you for saving me from being the vampire love slave to Lord Byron." She hesitated. "Actually, maybe I should be mad at you for that."

"I just don't know how I would tell Walter," Jane said. "Of course I *should* tell him."

"Are you kidding?" said Lucy. "Do you know what kind of pressure that would put on the poor guy?"

Jane shrugged. "Well, of course it would be difficult accepting the vampire issue."

"The vampire issue?" Lucy said. "I'm talking about the Jane Austen issue. How would you like to be the guy dating Jane Austen?"

Jane was confused. "Would that be a bad thing?" she asked. "I mean, apart from the obvious."

"Um, yeah," said Lucy. "And it's your own fault for coming up with Mr. Darcy. He's every woman's ideal. Some men's too. What man can live up to that? You ruined it for every man on the planet when you wrote him up."

Jane put her hands on her hips. "Are you accusing me of making it impossible for men to live up to an image?" she said.

"Yes," Lucy replied simply. "Don't deny it."

"I do deny it," Jane objected. "He's just a character in a novel."

Lucy looked shocked. "Just a *character*?" she said. "Just a *novel*?" She located a copy of *Pride and Prejudice* and waved it around. "This is only the greatest novel ever written," she said.

Jane blushed. "You're not the first to say so," she said, trying to sound modest.

"Trust me," said Lucy. "Do not tell Walter anything. At least not until you're married."

"Married?" said Jane. "Whatever makes you think I'm going to marry him?"

"I've read your books," Lucy said. "This is exactly like one of them."

"How so?" asked Jane. "I've never written about a vampire in my life."

"Forget the vampire thing," Lucy said. "You've got the lovely, kind man who adores you but whom you find a little bit boring."

"I do not," Jane denied.

"Yeah, you kind of do," said Lucy. "And that's okay. On the other hand, you have the incredibly sexy but totally-bad-for-you guy you can't quite get out of your mind."

"Go on," Jane said. Now that Lucy had pointed it out, she had to admit that it really was a bit like something she might write.

"Well, now you just have to realize that the nice guy is a much better match for you," Lucy concluded. "Then you marry him."

"He hasn't even asked me," said Jane. "Not exactly." She didn't tell Lucy that Walter had as good as done so several times, and that she had simply pretended he hadn't.

"Times have changed," Lucy said. "Why don't you ask him?"

"Times may have changed," Jane agreed. "But I haven't. At least not that much. Anyway, I don't know that I want to marry Walter."

"Don't tell me there's another hottie in the picture," said Lucy.

An image of Kelly's face popped into Jane's mind. "No," she said. "I just don't know that I'm ready for marriage. Then there's the whole . . . well, you know," she concluded. She pushed her teeth out, her canines protruding over her lower lip.

"If you ask me, he wouldn't care," said Lucy.

"I don't want to talk about this anymore," Jane said. "There's already been enough excitement for one day."

"That's true," Lucy agreed. "I guess I have to get used to being your Alfred."

"My what?"

"Your Alfred," Lucy repeated. "As in Batman?"

Jane looked at her blankly. "Batman?" she said.

"Alfred was Bruce Wayne's butler," Lucy explained. "He knew Bruce Wayne was Batman, but he kept it a secret."

"Ah," said Jane. "I see. I hadn't looked at it in quite that way."

"We need a Batcave," Lucy said. "A secret lair."

"I think this is it," said Jane, indicating the inside of the store. "I'm not a superhero."

"You must have *some* powers," Lucy insisted. "What are they? Ooh—can you fly?"

"No," Jane answered. "Nor can I turn into a bat, so you needn't ask."

"Come on," said Lucy. "Nothing? Really?"

"I don't get cold," Jane admitted. "I see very well, and I don't have to sleep, although I can and do. My body heals itself quickly, at least for minor injuries. I'm strong enough that I never have to ask for help getting the tops off of jars. Other than that, no, there's nothing extraordinary about me." She didn't mention her glamoring ability, and felt guilty about it, but she worried there might be a time when she would need to use it on Lucy.

"Except the part where you get to live forever," Lucy suggested.

"Yes, except for that," said Jane. "But believe me, it comes at a cost."

Lucy made a face. "Can we at least have costumes?" she suggested.

"I'm glad you're enjoying this," said Jane. "But do try to remember that this is my life."

"Sorry," Lucy apologized. "It's just that you're my first vampire. And you're Jane Austen. It's hard not to be a little excited."

"I may be those things," said Jane. "But I'm still your boss, and this is still a bookshop. Let's see if we can get some work done, shall we?"

She set Lucy to work reorganizing the children's section, and went into the office to collect her thoughts. Everything had changed overnight. For the first time ever, someone besides Byron and a few other undead knew her identity. She was putting herself at great risk trusting in Lucy to keep her secret. *She's young,* Jane thought. *She could make a mistake.* She wondered if maybe she should leave Brakeston after all. Then if Lucy said anything, everyone would just think she was crazy. *I couldn't do that to her,* Jane thought. She also couldn't leave Lucy or Walter exposed to the danger posed by Byron. Even if he really was gone, he could always come back.

No, she would have to stay and she would have to trust Lucy to keep her promise. It was the only honorable thing to do. But what about Walter? He knew nothing. Was it fair to keep the truth from him when Lucy knew? She knew it wasn't. Yet she also knew that she couldn't tell him.

"You're a coward, Jane Fairfax," she said. "You're afraid he won't love you if he knows."

It was true. Although she wasn't sure that she could ever marry Walter, she wasn't ready to give him up. It was a horrible thing to realize about herself, but there it was. Once more Kelly's face appeared in her thoughts. Yes, there was that as well. She did find him attractive, and she still believed that he was worldly enough to accept her for what she was. But he'd shown no romantic interest in her at all.

I really am living inside one of my novels, she thought.

Her moment of self-pity was interrupted by the arrival of the mail carrier. "Here you go, Jane," Paula said, handing her a stack of mail. She held up a white envelope. "This one was dropped in the box at the station. No stamp, and just your name on it. Technically, I should charge you the cost of the postage, but I'll let it slide this time." She winked as she gave Jane the envelope.

"Thank you, Paula," Jane said. She placed the stack of mail on her desk and looked at the envelope. As Paula had said, her name was written in black ink across the front of the envelope in spidery script. She slid her finger along the back and withdrew a single sheet of paper.

My dear Jane,

At the risk of sounding melodramatic, by the time you get this I shall be gone. I've mailed it rather than leave it on your doorstep or some other more obvious place because I don't want you to read it until I'm halfway back to England. My apologies for forgetting your address. I'm in a bit of a hurry. I'm sure this will find its way to you in due course.

You will of course be thinking that you have bested me. And perhaps you have. But this is only one battle. I am now determined more than ever that it is our destiny to be together.

For now I will leave you to the life you have
chosen. But know that I will be thinking of you,
and that one day I will return.

All of my love,

Byron's signature was scrawled across the bottom of the page.
Jane read through the note one more time, then crumpled it up
and threw it into the trash. *Only one battle,* she thought. *Who
does he think he is, Charles de Gaulle?*

Chapter 19

What kind of writer did she want to be? She had
never considered the question. Now that it had been
asked, she found that what she wanted was to tell
the stories of women. Not women whose primary
interest in life was marriage, but women like
herself, who wanted more than just a husband.

—Jane Austen, *Constance*, manuscript page 87

WINTER GAVE WAY TO SPRING, AND EVENTUALLY JANE STOPPED
looking for Byron everywhere she went. She still did not tell
Walter about herself, and after nagging her for weeks about it
Lucy stopped, but mostly because she had something else to
torment Jane about. The announcement of the publication of
Constance appeared in *Publishers Weekly* the first week of
March, with a full-page ad trumpeting it as "the must-read
book of summer." The cover was featured prominently, along
with a photograph of Jane, which against her objections Nick
Trilling had insisted they use. There were several flattering
blurbs, and a box at the bottom announced a fifty-thousand-
copy first printing.

"When were you going to mention this?" Lucy asked Jane the day the magazine arrived. "When I opened the box of books?"

Since then life had been a whirlwind. First the galleys arrived and Jane spent two weeks going over them. Several times she'd called Kelly in tears because she was convinced the novel was dreadful and should never be published. Each time he'd talked her down, assuring her that it was a very good book. After that had been the unpleasantness of the author photo, which Walter had taken with his digital camera and which Jane thought made her look like a woman who spent all her time knitting scarves and doing acrostics. Nick had proclaimed it just the thing, which did nothing to allay her fears.

There was a lull from March until the middle of April, when the first reviews began to appear. That was when people other than Lucy and Walter began to realize that there was an author in their midst. Soon Jane was something of a minor celebrity in town and could walk no more than a few blocks without someone stopping her to congratulate her on her first book. She quickly adopted a standard response ("That's so kind of you") and perfected the art of appearing thankful yet busy ("I'd love to chat, but I must get to the bank before it closes. Yes, we'll probably have a party when it comes out").

"If I'd known how exhausting this would be, I never would have sent the manuscript in," Jane complained to Walter one evening after dinner at her house. "Having to be relentlessly cheerful is making my face cramp." She massaged her cheeks and sighed.

"It's the price you have to pay for literary stardom," Walter joked.

Jane began to say something about how things had been easier when her books were published anonymously, but caught herself in time. It was becoming increasingly difficult to remember what she could and could not say, and to whom. She had begun to cherish the freedom she felt when she was talking to Lucy. Having to watch herself around Walter always put her on edge.

"Kelly sent me an early review," she told Walter. "From a newspaper in Chicago, I think. It's quite nice." She handed Walter the clipping, which he read silently.

"Nice?" he said when he was finished. "Jane, they compared you to Inez Gossford. That's not just nice, it's fantastic."

"I suppose it is," Jane admitted. "She's rather *popular*, isn't she?"

Walter wagged a finger at her. "Don't you start that," he said.

Jane looked at him. "Start what?" she said.

"The whole popular-versus-literary thing," Walter said. "I hate it when people try to say one is better than the other. Like books people enjoy reading are somehow beneath books that literary snobs approve of."

"Where is this coming from?" Jane asked. "I've never seen you so annoyed."

"Oh, it's just a particular peeve of mine. Whenever I mention that I like certain novels, someone has to say something snide about how although they may be popular, they aren't *real* novels. It's stupid. Then they get all put out when I remind them that some of the books we consider classics today were considered popular fiction in their time. Dickens, for instance. Even Austen."

Jane felt herself tense up, but Walter didn't seem to notice. He continued talking. "Where are all the 'literary' novels from that period?" he asked, using his fingers to emphasize the quotes. "And what about Trollope? His Barchester books are basically soap operas, yet today they're considered great English novels.

And do you know what the critics of his time said about him? They said that his work couldn't be taken seriously because he wrote *too much* and admitted that he wrote for money. Like authors are supposed to languish in drafty garrets waiting for inspiration to strike."

Jane didn't know what to say. Of course she *did* know what the critics had said about Trollope. She had been outraged when the man's delightful books had been so cruelly treated. She herself had weathered some terrible notices. But nobody remembered those now save for some academics who insisted on recording every tiny thing about a person's life. What people remembered was that her books were *read* and that they were *enjoyable.*

"I didn't mean to sound ungrateful," she told Walter. "I do like Gossford's books. I suppose I'm just afraid I won't be taken seriously."

"I take you seriously," said Walter. "Your friends take you seriously. Do you honestly care what some critic who doesn't even know you thinks?"

Jane thought for a moment. "Well, yes," she said. "I'm afraid I do. Oh, I know it's shallow of me, but I can't help it. I do care, Walter. This is my first novel. I want people to love it as much as I do."

"Well, so far no one has said a bad thing about it," Walter reminded her. "I'm sure someone will—"

"Thank you," Jane interrupted. "That makes me feel immensely better."

"But they'll be wrong," Walter concluded. "You just have to remember that."

She knew what he said was true. It was, however, difficult to keep herself from looking to see what was being said about her book. In addition to the reviews Kelly sent her, she had taken to looking herself up on the Internet. As the book was only available as a review copy, there was not a lot she hadn't seen, but she had found a handful of blogs and such in which she was mentioned. As with the reviews, most of the things written about her were positive, although a couple had been less than flattering.

One in particular continued to bother her. It was a blog called the Constant Reader. The writer was Violet Grey, the Brontë scholar, and she apparently fancied herself an expert on what she referred to as "novels of the heart." She had recently posted an item about *Constance*—which she admitted to not yet having read—in which she made snide comments about Jane's author photo and expressed doubt that "a woman with such a bland face could pen something filled with passion." In a fit of pique Jane had left an indignant comment (anonymously, of course) on the post, suggesting that Miss Grey confine her remarks to the work at hand. She had not received a reply.

"What do you want to do on the big day?" Walter asked, drawing her back to the moment.

"Big day?" said Jane, trying to remember if she'd forgotten an imminent birthday or holiday.

"The day your book comes out," Walter explained. "We should do something to celebrate."

"I haven't thought about it," said Jane. "I suppose we could make a display in the window."

"I don't mean at the store," Walter said. "I mean what do *you* want to do?"

"Let me think about it," Jane told him. "I may be all booked out by that point."

"You'd better not be," said Walter. "This is just the beginning."

"You sound like Kelly," Jane said. "He said almost the same thing to me this morning."

"He's right. You're going to be a star. I just know it."

Something in his voice troubled Jane. "You sound as if that might be a bad thing," she said.

Walter smiled briefly. "It's not bad," he said. "Not for you, anyway. Maybe for me."

"Why would it be bad for you?" asked Jane.

Walter sighed. "You'll be a big success," he said. "I'll be the small-town contractor who can't offer you anything."

Jane waited for him to laugh or tell her he was kidding. When he didn't, she said, "You really are worried about that, aren't you?"

"A little," Walter admitted. "As it is, you don't want to marry me. Why would you change your mind once you have the attention of people in the literary world? Then you'll want someone like . . . like . . . Kelly or . . . Brian George," he concluded.

Jane looked into his eyes. She could see he was serious. *Tell him the truth*, a voice in her head commanded. *Tell him now.*

"That's not it at all," she said, realizing immediately that it was the wrong thing to say. "What I mean is . . . marriage . . . you . . . me . . ."

"You don't have to say anything," Walter told her. "I know how things are. And I'm happy we've had this long together. I've always known it wouldn't be forever."

Jane reached for his hand. "No," she said. "You really don't understand. I do care for you. Very much."

"But?" said Walter.

Jane knew that if she was going to tell Walter the truth, it would be now. She closed her eyes. "But I'm . . . ," she began. She could sense Walter's nervousness as he waited for her to continue. *Just say it!* the voice in her head cried. *Just tell him already!*

"I'm celibate," she blurted out.

She opened her eyes a little and looked at Walter's face. *Celibate?* she thought. *That's what you thought of first?*

"Celibate," said Walter.

Jane nodded. "Yes," she answered. "Celibate."

"I see," said Walter. He cleared his throat. "That certainly explains some things. May I ask, is this a religious thing?"

"No," Jane said. "It's more of a . . . spiritual thing. I made the decision about twelve years ago. It just seemed . . . right. For me. Not for everyone, of course. Then we'd just die out." She clamped her lips shut, afraid she would say something even more stupid if she kept talking.

"Twelve years," said Walter. "That's a long time."

Jane nodded but said nothing.

"And that's why you don't want to get too serious?"

Jane nodded again. "It just wouldn't be fair to you," she said.

"Excuse me for saying so," said Walter, "but shouldn't that decision be mine? Suppose it doesn't matter to me anyway. Suppose there's some reason why I can't . . . you know," he said, making a vague motion with his hand toward his crotch. "Maybe I have physical problems in that area, or just don't like it, or have hangups about my body."

"But you don't, do you?" Jane asked.

Walter shook his head. "Well, no," he said. "But that's not the point. The point is that you've been keeping this from me because you thought it would upset me. You didn't give me the chance to tell you whether it would or not."

"Would it?" said Jane, forgetting that she had invented her celibacy precisely to prevent a similar discussion.

Walter leaned back in his chair. "I don't really know," he said. "I've gone without it this long. Maybe it doesn't matter."

Jane blushed. To her great relief, Walter had never attempted to do more than kiss her. She'd assumed he was too much of a gentleman to suggest more. The truth was she was afraid of what might happen if she coupled with a human. Should her hunger become too strong, Walter would be imperiled. As for herself, she wasn't certain that a mortal male could fulfill her in the way a vampire could.

"I need to think about it," he said. He gave a short laugh. "And all this time I thought I was the problem. Not that you have a problem," he added hastily. "I'm not saying that."

"I know what you're saying," Jane said. "It's all right. I should have told you sooner. I guess I was just embarrassed."

"Don't be," Walter said. "It's nothing to be embarrassed about."

Jane felt terrible. She'd lied in order to put off having to tell him the real reason for her reluctance to become serious. Instead he was reassuring her that there was nothing wrong with her. *Now how will I ever tell him?* she wondered.

"I should go," Walter said. "It's late, and I have to get up early to drive to Syracuse to pick up a sink."

"You're trying to be polite," said Jane. "I've upset you. I'm sorry."

"I'd be lying if I said I wasn't a little . . . perplexed," Walter replied. "But I'm not angry. We'll talk tomorrow."

Jane patted his hand. "All right," she said. "And thank you for being so understanding."

She walked Walter to the door, where he gave her an awkward kiss. Afterward, he laughed. "I feel like a teenager," he said. "I'm not sure what I can get away with."

Jane kissed him again, this time for longer. "Good night," she said.

She shut the door behind her and leaned against it. "What have I done?" she said. "I've made things even worse. Now he thinks I'm frigid."

She went into the kitchen and took a pint of chocolate ice cream from the freezer. Removing the lid, she began spooning it into her mouth. But after half a dozen bites she'd had enough. Instead of feeling better, she was feeling worse. *And if chocolate can't fix it,* she thought as she put the container back, *you know it's bad.*

She turned out the kitchen light and went upstairs, where she brushed her teeth, changed into a nightgown, and got into bed. She had to push Tom out of the way, as he was sleeping on her pillow. He meowed in protest and relocated to the other side of the bed.

"Don't you start," Jane told him.

She leaned back against the pillows and looked at the ceiling, vaguely noting that she ought really to vacuum the cobwebs out of the corners. She wanted to go to sleep, but she knew she would just keep thinking about how she was hurting Walter more every time she lied to him. She'd done so much to keep the truth from him that now she wasn't even sure whom she was trying to protect—him or herself.

Maybe you just don't want to be with him, she thought.

"I don't know!" she said in frustration. "I don't know what I want!" As always, she wished that Cassie were there to talk to. She had always given sound advice. Even when Jane had not been able to decide what choices her characters should make, Cassie had helped her work through the options. But Cassie wasn't there now.

"I wish I were dead," Jane complained to Tom. "I mean undead. No. Un-undead. Oh, I don't know what I mean."

Gripping the sheets in her hands, she began to cry.

Chapter 20

She stole glances at the other girls' dresses,
comparing them to her own. They all looked so
lovely, moving about the room like butterflies
riding warm summer breezes. She, however, was a
moth, drab and inconspicuous as she sat in the
corner, wearing a hole in the velvet of the sofa as
revenge for her invisibility.

—Jane Austen, *Constance*, manuscript page 11

"WHAT DO YOU THINK?"

Jane looked at the book she was holding in her hands. *Her* book. She'd just opened the overnight package from Kelly, which had arrived only minutes before. Now she was on the phone, thanking him for sending it.

"It's beautiful," said Jane, running her fingers over the glossy cover. The title and her name were in raised lettering. Her fingers traced the letters. "I can't believe it's mine."

"You should be getting a box of fifty copies later this week," Kelly told her. "But I couldn't wait for you to see it."

Jane opened the cover and looked at the title page. She turned the pages slowly, watching the words go by. The smell of the ink and paper floated up like the scent of a rare flower. She closed her eyes and inhaled it.

"Thank you for sending it," she said.

"It's my pleasure," said Kelly. "I also have some news for you."

"I don't think it can get any better," Jane told him. "What is it?"

"Nick sent a copy of the book to Comfort and Joy."

"Is that a bookstore?" Jane asked.

"Comfort and Joy," said Kelly. "You don't know who they are?"

Jane thought for a moment. "The television people?" she said.

"That would be them," Kelly confirmed.

Jane inhaled sharply. Comfort and Joy were the queens of daytime television. Joy, a perky blonde with conservative views and insufferably cute triplets of whom she spoke incessantly, was the polar opposite of Comfort, a liberal African American woman from Louisiana who doled out homegrown advice in a no-nonsense manner. They had been the winners of one of the endless reality shows that had taken over television in recent years, and their resulting talk show had been meant to last only a season. But to everyone's surprise, it had quickly become a hit, particularly with women, and it had now been running for five years. Several times a year they devoted an episode to a current book. They would interview the author and discuss the book with audience members. Almost invariably, the books they selected flew off the shelves. Lucy had made a prominent display of Comfort-and-Joy-recommended books, and browsers frequently came to the counter with at least one of the titles in hand.

"They want *me*?" said Jane.

"Nick is firming up the details," Kelly said. "I should have let him tell you, but I couldn't resist. He's going to kill me for ruining his surprise."

"I'm going to be on television?" said Jane.

"Not just television, Jane. Comfort and Joy. This is huge. Nick will call you later with the details."

They talked for a few more minutes before Jane hung up. She sat at her desk in a daze, staring at the novel in front of her. *This isn't happening,* she thought. *There's been a mistake. This is someone else's book. Somehow my name got on the jacket.*

"You got a copy!"

Lucy's voice startled Jane out of her thoughts. Lucy snatched the book from the desk and looked at it. She flipped it over and scanned the blurbs on the back, then opened it to read the author bio. She reminded Jane of a new parent checking the baby to make sure all of its fingers and toes were accounted for.

"Can I put it out front?" Lucy asked.

Jane shook her head. "Not yet," she said. "It's an advance copy. The main shipment will be here next week."

Lucy squealed with excitement. "Your first book!" she said. "This is so cool." Then she seemed to remember something. "Well, not your *first* book," she amended. "Oh, you know what I mean."

"I do," said Jane. "And it might as well be. I haven't published anything in more years than I care to think about. And back then it wasn't quite as exciting. There were no such things as publicists, or interviews, or television talk shows."

"Talk shows?" said Lucy. "Are you going to be on a talk show? What is it, some local thing? I hope it's not that *Book Talk with Bonnie* segment Channel Five does on Sundays. That woman is moon-bat crazy. Do you know she once asked Amy Tan to explain the difference between lo mein and chow mein?"

"No," Jane said, "it's not Channel Five." She told Lucy about Comfort and Joy. She covered her ears as Lucy shrieked in excitement.

"Wait until Walter—" Lucy began when she'd calmed down a little. "Sorry," she added a moment later.

Jane waved a hand at her. "It's all right," she said. Since her talk with Walter things had cooled between them. Although they still spoke, they hadn't had what Jane would consider a date, or even a dinner. She didn't know if he'd given up on her or was still thinking about things, and she hadn't pressed him for an answer. She of course felt guilty about this, but she told herself he was the one who needed time.

"I'm sure he'll be excited even though you two aren't . . . ," Lucy tried. She frowned. "I'll shut up now," she said, and handed the book back to Jane. "I'll be out front," she whispered. "Minding my own business."

As soon as Lucy left, the phone rang again. Jane picked up and heard Nick Trilling's voice.

"Bastard already told you," he said.

"Told me what?" said Jane.

"Don't try to cover for him. I heard him. I was just coming into his office to tell him you're confirmed for the show. I had to take a few minutes to tear him a new one, otherwise I would have called you right away. I can't let him get away with that shit. Pardon my French."

Jane tried not to laugh. Nick's blustery manner was one of his charms. "I confess," she said.

"You're going to be on next Wednesday," Nick informed her.

"The book is out Tuesday, so this is perfect. If we can get even one percent of the five million women who watch that show to buy the book, we'll sell out the first printing. Which reminds me, I'm going to get Kelly to double the run to a hundred thou."

"A hundred thousand," Jane said. "A hundred thousand copies?"

"Right," Nick said. "Oh, and Comfort and Joy are giving each of the audience members a copy. That should be good for word of mouth. I don't like to tempt fate, but I think you're looking at the top of the list."

"The list?" Jane asked, not understanding.

"The *Times* list," said Nick. "As in bestsellers."

"You're joking," Jane said.

"You got wood around there?" said Nick. "Knock on it. But from my lips to God's ears."

"A hundred thousand copies," Jane said dazedly.

"One with five zeros," said Nick. "Which reminds me, I have to go tell Kelly he's got to up the print run. If he gives me any shit about it, I'll remind him that my sister's an editor over at Random House and that I'm not above giving her your number. Does your contract have an option clause?"

"I don't know," Jane answered. "I guess it does."

"Too bad," said Nick. "That would put the fear of Jesus into him. Anyway, I've got to run. My assistant will call you later with your flight and hotel information."

He hung up before Jane could ask him any questions, such as what she should say on the show and what she should wear. *I should probably watch an episode,* she thought. She wondered if she should bring a gift.

The phone rang a third time, startling her. She was almost afraid to pick it up. "Hello?" she said.

"Jane, it's Kelly again. Nick is in here twisting my arm about your print run. I hate to admit it, but I agree with him. We're going up to a hundred thousand. Also, I wanted to let you know that I'll be in Chicago with you. Oh, and one more piece of news."

"Two," Jane heard Nick shout.

"Two," Kelly repeated. "I got a call from the organizer of the Romance Writers' Guild conference. It starts next Friday and they want you to sign books. That's in New Orleans. We'll fly you there from Chicago."

Jane's head was swimming with all of the news she'd received in the past hour. *Comfort and Joy. A hundred thousand. The* New York Times *bestseller list.* The words floated through her head like clouds. *Chicago. New Orleans. Sign books.* It was overwhelming. *I need to make a list,* she thought. Then she remembered what Kelly had said earlier.

"What's the second thing?" she asked. She was almost afraid to hear the answer.

"*Entertainment Weekly,*" Kelly replied. "They want to profile you in their book section. They're doing a big what's-hot-for-summer issue. You're their main fiction selection. As it happens, one of their writers lives in Chicago. She'll interview you at the hotel while you're there for the taping."

Jane heard Nick saying something in the background. "Nick says to tell you that they bumped Nora Collins for you," he said. "I gather she's none too happy about it."

Jane heard what sounded like "tired old cow" being called out in Nick's voice. Kelly laughed. "Anyway, I think that's all the news for today."

"I hope so," said Jane. "I don't think I could take any more. As it is, I'm not sure where to start to prepare."

"Don't worry. We'll walk you through it all," Kelly assured her. "You'll be fine. Remember, you're a superstar."

"A superstar," Jane repeated. "All right, then."

She hung up for the third time that morning. For the next ten minutes she sat staring at the phone, waiting for it to ring again. When it didn't, she took out a pad and started making a list of everything she had to do before leaving for Chicago. In the end it contained only two items.

1. Go over store business with Lucy
2. Find something to wear

"I guess there's not so much to do after all," she said as she looked at the list. She felt as if there should be more involved. Then she thought of something else.

3. Tom

Having a third thing made her feel oddly relieved, even though she knew full well that Lucy would be happy to stay with Tom and look after him. It gave her something to cross off the list and gave her a feeling of accomplishment. At the moment everything else in her life felt as if it were totally out of control. Her book was taking on a life of its own and dragging her along with it. After waiting so long to be published again, suddenly it was happening much too quickly.

She called Lucy in and gave her a brief rundown of what was happening. As she'd expected, Lucy was only too happy to stay with Tom for the week. Going over the store business took very little time as well, and at the end of fifteen minutes Jane had just one item on her to-do list.

"What does one wear on daytime television?" she asked Lucy.

"Nothing white," Lucy answered instantly.

"White?" said Jane. "Why not white?"

"In case you get your period," Lucy explained. When Jane looked at her with a confused expression, Lucy added, "I'm just saying. You don't want to be up there onstage and get a note from Sally."

"Where do you come up with this stuff?" Jane asked. "Aunt Flo? A note from Sally? You're like a gynecological thesaurus."

"Blame my mother," said Lucy. "She never called things by their real names. Until I was seventeen I called my vagina my weet-woo."

"I suppose that's better than calling it your lady garden," Jane mused. "Anyway, apart from not wearing white, we haven't narrowed down my fashion options."

"I'll come over tonight," said Lucy. "We'll go through your closet and see what you have. I'm sure something will work. And if not, we can always go to the mall."

Jane shuddered. "The mall," she said, pronouncing the word as if it were an incurable disease.

"Yeah, well, you might just have to suck it up," Lucy told her. "I'm not letting you meet Comfort and Joy looking like you usually do."

"Like I usually do?" Jane said. "What does that mean?"

Lucy indicated Jane with a wave of her hand. "Like this," she said.

"It's not that bad!" Jane exclaimed.

"Sorry," said Lucy. "It kind of is."

"Byron didn't seem to think so," Jane said, her dignity bruised. "Walter doesn't think so."

"Byron would make it with anything on two legs," Lucy reminded her. "And Walter is . . . Walter. Trust me on this. You need a makeover."

Jane looked at herself in the small mirror that hung on the wall. She did look tired, and her hair *was* a bit on the dull side. "I suppose I could use some freshening up," she admitted.

"We'll start right after work," said Lucy. "It'll be fun."

The bell over the front door jingled, and Lucy went out to help the customer. Jane remained in the office, looking at her reflection in the mirror.

"It'll be fun." She repeated Lucy's promise, trying to sound as if she believed it.

Chapter 21

Charles touched her cheek. "You're like the thrush,"
he said. "It is not the loudest. It does not have the
brightest plumage. But its song is the most
beautiful. Beautiful enough to break your heart."

—Jane Austen, *Constance,* manuscript page 246

"WHAT ARE WE GOING TO DO WITH THIS?"

Jane looked at herself in the mirror. Behind her, Lucy stood with a stunning Japanese woman dressed in a black turtleneck and stylish black pants. The woman was looking down at Jane's hair with a bemused expression, as if it were an accident she had just come across and she was deciding whether or not the victim could be saved.

"Don't worry," Lucy said to Jane, patting her on the shoulder. "Aiko can do miracles."

Jane smiled wanly. She was already regretting letting Lucy talk her into visiting her hairdresser. But according to Lucy, Aiko had graciously agreed to see Jane on short notice. Now Jane was ensconced in the woman's chair, awaiting her verdict.

Aiko poked at Jane's hair with a comb. "Limp," she said.

"Sorry," Jane apologized.

Aiko shook her head. "Horrific color," she said.

"I did it myself," Jane explained.

"I know," said Aiko. She sighed deeply.

"Can you help her?" Lucy asked.

"I don't know," Aiko answered. "It's bad."

"But you'll try?" Lucy said hopefully.

Aiko picked up a pair of scissors and snapped them open and closed several times while staring at Jane in the mirror. "I'll try," she confirmed.

She spun the chair around so that Jane was no longer looking at herself in the mirror.

"Aiko doesn't like you to see what she's doing," Lucy explained to Jane. "It disturbs her process."

"As long as it's nothing too drastic," said Jane.

Lucy put a finger to her lips. "Don't say anything," she whispered in Jane's ear. "She's a little temperamental. Just trust her. She's a genius."

Jane watched as Aiko pulled a pair of black latex gloves over her slim hands. "Color first," she announced.

Jane decided that the best course of action was to close her eyes and think of England. She didn't want to know what Aiko was doing to her head. *It's going to be fine,* she repeated to herself. *It's going to be fine.*

She pretended she was having a dream in which she was moved from one chair to another. Things were applied to her head, then rinsed off. Scissors snapped around her ears. Hot air blew in her face.

Then Aiko said, "Done."

The chair was spun around, and Jane saw her new self in the mirror. She gasped. "I'm beautiful," she said breathlessly.

"Yes," Aiko said. For the first time since Jane had entered her salon, the woman smiled. "Beautiful."

Jane didn't know if she was referring to her haircut or to Jane herself, but she didn't care. She couldn't believe how she looked. Her hair was now a rich golden brown. Aiko had removed a great deal of it, so that it now framed Jane's face rather than circling it like a tired holiday wreath. It was modern, natural-looking, and perfect, Jane thought.

"It's a miracle." Lucy was standing beside Jane, staring at her head.

"I know," Aiko said.

Jane reached up and touched the hair where it brushed against her cheek. It felt like she was touching someone else's face. "It's really me," she said.

"Now for your makeup," said Lucy.

"No makeup," Aiko said. "Just hair."

"No, no," said Lucy. "We're doing makeup at home."

"Good luck," Aiko said, and walked away.

"Thank you," Jane called after her. She looked at Lucy. "Am I done?" she asked.

Lucy nodded, then helped Jane out of the chair. Jane paid for her haircut at the front desk, where a thin young man dressed all in black said nothing as he handed Jane the credit card slip for her to sign.

"They're very quiet, aren't they?" Jane asked as she and Lucy left the salon.

"Aiko is all about minimalism," said Lucy. "I think she likes you," she added as they got into Jane's car. "She doesn't normally talk so much."

Jane drove back to her house, making a stop at a drugstore so that Lucy could pick up some cosmetics she declared they needed for the second part of Jane's transformation. Lucy made Jane wait in the car as she shopped. Jane spent the time looking at herself in the rearview mirror. She still couldn't believe she was looking at her own reflection, and had to resist the urge to turn around and search the backseat to see if some other woman was sitting there.

When Lucy returned, she was carrying a large bag. "Is that all for me?" Jane asked. "Am I that bad?"

"It's just a few things," Lucy said unconvincingly.

Her lie was revealed twenty minutes later when, in Jane's bedroom, she upended the bag and unleashed a torrent of tubes, compacts, brushes, jars, and various other items Jane didn't recognize.

"I didn't know you were a cosmetologist," Jane joked.

"I had to do all the makeup for the band," said Lucy. "I picked up a few techniques."

Like Aiko before her, Lucy didn't allow Jane to see herself as her face was done. However, she did explain to Jane what she was doing, as well as show her the different brushes and curlers and lip liners she used.

"Apply the darkest shadow to the inside corner of your eye," she said. This was followed by "Use liner to give your lips shape," "Hold the eyelash curler in place for at least ten seconds," and "Put the blush on the apples of your cheeks." "Are you getting all this?" she asked in between pronouncements.

"I think so," Jane said anxiously.

"I'll write it down," Lucy said, shaking her head.

"It's all so complicated," said Jane. "In my day we just bit our lips to bring a little color to them."

"Don't use the 'I was born before Maybelline was invented' excuse," Lucy said. "You've had a thousand years to learn how to wear makeup."

"Don't exaggerate," said Jane. "I just never saw much use in it."

"Well, you should have," Lucy said. "You look amazing." She picked up a hand mirror and held it in front of Jane's face. "See?"

Jane had been stunned by her new hair; now she was equally amazed at the transformation her face had undergone. It was still her, just a new and improved her. Best of all, she wasn't all tarted up like some courtesan.

"I was afraid I was going to look like Marie Antoinette," she told Lucy.

"The bird-shit-facial look went out a few years ago," Lucy teased.

Jane touched her face. "I had no idea I could look like this," she said. Then, to her immense surprise, she began to cry. "I had no idea," she said again.

Lucy put her arms around Jane. "You've been a lady for two hundred years," she said softly. "But somewhere along the line, you forgot how to be a woman."

Jane laughed as Lucy tried to keep a straight face. "That line is worthy of Bulwer-Lytton," said Jane. "But I appreciate the sentiment. Thank you." She dried her eyes with a tissue Lucy produced from a pocket. "I'm never going to be able to do this on my own, you know."

"It's really not that difficult," Lucy said. "Now, let's see what you have in that closet."

"Wait a minute," Jane said. "Just sit with me for a little bit."

Lucy sat back down on the bed. "Is something wrong?" she asked.

"Not wrong," said Jane. "Just a little overwhelming. It really *has* been a long time. For everything. But now I'm a writer again. It's all happening so quickly."

"You didn't think it would, did you," said Lucy.

Jane shook her head. "No," she admitted. "I sort of . . . well, I gave up hoping."

Lucy hesitated a moment. "Have you really not . . . been . . . with anyone since Byron?"

"Oh, I have," said Jane. "I mean, I'm no Marie Duplessis, but I've had a number of affairs of the heart."

"Affairs of the heart," Lucy repeated. "In other words, you haven't had *sex*."

"Don't be vulgar," Jane said primly.

"Not even with other vampires?" asked Lucy.

"Especially not with them," Jane said.

"You never talk about any of that," Lucy said. "Why not? Don't you have any vampire friends?"

Jane gave a little laugh. "You make it sound like a garden club," she said. She thought for a moment, trying to decide how much she wanted to say. It was not a topic she was particularly comfortable speaking about. "I did associate with others," she said. "For the first fifty or sixty years, I found it pleasant to be with them."

"Were there a lot of you?" Lucy asked. "*Are* there a lot of you?"

"Not so many," said Jane. "But at that time we banded together more than we do now. I did have friends," she continued. "Some of them you've even heard of. And no, I'm not going to tell you who they are," she added before Lucy could ask. "One of the rules is that we don't expose one another unless it's absolutely necessary. Anyway, when you first turn, you want to be with those like yourself. It's comforting. But over time, I found that beyond *what* we are, we had little in common. I spent less and less time with the others. For the last hundred years, I've had virtually no contact with that world."

"Until now," said Lucy. "Until Byron showed up."

"Until Byron," Jane agreed. "But I'm not doing this for him," she added. "I'm doing it for me."

"And maybe a little bit for Walter?" Lucy teased.

"Don't ruin a lovely moment," said Jane. She took Lucy's hand. "You really are very special to me," she told her. "I hope you know that."

"I do," Lucy said. "And you're special to me." She stood up, pulling Jane with her. "Which is why I'm going to make sure you don't wear anything tragic on national television."

Chapter 22

She looked out into the garden. There, by the rose bushes, stood the figure of a man. He looked up at the window, unmoving. Was it Charles? She tried to make out his features, but the rain obscured them. She ran down the stairs and through the kitchen door. Her feet slipped on the wet grass as she made her way to the back of the house. But when she reached the garden, the man was gone. A single red rose lay in the place where he had stood.

—Jane Austen, *Constance*, manuscript page 193

JANE WATCHED THE BAGS GOING AROUND ON THE CONVEYOR BELT. One by one they were picked up by waiting passengers and wheeled away. They had stopped coming out from the depths of the airport's underbelly some time ago, and now only three forlorn bags and one box marked FROZEN FISH remained. They slowly circled the baggage claim until with a *chunk-chunk-chunk* the machinery ground to a halt.

"Looks like we've been stranded on the Island of Lost Luggage," said a man standing next to Jane. "Might as well get in line."

He turned and walked away. Jane followed his path and saw that he was heading for a line of about twenty people. They were queued up outside the airline's baggage claim office, and all of them wore a look of resigned frustration on their faces. Scanning the remaining bags once again in the hope that she'd somehow overlooked her suitcase, Jane gave up and joined them.

Half an hour later she stood in front of a grim-faced woman who didn't look at her as she said, "Claim ticket."

Jane handed over the sticker that was stapled to her ticket folder. "Do you know when I can expect my bag?" she asked.

The woman's grunt held more than a hint of mean-spirited glee, Jane thought. She wondered what kind of person could do such a job day in and day out, dealing with miserable travelers and wayward luggage for hours at a time. *Sadist,* she thought as the woman typed something on a keyboard with undisguised hostility.

"There's no record of it," the woman said. "Sorry."

"No record?" said Jane. "I don't understand. I have a claim ticket." She nodded at the ticket, which was still in the woman's hand.

"There's no record of it," the woman repeated.

Jane gave the woman her sweetest smile. "Surely there must be *some* record," she said.

The woman sighed deeply. "It could be anywhere," she said in a weary voice. "Albuquerque, New Delhi, Paris. Take your pick. If it's not in the system, it officially doesn't exist."

"But surely—" Jane began.

"Fill this out and send it in," the woman interrupted, sliding a form toward Jane. "We'll reimburse you up to a hundred and fifty dollars." She looked past Jane. "Next," she said.

Jane started to argue but, sensing the growing irritation of the people behind her, decided there was no point. The woman was clearly not going to be of any further use. Besides, Jane was already going to be late getting to the hotel. It was half past nine, and her interview with the *Entertainment Weekly* reporter was at eleven. Feeling more than a little put out, she headed out the door to the taxi stand.

The trip from O'Hare to the hotel took much longer than Jane expected, and when she finally reached her room after ten minutes at the registration desk it was a quarter to eleven. She barely had time to use the toilet and wash her face before there was a knock on the door.

She opened it to find a woman who seemed impossibly young to be a journalist. Thin as a willow, she was dressed impeccably and her makeup was flawless. Her auburn hair fell about her shoulders in waves and perfectly complemented her green eyes. Jane hated her immediately.

"Hi," the woman said cheerfully. "I'm Farrah Rubenstein."

"Farrah," Jane repeated.

Farrah laughed. "I know, right? My mother was a huge *Charlie's Angels* fan. My sisters are Kate and Jaclyn. It's all too retro." She entered the room without further invitation. "What a great room!" she enthused. "It's so red!"

"Yes," Jane said. The young woman's manner had caught her off guard. She'd been expecting someone older, someone more reserved. *I probably should have looked at the magazine,* she thought. She'd bought a copy to read on the plane, but had fallen asleep shortly after takeoff and woken up just before landing in Chicago.

"I was so excited when I got this assignment," Farrah said as she removed her jacket and sat down on one of the chairs in the suite's living room area. "I love books."

"Do you?" said Jane politely.

Farrah nodded. "I was a *huge* fan of the Cherry High Gossip Club series when I was in high school," she said.

Jane suppressed a laugh. The Cherry High books were some of the most vapid books she'd ever come across. They centered around a group of girls who published an anonymous gossip magazine about the goings-on at their upper-class high school. Not surprisingly, the series sold millions of copies, particularly after the television show based on it became a hit.

"Do you know Felicity Bingham?" Farrah asked, naming the author of the series.

"I'm afraid not," said Jane.

Farrah took a small tape recorder from her bag. "Too bad. I assumed all of you writers know each other," she said.

Jane sat down on the couch opposite Farrah. "Brakeston isn't exactly the literary capital of the world," she said.

"Brakeston?" Farrah repeated, a frown creasing her flawless brow.

"Where I live," said Jane. "It's in New York."

Farrah nodded. "I remember now. Sorry. I've been crazy busy this week."

"It's quite all right," Jane said.

Farrah fussed with the tape recorder for a minute while Jane waited. Then she placed it on the table between them. "Okay," she said. "Let's start. You're English, right?"

Jane repeated the story she'd rehearsed in preparation for the interview, and for all the interviews Nick assured her she would be doing. She was from England but had moved to the United States at a young age when her father, a diplomat, was transferred there. She had no siblings. Her parents were both dead. It was tragic and convenient, and Jane told it well.

"That's pretty much what the bio your publisher sent over said," Farrah told her. "I tried to find out more on the Internet, but there isn't anything. Don't you have a website?"

Jane shook her head. "I'm afraid I'm not terribly up-to-date on technology," she said. "I'm old-fashioned that way."

"Old-fashioned," Farrah repeated. "That's kind of sweet. Usually when I interview people they're texting and checking their email at the same time."

She asked a few more tedious questions (What did Jane do for fun? What was her writing day like? How did it feel to have her first novel come out at her age?), all of which Jane answered with what she hoped was charm and wit. Then Farrah cleared her throat and adopted a more serious demeanor.

"Where did you get the idea for the novel?" she asked.

"It's something I've worked on for a number of years," Jane told her. "The idea first occurred to me when a friend was having a new house built. I started thinking about how intimate the relationship between the builder and the homeowner is. It's almost a marriage of sorts. Then I came up with the characters of Constance and Charles, and the rest grew from there."

Farrah nodded vigorously. "I see," she said. "So they're real people?"

"Well, no," Jane replied. "They're fictional characters based on the experience of a friend."

"What's your friend's name?" asked Farrah.

Jane hesitated. "I don't think she'd want to be mentioned by name," she said.

"If it was someone else's experience, don't you feel like you—I don't know—stole it?" said Farrah.

"Stole it?" Jane said, shocked. "No."

"But it isn't your story," Farrah persisted.

"It's *fiction*," Jane said. "All fiction is based on some kind of truth. My book is not literally about my friend. It is *inspired* by her."

"I see," said Farrah. "Still, don't you think you should have come up with something of your own?"

Jane looked at the reporter for some time, unsure how to respond. Finally, Farrah spoke again. "I'm sorry for asking these questions," she said. "But I think we journalists owe it to our readers to print the truth."

"The truth?" Jane said. "I don't understand."

Farrah turned off the tape recorder. "I shouldn't do this," she said. "But I love your book, and you seem like a nice person." She pursed her lips, as if she were trying to solve a math problem. "I got an email," she said eventually. "A couple of days ago. I don't know where it came from. It was anonymous. Whoever sent it said that you . . . borrowed the idea for your book from someone else."

"Borrowed it?" said Jane. "You mean plagiarized it?"

"I don't like to use that word," Farrah said. "But yes, that's more or less what it said."

Jane was at a loss for words. Who would accuse her of such a thing? She hadn't the faintest idea. She had no enemies that she knew of. *Except possibly Byron,* a voice in her head said.

Byron. Would he really do such a thing? She could think of no one else who would want to. But this was low even for him. Did he really despise her so much? *You did wound his manly pride,* the same voice reminded her.

She could sense Farrah waiting for an answer from her. But how should she proceed? She could protest all she wanted to, but the accusation had already been leveled. Anything she said would sound disingenuous, especially to someone like Farrah, whose idea of investigative journalism was based on the reporting skills of the girls of Cherry High.

"I think it's important that I address this," Jane said carefully. "But would you excuse me a moment? There's something I have to attend to. It will only take a few minutes."

"Sure," Farrah answered. "No problem."

Jane stood up. "I'll be back shortly," she told the young woman. "Please, help yourself to a beverage from the minibar." She smiled graciously as she went to the door.

Once she was in the hallway she ran as quickly as she could to the elevator. She paced as she waited for it to arrive, then practically leapt inside when the doors finally opened. Hitting a button on the control panel, she rode down a floor and got out. She looked for the numbers painted on the hallway wall and followed the arrow to number 1822. She rapped on the door and waited for Kelly to answer. A moment later the door opened.

"You have to help me—" Jane began. Then she realized that the man standing before her wasn't Kelly. It was someone she'd never seen before. And he was wearing nothing but a towel wrapped around his waist. "I'm sorry," Jane fumbled. "I must have gotten the number wrong."

"Who is it, Bryce?" Jane heard Kelly's voice. "Is that my laundry?"

"No," the man Jane now assumed to be Bryce said. "I believe

it's your author." He moved out of the way as Kelly appeared in the doorway.

"Jane," he said. "Aren't you supposed to be doing your *Entertainment Weekly* interview?"

Jane nodded. "That's why I'm here," she said, glancing inside the room where Bryce was looking through the wardrobe.

Kelly noticed her stare. "I'm sorry," he said. "I should have introduced you first. Bryce, this is Jane. Jane, this is Bryce. My partner."

The last word hit Jane like cold water. *Partner,* she thought numbly as she realized what it meant.

"I forgot you two have never met," Kelly continued, oblivious to her shock.

Bryce slipped a shirt on. "I *love* your book," he said.

"Thank you," said Jane. She turned her attention back to Kelly. "We have a problem," she said. She then explained the situation.

"Is that all?" Kelly said when she was done. "Don't worry. This happens with every big book. Some crackpot starts a rumor that the author plagiarized the book. He fires off letters to various magazines and tries to cause trouble. Usually it's some wannabe who thinks he'll get attention or money by causing a stink."

"But she says she doesn't know who sent the email," said Jane.

"That's actually good news," Kelly told her. "That means it's just someone with nothing better to do. Here's what you do. Tell this woman—what's her name?"

"Farrah," said Jane.

"Farrah?" Kelly and Bryce said in unison.

"Something about her mother," said Jane. "So, what do I say?"

"You tell her that we're aware of the emails and that they're being sent maliciously by someone who has a grudge against you. Tell her our legal department is handling it. That will shut her up. She won't write anything about it if she thinks she might get in trouble for spreading unfounded claims."

"That's it?" said Jane.

"That's it," Kelly said. "Sometimes living in a litigious country works to your advantage. Now go, before she gets even more suspicious. Here, take this so she thinks you really did have something you needed to do." He handed Jane a copy of her book. "She's only read a bound galley. Tell her you wanted her to have a signed copy of the real thing."

Jane took the book. "*Go,*" Kelly ordered. "We have to be at the studio by one-thirty."

"Bye!" Bryce called out as Jane left. Jane didn't answer. As she headed for the elevator, she wondered how she could have been so foolish regarding Kelly's preference for men. *He's smart, handsome, and cultured,* she thought. *I should have known. You'd think I would have learned my lesson after what happened with Percy Shelley.*

Back at her room, she paused at the door and caught her breath. She looked at her watch. She'd been gone only five minutes. Now she simply had to get through the rest of the interview. She would tell Farrah that she'd had to get permission from her editor to tell her about the claim of plagiarism, as it was now a legal matter. That should take care of it.

She opened the door. "I'm sorry about the interruption," she said. "I wanted to get you—"

She stopped mid-sentence. Farrah was lying across the bed. Her eyes stared up at the ceiling, unblinking.

Chapter 23

Mrs. Eleanor Burnham regarded Constance icily.
"You should be commended on your successful
entry into our company," she said. "It isn't
often that a young woman of your
background rises above it."
"I wonder if that is indeed the case," Constance
replied, smiling sweetly. "Or perhaps it is not I who
have risen but you who have fallen."

—Jane Austen, *Constance*, manuscript page 115

"FARRAH?"

Jane approached the bed slowly. The reporter didn't respond, and her eyes remained open. Then Jane noticed the two small wounds on her neck. The blood around them was still fresh.

"No, no, no," said Jane, shaking the young woman. Her limp body rolled beneath Jane's hands. Her head turned and she looked, unseeing, into Jane's face.

"Damn," Jane said firmly. The girl was gone.

Clearly, she had been bitten. But by whom? As far as Jane knew, she was the only vampire in the hotel. Then again, she had never been particularly good at sensing her own kind; it was as if her vampire radar had fizzled out from years of disuse. Certainly there were likely to be others of her kind in Chicago, but she didn't know any of them. The only other possibility was Byron.

It all became clear. Byron was the one who had sent the reporter the email. Now he had killed her in order to frame Jane not only for plagiarism but for murder as well. *I knew he left too easily,* she thought bitterly. *He was planning his revenge.*

Well, he'd done a good job of it. She looked at Farrah's lifeless body. Then she lifted the girl's lips with her finger, recoiling at the sensation. There was no blood on her teeth. That, at least, was good. It meant that Byron hadn't turned her. She was merely dead. *Which isn't much of a relief,* Jane thought as she closed the girl's mouth and reached for a tissue with which to wipe her finger. As she did, she noticed the clock on the bedside table. It was almost noon.

She remembered Kelly saying that they had to be at the studio by one-thirty. And she still had nothing to wear. She'd dressed comfortably for the plane, and what she had on was not at all acceptable for appearing before millions of viewers. She had to find something. But she couldn't just leave Farrah lying on her bed. Anyone who came in would see her, and that would be disastrous.

There was no way she could get the body out of the room. Even if she could drag it into the hall, what would she do with it? And she couldn't ask Kelly for help with this particular problem. Apart from the whole murder thing, it would bring up other questions Jane was not prepared to answer.

The longer she worried, the less time she had to shop for an outfit. She looked around the room. The closet was impractical, as was the bathtub. She would have to stow Farrah under the bed for the time being.

Taking the girl by the shoulders, she pulled her off the bed and laid her as gently as she could on the carpet. One of Farrah's shoes fell off in the process, and Jane tried slipping it back on the bare foot. But it wouldn't quite go, and so finally she shoved it under the bed. She followed it with Farrah's body, first pushing it as far as she could, then going to the other side and pulling it the rest of the way.

That's better, Jane thought as she straightened the bedspread. *Now for the shopping.* She located her purse and looked inside for the notes Lucy had written up for her. Lucy had written out what pieces should be worn together, and had outlined the makeup regimen Jane should follow.

Now, however, the list was useless. All of Jane's clothes and makeup were who knew where. She had to start all over, and this filled her with panic. She didn't even know where to begin. But the clock was ticking, and she had to move. Grabbing her key card, she left the room and headed down to the lobby, where she approached the concierge desk.

"Excuse me," she said, trying to keep the hysteria from her voice. "Where's the best place to look for shoes? I seem to have forgotten to pack my good ones."

The man behind the desk answered instantly. "Macy's," he said. "It's only three blocks away. Or you could try Nordstrom, but that's farther away."

"Macy's will be fine," said Jane. "Thank you."

She rushed from the hotel and practically ran in the direction the concierge had indicated. Arriving at Macy's breathless and exhausted, she looked anxiously at her watch. She had less than forty-five minutes to get everything she needed, get back to the hotel, and get dressed in time to meet Kelly for the ride to the television station. She unfolded Lucy's list and read the first item.

"Black pants," she said aloud. "Red blouse. Right."

She consulted a directory and made her way to the women's department. Once there, she looked about helplessly. There were at least twenty different kinds of black pants, and almost as many red blouses.

"May I help you?" A young woman who looked disconcertingly like she could be Farrah's sister approached Jane.

"I need some clothes," Jane said unhelpfully. "And I'm in a hurry." She thrust the list at the associate.

The woman looked over the list and nodded. "I think I know just what you need," she said. "Come with me. My name is Sandra, by the way."

"Jane," Jane said curtly. She cast her eyes at the makeup counter as they went past. *Eye shadow,* she thought vaguely. *Lipstick. Pink, not coral.*

"Let's try these," said Sandra as she stopped in front of a rack of pants. "I think these will fit. Why don't you try them on, and I'll bring you some more options."

"I don't think I have time to—" Jane began.

"The fitting rooms are right over there," said Sandra. "Go on. I'll be right with you."

Jane, cowed, obeyed. She took the pants with her into one of the little changing rooms and dutifully tried them on. To her surprise, they actually fit. She started to take them off, relieved that things were going so smoothly, when Sandra's voice came through the door. "Here are some more pants," she said.

"These will be—" Jane started to say.

"Here," said Sandra, opening the door and thrusting an armful of pants at Jane. "I'll be right back."

Before Jane could object further, the girl was gone. Jane looked at the pile of black pants, all of which looked to her to be exactly like the first pair, and groaned. A quick look at her watch increased her feeling of panic. *I have to get out of here,* she thought.

Opening the door to the dressing room, she crept to the door of the fitting room, the first pair of pants clutched in her hand. She peered out, looking for signs of Sandra. The girl was halfway across the sales floor. She had an armful of red blouses draped over one arm.

Go! a voice in Jane's head shouted. *Go now! Before she sees you!*

Ducking down, she moved between the racks, keeping her head low in case Sandra spied her. Only when she was concealed behind a display of sundresses did she dare look around. Sandra was heading for the fitting rooms. Jane took the opportunity to rush over to one of the racks of blouses Sandra had been looking at. She grabbed one of the red ones, checking only to make sure that it was the right size, then fled toward the shoe department.

Minutes later, clutching a pair of black pumps, she left a stunned shoe salesman still kneeling on the floor surrounded by boxes. Next she tackled the makeup counter. "Eye shadow, lipstick, blush," she shouted at the surprised clerk. "I don't care what colors as long as it matches."

The girl stared at Jane with wide eyes. "What brand would you like?" she asked. "We have a special on—"

"I have five minutes!" Jane shrieked, pounding her fist on the glass countertop.

The girl opened the cupboards beneath the counter and started pulling things out. As she worked, Jane craned her neck, hoping Sandra had given up on her. To her horror, she saw the girl wandering through the racks, apparently looking for her.

"This all looks wonderful," Jane said to the makeup associate. "And I'd like to pay for all of this as well." She loaded the counter with her clothes and shoes and practically flung her credit card at the girl, who ran it through the machine and handed Jane the sales slip to sign.

"I'll just fold these for you," the girl said, opening a bag and picking up the blouse.

"No time!" Jane said. She snatched the blouse from the girl's hands, threw it into the bag, and swept everything else on the counter after it. "Thanks for all your help," said Jane as she ran off. "Tell Sandra I'm sorry."

She arrived back in her room at five minutes to one. Through the door she could hear the phone ringing. She went inside and snatched up the receiver. "Hello?"

"It's Kelly. I just wanted to make sure you're almost ready. We'll be downstairs in fifteen. As usual, Bryce is running late. He has to make himself pretty for Comfort and Joy. But we'll be at the station in plenty of time. It's not far away."

"Fine," Jane said, keeping her voice as calm as possible. "That's fine. I'll see you in fifteen minutes."

Hanging up, she emptied the contents of the shopping bag onto the bed and set to work. Getting the clothes on was easy enough, but doing her makeup was another matter. She'd left Lucy's note in Sandra's hands, and so she had to try to remember exactly what Lucy had said to do. Opening the eye shadow, she saw that the girl had chosen a peculiar shade of purple. When

Jane dabbed some on her eyelid it gave her the appearance of having a bruise.

She tried to ignore the color and applied it as well as she could. Then she added lipstick and blush to her face and sat back to look at the results.

"I look as if I've been dragged backward through a hedge," she muttered. But there was no helping it. She was due downstairs.

As she put on her new shoes, she accidentally kicked one under the bed. Kneeling, she felt around for it. Her fingers closed on the heel almost immediately. Then, as she pulled the shoe out, she realized that there was something her fingers had *not* touched.

Lifting the bedspread, she looked under the bed. Farrah's body was gone.

Chapter 24

The cottage was small and plain, but it had a lovely
garden and a pond. It would do very well. She
imagined herself sitting in the small study, looking
out at the flowers and writing for hours at a time.
"With persistence and six months' time," she told
herself, "you will complete your first novel."

—Jane Austen, *Constance*, manuscript page 278

"Girl, what drag queen did your eyes?"

Comfort took one look at Jane and hauled her away to her own dressing room. "Sit," she said, practically pushing Jane into a salon chair. "Tomboy, where are you?" she bellowed.

A moment later a tall Latino man ran in, drying his hands on a towel. "Settle down, woman," he said. "I was spackling up Miss Joy. You know how long that takes."

He and Comfort cackled over the joke while Jane sat silently, looking at her peacocked eyes in the mirror. Kelly and Bryce had been kind in their compliments; she looked awful, like a prize-fighter on the losing end of a punch.

"Jane, this is Tomboy," said Comfort. "He does our makeup, so you *know* he's a genius. Tomboy, this is Miss Jane Fairfax."

"*The* Jane Fairfax?" Tomboy said, putting his hands on his hips.

"I let him read your book," Comfort told Jane. "Bitch still hasn't given it back to me."

"And I'm not going to give it back," said Tomboy. He put his hand on Jane's shoulder. "I *loved* it," he enthused.

"Sweetheart, do something about Miss Jane's face," Comfort ordered. "Make her pretty like you do me and the gargoyle."

More cackling ensued, then Comfort strode out of the dressing room. Jane could hear her talking to Kelly and Bryce in the hallway. Her deep, rich voice was occasionally broken by laughter.

"She seems nice," Jane said as Tomboy draped a white cloth around her neck.

"As nice as the other one is nasty," said Tomboy. He picked up a cotton pad and dipped it in some cold cream. "Close your eyes," he said.

Jane did as she was told, and a moment later she felt cream being applied to her eyelids. Tomboy's touch was gentle, and it relaxed her frayed nerves. "Is Joy really that bad?" she asked.

Tomboy let out a low whistle. "Let's just say her mama didn't give her the right name," he said. "Maybe if she'd waited until that girl was five or six she would have called her something like Crabapple. Isn't there an actress just named her baby Apple?"

"I think so," Jane said, not knowing whether this was true or not. "Joy always seems so nice on the show." This too was a lie. She'd only watched one episode, and that was to prepare her for her visit. But Joy *had* seemed, if not exactly joyful, at least pleasant.

"They drug her up before the taping," said Tomboy.

"You're joking," Jane said.

"Oh, nothing serious," Tomboy replied as he wiped her eyelids with a warm cloth. "Just a couple of Valium. It keeps her from freaking out."

"I had no idea," said Jane.

"It's for the good of the world," Tomboy assured her. "Now look at me."

Jane stared into his eyes, which were a lovely dark brown. His face was only inches from hers. He reached out and suddenly she felt a sharp pain in the vicinity of her brow. "Ouch!"

"Just tweezing these caterpillars," said Tomboy. He plucked another hair, then another. Jane tried not to wince. When he finally stopped she found that she had been clutching the chair arms in a death grip. This in turn reminded her of Farrah's missing body, and she became anxious all over again.

"Close your eyes," Tomboy said.

Jane felt something—presumably eye shadow—being applied to her lids. She wondered what color it was, although anything would be better than the purple she'd smeared on.

"I really did love your book," Tomboy said as he continued to work. "It's so much better than most of the stuff out there. The characters seem like people you can actually believe exist, not like soap opera actors. It reminded me of Jane Austen."

"Austen," said Jane. "Really?"

"Mmm-hmm," Tomboy murmured. He was running what felt like a pencil along her lower lid. "She's my favorite. I must have read *Mansfield Park* at least a dozen times."

"*Mansfield Park*? Really?" Jane was surprised. It was her own favorite out of all her books, but she was used to people disliking it. "Not *Pride and Prejudice*?"

"Oh, I like that one too," said Tomboy. "But *Mansfield Park* has more, I don't know, depth to it. Fanny's a real person, you know? She basically can't do anything right. Your novel kind of reminds me of that."

He stepped back and looked at his handiwork. After applying a few more touches and adding some blush he said, "Take a look and see what you think."

Jane was amazed. Tomboy had transformed her face. Instead of looking tired and stressed out, she looked fresh and alive. "I can't believe that's me," she said. "Thank you."

Tomboy smiled. "My pleasure," he said. "Now go out there and knock them dead."

As if on cue, Comfort walked in, took a look at Jane, and clucked her tongue. "He went all out on you, girl," she told Jane. "I don't know if I like you showing me up like this."

"I don't think that's possible," Jane told her. "But thank you."

"Come on," Comfort said, taking Jane's hand. "Time to introduce you to the dragon lady." She led Jane down the hallway to another dressing room. Joy was in there, speaking to a rabbity-looking young man who was writing on a pad as Joy spoke.

"And six bottles of gin," Joy said. "But not that crap you got last time. Now go."

The assistant ran out as Joy turned to see who had come in. When she saw Comfort and Jane, she beamed. "Hello," she cooed as she stood and embraced Jane. "I'm soooo pleased you could come."

"Thank you for inviting me," said Jane. Joy was looking directly at her. Jane looked back. There was something odd about Joy's eyes. They looked slightly dull. Then Jane remembered the Valium.

"This is going to be soooo much fun," Joy said. "Isn't it, Comfort?"

"Of course it is," Comfort said cheerfully. "Jane, let me show you to the greenroom. Joy, I'll see you in a minute."

"Bye," Jane called over her shoulder as Comfort hustled her out.

"Lord have mercy," said Comfort. "That girl is mellower than a hound dog on a front porch on a warm day in July. Thank God. All I need is for her to freak out during the cooking segment."

"Cooking segment?" Jane asked. She'd thought she was the only guest.

"Quick and easy quesadillas," Comfort replied as they walked. "It's only ten minutes, but sometimes Joy gets spooked when fire is involved. Anyway, our first guest is this family who collected five thousand dollars just by picking up spare change for a year. Between you and me, I think they looted a couple of wishing fountains, but the kids are cute and it makes the audience feel good. Then you'll be on for the main part of the show, and we'll finish up with the quesadillas."

They arrived at the greenroom. "I've got to go get ready," Comfort said. "You wait here and someone will come get you when it's your turn. You can watch the show on the monitor if you want to."

Jane opened the door to the greenroom. Kelly and Bryce were there, along with a family of five who Jane assumed were the change collectors. Seeing her, Kelly leapt up. "There you are," he said. His tone suggested that he'd had more than enough of the thrifty family, all of whom stared at Jane with broad smiles on their faces.

"I'm Tammy Tucker," the mother of the family said, waving. "This is my husband, Ted, and these are our children. Tracy and

Tina are the twins, and this is Ted junior." All three children waved at Jane in unison.

"Hello," said Jane.

"Do you want to see my change jar?" One of the girls (she couldn't tell which) came up to her holding out a plain glass jar filled with coins. "There's over two hundred dollars in here!" she said proudly.

"Well," Jane said. "Isn't that wonderful!"

"Tina, don't bother the nice lady writer," said Tammy. "Let Mommy fix your hair. We're going to go on soon."

Leaving Tammy to ready her family, Jane and Kelly joined Bryce, who was standing at the back of the room studiously looking over a table heaped with food. "Are they gone?" he whispered.

"No," Kelly replied. "But almost." He turned to Jane. "They showed us the funnel they use for filling coin wrappers," he said.

"I just couldn't take it," Bryce said. "If that kid said 'Canadian pennies aren't real money' one more time, I was going to slap him."

Kelly picked up a bagel. "Do you want something?" he asked Jane.

Jane shook her head. "I don't think I should," she said. Her stomach had already been in knots because of the Farrah problem. Now she could feel it starting to cramp. *Oh, no*, she thought as she realized what it meant. Not only was she nervous, she was going to need to feed soon. All of the anxiety and rushing around had used up her energy. She found herself looking at the three Tucker children. *Surely they wouldn't miss one*, she thought.

Fortunately for the twins and their brother, a show staffer arrived to take them to the set. When the door was shut again, Bryce returned to the seating area. "What a horror show," he announced. "How much money did they say they'd 'found' last year?" He used his fingers to indicate his doubt as to the Tuckers' claim.

"Five thousand, I think," Jane said.

Bryce counted on his fingers. "That's like fourteen bucks a day," he said. "Unless those kids are turning tricks at a truck stop, I don't buy it."

"Stop it," said Kelly, laughing. "Maybe they're just savants. Instead of playing the cello they can spot loose change."

Jane joined them, seating herself in a chair. She tried to ignore the gnawing sensation that was quickly taking over her stomach. *Just make it through the show,* she told herself.

A few minutes later the show began. Jane could hear the audience through the walls, and she could watch it on the monitor. First Comfort and Joy came on and engaged in some banter. This was followed by a commercial, and then the Tucker family was on. Jane tuned them out. Her stomach hurt, and she couldn't stop thinking about Farrah's missing body. More and more, she was sure that Byron was behind it.

"Jane?" A voice woke her from her thoughts. The same fellow who had come for the Tuckers was motioning for her to come with him. Jane stood up.

"Break a leg," Kelly said, squeezing her hand. "You'll be great."

Jane followed the staffer down the hall. As they turned a corner they ran into the Tuckers being escorted back to the greenroom by someone else. "Are we famous now, Daddy?" Ted junior asked his father as Jane passed them.

"We're at commercial," the young man told Jane as he led her onto the set. "We'll be live in ninety seconds."

The Comfort and Joy set was decorated to look like a living room. The two hosts sat on a couch, while their guests sat in the armchairs positioned across an oval coffee table. Jane was put into one of the chairs and someone came from behind and attached a microphone to her blouse.

"It's so nice to meet you," Joy, who was closest to Jane, said. Jane looked at Comfort, who rolled her eyes in sympathy.

"And we're on in five . . . four . . . three . . ." Somewhere to Jane's right someone counted down to the return of the show.

"As y'all know, I'm a readin' fool," Comfort announced. Applause erupted from the audience, but Jane was confused. Comfort sounded like another person, as if she were playing a character.

"Today it is my pleasure to introduce you to Jane Fairfax," Comfort continued. "Jane's book is called *Constance*. Now, I don't want to say this book is better than getting some lovin' from my man, but I was up all night and my husband was asleep next to me."

The audience roared its approval. Comfort's voice was getting on Jane's nerves. Worse, her ears were beginning to ring and she felt herself begin to sweat.

"Comfort, I have to agree with you." Now Joy was talking. Her voice was almost monotone, robotic and distant. "I think this book is maaaarvelous."

"Jane, tell us how you came up with the idea for this novel," Comfort said.

A camera swung toward Jane and she looked right into its blinking red eye. A production assistant motioned soundlessly for her to look at Comfort and Joy instead. Jane turned her head and looked at Comfort's smiling face.

She started speaking, but she didn't hear what she was saying. Her words sounded like the mumbled ramblings of someone speaking through a pillow. She found herself staring at Joy's head. It was bobbing up and down as Joy apparently agreed with whatever Jane was saying. Jane saw Comfort's mouth open and close as she asked a question, and she heard what sounded like the buzzing of bees as she answered. She heard herself laugh, and in the distance the audience laughed back. She had no idea what she'd said. *Don't forget to smile,* she told herself, and pulled her lips back in what she hoped looked like confident enjoyment.

A bead of sweat ran down her back. Why was she so hot? A change in the light caught her eye, and she realized that she was sitting directly under the studio lights. Brighter than normal, they were also hotter, and her sensitive skin was reacting badly to the increased temperature. Already her hands were reddening, and she knew the rest of her would soon follow suit. She put her hands in her lap, trying to cover one with the other to slow the burning.

When finally they came to a commercial break, Jane waited for the all-clear from the stage manager and stood up. Joy remained seated while an assistant fixed her makeup, but Comfort stood up and came over to Jane.

"You're doing great, sweetie," she said. "I apologize for the down-home bullshit. The audience loves it." She glanced over at Joy. "At least that one isn't slurring her words today. I count my blessings. Now look, when we come back we'll wrap this up, I'll announce that everyone is getting a copy of the book, and you can get out of this freak show."

"It's not so bad," Jane said. "I'm having fun."

"I'm glad one of us is," said Comfort. "Now sit down. We're on again in ten."

The second half of the interview went smoothly, at least as far as Jane could tell. The heat from the lights was really starting to bother her. Her skin was itching and she felt as if her makeup had hardened into a mask. When Comfort announced that everyone was getting a copy of Jane's novel, Jane feigned surprise and beamed at the audience. *It's over,* she told herself. Then she heard Joy speak.

"When we come back, chef Juan Fernandez will be showing us how to make quesadillas!" she shrieked. "Jane, why don't you stick around and help us out with that?"

"Well," Jane began. "I really ought—"

"Don't you want Jane to stick around?" Joy shouted at the audience. "Wouldn't that be greeeeat?" They responded by screaming back.

"I suppose I could," said Jane weakly.

"All right, then!" Joy said. "We'll be back in a few minutes."

The show went to a break and the stagehands rushed the stage. Jane jumped up as someone whisked away her chair and another rolled a makeshift kitchen onstage. Someone put an apron around Jane's neck and tied it in the back, and then she was shaking hands with a cranky-looking man in chef's whites. *That would be Juan,* she thought as the man inspected the ingredients that had been laid out on the counter.

"What do I do?" Jane asked him.

"Stay out of the way, and when I tell you to, sprinkle cheese on the goddamn quesadilla," Juan said, his voice heavy with irritation.

Jane huddled beside Comfort, who stood on Juan's left while Joy stood on his right. "Showtime," Comfort said as the stage manager once more counted down from the break.

Jane's head felt as if it were on fire. Her scalp burned, and she feared that at any second her hair might burst into flame. She tried to look interested as Chef Juan explained the finer points of making a quesadilla, but she really had no idea what was happening. The various smells coming from the bowls on the counter were combining in her nose, making her ill. She felt like she might retch.

Then she heard a muted cry of pain and smelled something sharp and metallic. She looked over and saw that Joy, who had been slicing a tomato, had managed to cut her finger. A few drops of blood speckled the counter, and more was seeping from the wound on Joy's hand.

Jane felt her fangs click into place. Her senses sharpened as the scent of the blood kicked her need into high gear. She felt herself being drawn toward Joy's injured finger.

"Whoops!" Joy said gaily. She wrapped her finger in a dish towel. "It's okay. It's just a little nick," she assured the audience.

Jane continued to stare at the blood. She could practically taste it. Her head was swimming. The lights above her felt like burning suns. Her skin was on fire, and her eyes ached. But all she could see was the drops of blood.

Then all of a sudden Joy was thrusting a bowl of grated cheese at Jane. She looked at it dully, then remembered what Juan had told her to do. Taking a handful, she leaned over and tried to sprinkle it on the waiting quesadilla. But the heat from her hands turned the cheese into a gloopy mess that plopped onto the tortilla and sat there like a recalcitrant toad. Chef Juan looked at it, then glowered at Jane.

"Okay," Jane heard Comfort say. "Now we'll put this in the oven." She grabbed the baking sheet with the quesadilla on it and hurried it into the nonfunctioning oven behind them. Then she removed a completed quesadilla from the top rack and displayed it to the audience. "Doesn't it look great?" she asked.

"I just loooooove Mexican food!" Joy proclaimed, while Chef

Juan smiled crookedly and flicked a stray piece of cheese from his fingers onto the carpet.

It was all over a minute later. As soon as the stage manager called break, Jane rushed offstage. Away from the lights she felt a little better. She had just started back toward the greenroom to get some water when Joy walked by.

"Goddamn knife," she muttered as she went past. "Why didn't somebody *tell* me it was sharp?"

The smell of blood trailed Joy like the tail of a kite. Jane's nose twitched. She really *had* to get something to eat. She watched as Joy went into her dressing room. Then she looked around. Everyone involved with the show seemed to be busy. Even Comfort was signing autographs and talking to some audience members. Jane looked again at Joy's dressing room door.

I'll just have a little something, she told herself. *Just to tide me over.*

Chapter 25

She looked at the page before her. Line after line of
words written in her hand covered the creamy
paper. It had taken her the better part of the
evening to compose them. Now, in the light of the
fire, she read them to herself. They were fine words,
filled with meaning and beauty, and they brought
her story to a most satisfying conclusion.

—Jane Austen, *Constance*, manuscript page 356

IT WAS RAINING LIGHTLY WHEN JANE ARRIVED AT LA MAISON DES Trois Soeurs in the French Quarter. The damp air carried a faintly swampy smell, which, combined with the warmth of the day, made Jane feel as if she were wrapped in a very wet wool sweater. Worst of all, it was doing nothing for her hair, which hung limply around her shoulders.

She paid the cabdriver and carried her two bags into the hotel. At the check-in desk a round-faced young man wearing small steel-rimmed eyeglasses greeted her with a sleepy "Afternoon. May I help you?"

"I'm checking in," Jane informed him. She gave him her name and waited as he looked through an old-fashioned ledger book filled with handwritten notations. There wasn't a computer in sight, she noted. In fact, everything in the lobby was a hundred years out of date. Gaslights flickered on the walls, and the solid wood furniture squatted atop the well-worn carpets like enormous beasts wearing pink velvet saddles. *It's really quite lovely,* Jane thought.

"Here we are," the clerk said, making a star next to what Jane assumed was her reservation in the book. "I see that you're in town for the conference."

Jane nodded. "Are there many of us staying here?" she asked.

"A few," the man answered. "Most of the attendees stay at the conference hotel. But some like to stay here because it's more out of the way. Also, they enjoy the authentic atmosphere."

"It certainly is lovely," Jane remarked as she was handed an actual key instead of the electronic card she was used to getting in hotels. Like everything else in La Maison des Trois Soeurs, it was old, its metal worn smooth from unknown fingers.

"You're in room number nine," said the clerk. "It's through the drawing room and up the stairs. Second floor. Would you like some help with your bags?"

Jane shook her head. "I can manage," she said. "But thank you."

"I'm Luke," the man said. "Let me know if there's anything you need."

Slipping the key into her pocket, Jane picked up her bags and walked through the lobby and up the stairs to the second-floor landing. The stairs continued up to the third floor, but a hallway lined with doors stretched out to the right. Jane walked along it until she came to a door with a small brass 9 affixed to its mullion. The key in her pocket fit neatly into the waiting keyhole, and the door swung open with only the faintest groan of protest.

The room was larger than she'd expected. Against one wall was a brass bed covered with an antique quilt in the traditional Jacob's ladder pattern, all in shades of blue. Directly opposite it was a dresser with a large mirror atop it, as well as a comfortable-looking armchair upholstered in deep blue. To the left a door led into what Jane assumed was the bathroom. The far wall was lined with floor-to-ceiling windows, all of which were shut against the rain. Outside was a small balcony of wrought iron that looked over the street below.

Placing one suitcase on the bed and the other beside the dresser, Jane went to the windows and opened one of them. The rain had slowed and now steam was rising from the cobblestones below. The smell of earth and rot was stronger now, but not unpleasant. *It's as if the whole city is decomposing,* Jane thought.

She had not been in New Orleans in almost a century. She'd once known several of her kind who lived there, but she'd ceased corresponding with them long ago. At first their obsession with the past had appealed to her, particularly as things in the world were changing so quickly at that time, making her feel as if the world she knew was disappearing. But eventually she'd tired of their mannered speech and morbid fascination with sleeping in coffins and holding masquerade balls, and had bid them adieu. She was certain that they lived here still, but she had no intention of looking for them. They would only depress her.

She returned to the bed and opened the suitcase. Another shopping excursion in Chicago prior to leaving had provided her with more clothes and other necessities. Removing several items of clothing, she hung them in the narrow closet. She was just carrying her toiletry bag into the bathroom when the chirping of her cell phone interrupted the quiet. Jane retrieved it from where she'd laid it on the dresser.

"Hello?"

"Ms. Fairfax," said a woman's voice, "this is Farrah Rubenstein. From *Entertainment Weekly*," she added when Jane didn't reply.

"Yes," said Jane, startled. She knew who Farrah was. She just hadn't expected to hear her voice. *You're supposed to be dead*, she thought. "It's good to hear from you," she told the waiting reporter.

"I'm sorry to bother you," Farrah said, apparently oblivious to any surprise in Jane's voice. "I just have a couple of follow-up questions about the book."

Jane sat on the edge of the bed. "Of course," she said. She very badly wanted to ask the young woman if she was okay. *Like, have you had any urges to bite people in the neck?* she thought. But she couldn't say anything without admitting that something peculiar had occurred, and part of her didn't want Farrah to know that she had left her stowed beneath the bed while she went shopping. She noticed that she was holding in her hand the red blouse she'd purchased, and she shoved it beneath one of the pillows on the bed lest Farrah somehow know she had it.

"Okay," said Farrah. "I forgot to ask you if the names of your characters are meant to symbolize anything."

Jane answered the question, not listening to a word she was saying. Farrah had several more questions, all of which Jane replied to in the same way. She couldn't get the image of the girl lying on the hotel room bed, her eyes staring up lifelessly at the ceiling, out of her mind. What had happened to her?

"Farrah," she said when she could stand it no longer, "are you feeling all right?"

"Me?" said Farrah. "Yes. Why?"

"Just asking," Jane said, thinking quickly. "I seem to have caught a little bug while I was in Chicago. I think it was the air in the hotel. I wondered if you had experienced any . . . symptoms after our meeting."

"No," said Farrah. "In fact, I feel great. Maybe you're sensitive," she added helpfully.

"Maybe," Jane agreed.

Farrah started to ask Jane a question about the plot of her novel. "You're *sure* you don't feel at all unusual?" Jane interrupted. "Forgetful, maybe? Or tired? Maybe you find yourself craving rare meat?"

Farrah laughed. "Eww," she said. "I'm a vegetarian. No, I feel great. Now, if I could just ask you a few more questions . . ."

They talked for another ten minutes before Farrah thanked Jane for her time and told her when to expect the issue of the magazine to be on the stands. She hung up and Jane turned her phone off. Jane continued to sit on the bed, looking at the phone in her hands and wondering what was going on. *I saw her,* she thought. *That girl was dead.*

But clearly she wasn't. Somehow she had left that hotel room and now either didn't remember a thing or was lying about it. Either way it was distressing. Why would someone go out of their way (out of *his* way, Jane suspected) to drain the reporter and set Jane up for murder, only to then get rid of the body? It didn't make any sense.

Unfortunately, she didn't have time to dwell on it. There was a cocktail reception for conference attendees beginning in an hour, and Jane was expected to make an appearance. Although she felt hot, damp, and now thoroughly confused, she had to go. She forced herself up and into the bathroom to see if she could do anything about her hair.

At a quarter past six she walked into a second-floor ballroom at the conference hotel. It was packed with people—mostly women—talking loudly and taking finger food from trays being carried around by bored-looking waitstaff. Jane noted with some alarm that there was a lot of pink clothing to be seen.

She located the sign-in desk and approached two women whose name tags identified them as organizers. Before she could even say a word one of them shrieked. "Jane Fairfax!" she exclaimed. "I *love* your book." She extended a hand as the people around Jane turned to look at her, clearly wondering who she was to command such enthusiastic attention. Jane, blushing, took the proffered hand.

"I'm Sally Higgins-Smythe," the woman said. "With a *y*," she added, underscoring her name tag with one pudgy finger. "I'm the one who invited you to the conference."

"Then I owe you a great deal of thanks," said Jane. Sally Higgins-Smythe had a wild look in her eyes, bordering on hysteria, and Jane suspected she had been running for the past twenty-four hours on caffeine and sugar.

"Here's your badge," Sally said, pinning on Jane's chest a name tag in the shape of a large heart. "And here's your schedule." She thrust a piece of paper at Jane. "I have to work the table right now, but I can't wait for your talk."

"Yes," said Jane. "I—" She stopped. "My talk?" she asked, registering what Sally had said.

"Didn't they tell you?" Sally said. "You're going to be on a panel about what women want from romance novels. It's you, Penelope Wentz, and Chiara Carrington."

"Nobody mentioned anything about a panel," said Jane. "Is it possible for you—"

"You'll be *fine*," Sally interrupted. "All you have to do is say a little bit and then answer questions."

Jane began to rebut, then thought better of it. She didn't want to cause trouble at her very first conference. *Isn't it enough that you almost got a reporter killed?* she asked herself. *You don't need to add to it by getting a reputation for being difficult.* "You're right," she told Sally. "It *will* be fun."

She left Sally to greet the other arrivals, and made her way to the far corner of the room, where she hoped she could keep out of the way. On her way she lifted a glass of wine from a passing tray and downed most of it before she'd gotten even halfway across the floor. She wished Kelly were there, or Nick. Alone, she felt like the new girl at school. She recognized no one, and everyone was looking at her chest as they tried to figure out who *she* was.

She found a spot next to a potted palm and tried to blend into the crowd. With a little luck, no one would notice her and she could skip out early. Then she could worry about what she was going to say at her panel. *What women want from romance novels*, she thought. *Honestly*.

"Jane?"

Jane looked up to see a tall, lovely woman standing before her. The deep brown of her skin was set off by the gorgeous amber-colored dress she wore. A simple diamond necklace circled her slender throat, and her hair was done up in a tight, shiny knot. Jane racked her brain, trying to identify which movie star she was.

"Chiara Carrington," the woman said, flashing Jane a stunning smile. "I thought I'd introduce myself before our panel tomorrow."

"Oh!" said Jane. "I'm so pleased you did. I just now found out that I'm even doing it."

Chiara laughed. "So did I," she said. "Sally has a way of forgetting to tell authors little details like that. You'll get used to it after a couple of conferences."

For several minutes Jane and Chiara made small talk. Then Chiara said, "I'm ashamed to tell you this, but I haven't read any of your books."

Oh, I bet you have, thought Jane. "It's all right," she told Chiara. "This is my first. And since we're confessing, I haven't read yours either. Is it your first as well?"

"My fifteenth," Chiara answered. A chill had crept into her voice, and Jane realized immediately that she'd made an error. "So many?" she said quickly. "You can't possibly be old enough to have—"

"Excuse me." Another voice interrupted Jane's attempt at an apology. Jane turned to see a woman, small and dressed all in gray, standing beside her. Her skin was fair and her eyes were the same gray as her dress. Her brown hair was gathered into a severe chignon at the nape of her neck.

"I'd like a word with you if I might," the woman said to Jane. She glanced at Chiara. "Alone."

"It's all right," Chiara said. "I was just leaving." She gave Jane an icy look. "I suppose I'll see you tomorrow," she said as she walked away.

Jane turned back to the new arrival. "I didn't get your name," she said.

"Violet," said the woman. "Violet Grey."

Jane, about to shake hands with the woman, kept her hand at her side. "Oh," she said. "I've read your work."

Violet smiled grimly. "I'm sure," she said. "And I yours."

Jane wasn't sure how to proceed. She already knew what Violet thought of her book. Was she supposed to confront her? Or was she expected to just stand there while Violet got some sort of perverse enjoyment out of seeing her squirm?

"I've no intention of making a scene," said Violet, as if reading Jane's mind. "I don't think either of us wants that."

"No," Jane said. "No, we don't."

Violet nodded curtly. "Then I'll say what I've come to say. I intend to expose you."

"Expose me?" Jane said. "I don't know what you mean."

"I imagined you would say that," said Violet. "What I mean is that I can prove that you are not who you say you are."

Jane hesitated. Did Violet know about her? And if so, how? She started to reply.

"Don't bother denying it," said Violet, stopping her. "I have all the proof I need."

"Proof?" Jane repeated.

"That you plagiarized your novel," said Violet.

Jane heard herself laugh with relief. The woman didn't know about her after all. Then her words sank in.

"You think I stole someone else's work?" she said.

"Not just someone's work, Miss Fairfax," said Violet. "Charlotte Brontë's work."

"Brontë?" Jane said. "What in the world makes you think that I stole from Charlotte Brontë?"

"As it happens, I am in possession of the original manuscript that you call *Constance*," Violet informed her.

"That's impossible," said Jane.

"And yet I do have it," Violet insisted. "I also have a witness— an expert in nineteenth-century manuscripts—who will testify to its authorship."

Jane thought for a moment. What *had* happened to the original manuscript for the novel? She tried to remember. Then it came to her—she'd given it to Byron. She had, in fact, written the book as a love letter of sorts to him, keeping it a secret from her family, unlike the works in progress she usually read aloud to them. The thought sickened her now, but at the time she'd thought it the perfect way to show Byron how much she adored him. Then, after what he did, she'd fled his house without the manuscript. She'd had a copy hidden at Chawton, of course, but the original had remained in the house on the shore of Lake Geneva.

"I don't know how you obtained a copy of the manuscript," Violet continued. "I suppose there could be several of them in existence. Brontë was known for always having two or three, in case one was destroyed. But you *do* have one, of this I'm certain. And I intend to prove that you used it as the basis for your book."

"There's been some kind of mistake," Jane said.

Violet snorted. "A very large one, I would say. What do you think the literary world will say when they find out that not only have you plagiarized your novel, but you've prevented the world from knowing that another Charlotte Brontë novel exists?"

"You don't understand," Jane said.

"Oh, I do understand," said Violet. "I understand that unless you stand up tomorrow at your panel and admit to what you've done, I will be forced to expose you."

"What?" Jane said. "I can't do that. It's not true."

"Tomorrow," said Violet, turning to leave. She looked back at Jane. "If you don't do it, I will."

Chapter 26

Charles arrived at the cottage in October, after the first hard frost had brought death to the last of the apples and the few leaves clinging stubbornly to the trees had withered. He came on a bright, cold afternoon, carrying a small suitcase and his favorite ginger tom in a wicker basket. Constance, returning from a walk to the pond to see if the bank ducks had finished building their nest, saw him standing near the front door. But instead of running to him at once she stood very still for a long moment, admiring the way the sunlight dappled his hair.

—Jane Austen, *Constance*, manuscript page 372

JANE WISHED IT WERE DARKER. ALTHOUGH TWILIGHT HAD DE-scended and rain continued to fall, it was still bright enough for Violet to see Jane if she happened to turn around. But so far she hadn't so much as paused, walking briskly through the French Quarter in a peculiar zigzagging route that made Jane wonder if the woman knew she was being followed.

Which of course she was. Jane had waited only long enough for the shock and anger cause by Violet's demand to subside, then had trailed her as she left the hotel. She wasn't sure why, or what she was going to do, but her instinct told her to keep Violet in her sight. And so she followed, staying a block behind in the event she needed to duck into a doorway to escape being seen.

So far Violet had traversed Chartres Street until reaching Jackson Square, on the far side of which she turned onto St. Ann and headed northwest. Turning again, she headed in an easterly direction down Dauphine, eventually crossing the Esplanade and entering the Faubourg Marigny. She continued past Washington Square, crossed Elysian Fields, turned onto Mandeville, and a block later made a final turn onto Burgundy. Halfway down that block she stopped in front of a small red house on the west side of the street, walked across the porch to its front door, and went inside. Jane stood in the shadows across the street, wishing she had worn sensible shoes. Her feet ached, and she could tell that a blister had already formed on her right big toe.

A light went on in the house Violet had entered, shining through the slatted wood shutters and casting watery yellow stripes across the white-painted floorboards of the porch. Jane could see nothing because of the shutters, and so she quickly crossed the street and ducked into the space between Violet's house and the next. There was another window there, but it was covered by heavy drapes, preventing Jane from seeing inside. She continued on, hoping to find a more revealing opening.

She found it at the back of the house. The yard was small, and its garden had been allowed to grow wild, so it now resembled a jungle of flowering plants that perfumed the air. There was a smaller version of the front porch outside a simple door that Jane assumed led to the kitchen. A narrow window on one side of the door glowed faintly in the gloom. Jane thought grimly of snakes as she made her way to the porch and peered through the glass.

She'd been right about the kitchen. It was a fairly large one, shabby but clean. The appliances were quite old—almost antique, Jane thought—and the wallpaper had worn away in several spots due to water damage. *She really ought to have the roof looked at,* Jane thought. *Walter would be appalled if he saw this.*

To one side of the room was a table, rectangular in shape and painted a kind of celery color. Four chairs were arranged around it, one on each side. Three of the chairs were occupied by seated figures. Seeing them, Jane stepped back, afraid that she would be detected. But when after a full minute had passed with none of them moving, she took a second look.

Two of the figures were female. They were dressed in somber dresses much like the one Violet wore. Their hair too was done up like hers, and their faces were equally pale. The third figure was male. He wore a suit, and his hair was parted neatly on one side. His back was to Jane and so she could not see his face. All three of the figures held their hands neatly in their laps.

A moment later Violet entered the room. "I'm back," she said. "And I believe our plan has worked."

None of the others answered her, but Violet didn't seem to notice. She moved about the kitchen, taking items from the refrigerator and putting them on the table, pouring wine into four glasses and setting one at each place. When she was done she took the final seat, across from the man. She lifted her glass.

"To revenge," she said. She laughed and took a sip of her wine. She closed her eyes for a moment. "Isn't it delicious?" she asked.

No reply came from the other three diners, none of whom moved even a finger. Their glasses sat untouched before them.

Still seemingly unaffected by their silence, Violet picked up a platter of meat and lifted a piece from it.

"Anne?" she said, looking to her right. "Oh, of course. You prefer the end cut. I'm sorry." She turned to her left and laid the meat on the plate there. "It's Emily who prefers it rare."

Anne and Emily seem to be keeping their opinions to themselves, Jane thought as she watched Violet load the plates with food. The strange tableau made less and less sense.

"Will you say the blessing?" Violet said, appearing to address the man across from her. She bowed her head. Jane heard no voice come from the man's mouth, but after a few moments Violet raised her head. "Thank you, Branwell," she said.

Branwell? Jane thought. *Anne? Emily?* Realization dawned on her. She looked at Violet, who was talking animatedly as she ate. *They're dolls,* thought Jane. *Mannequins or something. She's dressed them up and thinks they're the Brontës.*

Suddenly it all made sense. Violet wasn't just a Brontëite; she was obsessed with them. No wonder she wanted to believe that Jane's manuscript had been written by Charlotte. *She even pretends that she is Charlotte,* Jane thought. That's why the others were called Anne and Emily. *Of course she picked the most successful one for herself,* thought Jane. *She may be nuts, but she's at least clever.*

Jane had met any number of Brontë fanatics, but Violet took the cake. Not only had she created her own little family, she had somehow managed to unearth Jane's manuscript and convince herself it was really Charlotte who had penned it. It was actually kind of sad, and Jane felt a little bit bad for the girl.

Then again, she's trying to blackmail me, she reminded herself. The question was what to do about it. She could deny Violet's claims, but as long as Violet was in possession of the manuscript there would always be evidence that Jane had copied *someone's* work. Whether it was deemed by experts to be Charlotte's or not, Jane would be charged with plagiarism.

I have to get it back, Jane thought. *It's the only way.*

But how? She couldn't just walk in and demand that Violet give it to her. *You could always drain her,* a voice in her head suggested.

It wasn't a bad idea. She could easily do that, then look for the manuscript while the girl was out cold. With a bit of luck Violet wouldn't remember any of it the next day. But she would still remember the manuscript, which would defeat the whole point. The only sure way to handle her was to drain her completely. To kill her.

Jane was tempted. After all, Violet was threatening her. Worse, she was accusing her of stealing her own work. *She really does sort of deserve it,* Jane thought. But what if she'd told someone else? A friend, perhaps? Or the manuscript expert she'd mentioned. Who was he? Jane had no idea. If she took out Violet, there were still people who could implicate her.

No, the only solution was to get the manuscript itself. Hopefully, Violet had only the one copy. If Jane could get it back, then Violet could make any accusations she wanted to, but without the proof to back them up she would never be taken seriously. She might be able to cause some irritation, or even speculation, but it would be short-lived. And if anyone looked hard enough, they would certainly see that Violet was as mad as a basket of rats.

Jane's challenge, then, was to find the manuscript. If need be, she would bite the girl and incapacitate her, but she hoped that would not be necessary. She would prefer that Violet not see her at all. But she was prepared to do as she must.

She obviously could not enter the house through the kitchen, so she looked for another way. The front door was risky, but she thought a side window might do nicely. Unfortunately, the one she'd passed was locked. She went to the other side and found a second, smaller window. The glass was rippled and difficult to see through. *This must be the bathroom,* Jane thought.

She tried the window, and to her immense relief it slid up, revealing the bathroom Jane had suspected would be there. The door to the room was closed. Now Jane just had to get inside. She put her hands on the sill and gave a little jump. Her head passed into the room and she hung there for a moment, balanced on her stomach as she teetered like a seesaw. Then she was able to grasp the lip of the clawfoot bathtub over which she hovered and pulled herself in. She tumbled into the large tub and lay there, catching her breath and listening for the sound of footsteps.

When none came, she climbed out of the tub and went to the bathroom door. Peering through the keyhole, she looked into a long hallway. It was mostly dark, but from the far end came the glow of the kitchen lamp. *So far, so good,* thought Jane as she eased open the door. She stepped into the hall and looked around. There were two other doors, both of them closed. One of them, she hoped, led to the room where her manuscript was being stored.

She went to the first door and tried the knob. The door opened onto a closet filled with old coats. The smell of mothballs clung heavily to them. Jane stifled a cough as she closed the door and moved on. From the kitchen came the sound of running water. *Dinner must be over,* Jane thought. *I'll have to hurry.*

The second door opened onto what appeared to be a study. A large desk faced one wall, and built-in bookcases that ran from floor to ceiling were filled near to bursting with volumes of all kinds. Oddly, given the time of year, a fire was burning in the small fireplace at the side of the room opposite the desk. An armchair sat in front of it, facing the fire. And before the hearth a small brown and white spaniel was stretched out, its paws twitching as it slept.

Great, thought Jane as she entered the room and shut the door carefully behind her. All she needed was for the dog to wake up and start barking. She eyed it warily as she went to the desk, which seemed the most logical place to look for her manuscript. She pulled open the center drawer. It was filled with the usual assortment of odds and ends: pens, erasers, stamps, a few sheets of stationery. Jane closed it again.

She went through each drawer as quickly and silently as she could. Each time she came up empty-handed. If Violet indeed had a manuscript, she had hidden it somewhere else. Jane stepped into the center of the room and looked around. *Perhaps she's secreted it inside one of the books,* she thought, eyeing the shelves that were groaning beneath the weight of their holdings. There was no way she could look through each of them.

The dog gave a yip, making Jane flinch. She looked over at it and saw that it was still asleep. She wondered idly what it was dreaming about. Then she noticed that there was something on the chair beside it. A stack of papers. *It couldn't be that easy, could it?* she wondered.

She crept over to the chair and looked. Leaning down, she picked up the papers and looked at them in the firelight. *She watched him leave the house with a feeling of great triumph diluted by the bitter taste of despair,* she read. She recognized it as the opening sentence (since revised) of chapter 17 of her novel. She recognized too her own hand. The manuscript appeared to be her original.

A single page fluttered to the floor. Jane picked it up. It was the title page. *Constance,* it read. *By Jane Austen.* Only her name had been crossed out and the name of Charlotte Brontë had been written above it.

Violet really had found it after all. And she knew that Jane was the true author. Not Brontë. "Then why?" she heard herself say.

"Because it's the book I should have written."

Jane whirled around to find Violet standing behind her in the doorway. She was looking at Jane with an expression of pure hatred.

"I should have known you would come after it," she said as she turned and shut the door to the room. "I suppose I did know."

"What do you mean, it's the book you should have written?" Jane asked. "Do you write?"

Violet laughed. Her tone was icy. Jane noticed the spaniel wake from its dream and sit up. *Now I have two of them to worry about,* she thought.

"Do I write?" Violet said. "Yes, I do. And far better than Austen. At least until she wrote that." She nodded at the manuscript in Jane's hand. "That is a masterpiece."

"Thank you," Jane said, her manners trumping her fear and confusion.

Violet shook her head. "Only no one will believe you wrote it," she said. "They'll think I did."

"You?" said Jane. "You said you believe that Charlotte Brontë wrote it." She held up the title page and shook it.

Violet scowled. "Are you really so stupid?" she said. "Haven't you figured out who I am?"

"I know who you think you are," said Jane carefully. She thought about the figures seated around the kitchen table. "You think you're Charlotte Brontë. Which is fine," she added quickly. "There's nothing wrong with that."

"You idiot!" Violet snapped. "I don't think I'm Charlotte. I *am* Charlotte!"

As Violet opened her mouth in a roar, Jane saw the two fangs that had descended from her upper jaw. *No,* she thought. *It can't be.*

"Give me the manuscript and I might let you live," said Violet. She took a step toward Jane.

Let me live? Jane thought. *What is she talking about?* Then it dawned on her—Violet didn't know who she was. *She thinks I'm ordinary Jane Fairfax,* she realized.

"Wait!" Jane shouted, stalling for time. "I'll give it to you. Just tell me where you found it. I . . . I thought I'd found the only copy."

Violet laughed. "Of course you did," she said. "How would you know that I got this one from Lord Byron? Well, I stole it from him, anyway."

"Byron?" said Jane. She thought for a moment. "He turned you, didn't he?"

It was Violet's turn to look confused. "How do you know that?" she hissed.

Jane rolled her eyes. "For heaven's sake, Charlotte, who do you think *I* am?" She bared her teeth and let her fangs slip into place. "That bastard seems to have slept his way through all of English literature."

"No," said Charlotte, stepping back. "It can't be. You can't be."

"Yes, well, it seems we both *are,*" Jane informed her. "So what do we do now?"

"Jasper!" Charlotte yelled in response. "Sic her!"

The spaniel leapt to its feet, ready to obey its master. Jane, seeing it coming for her, knew that she couldn't get out of the room, especially with Charlotte standing in the way.

"Jasper, sit!" she said sternly.

To her surprise, it worked. The dog sat and looked up at her expectantly.

"Jasper!" Charlotte cried.

Before Charlotte could complete her command, Jane rushed to the fireplace and threw the manuscript into it. The aged paper caught fire immediately and began to crumble.

"No!" Charlotte screamed. She ran over and pushed Jane out of the way, reaching into the fireplace to retrieve the papers.

Jane scrambled to her feet and backed away, watching as Charlotte tried to salvage what was left of the manuscript. *It really is her,* she admitted.

Charlotte had removed some of the papers and was trying to beat out the flames with her hands. As she did, a tongue of flame leapt up and kissed the sleeve of her dress. Instantly it blossomed with fire, which quickly consumed the material. Charlotte screamed in pain.

"Help me!" she shouted, beating at herself with her hands. This succeeded only in helping the fire to spread, and in a moment her torso was engulfed in flame.

Jane, horrified, could only stand and watch as Charlotte spun around like a dervish, trying to put herself out. Then Jane realized that the fire was spreading to the room. Already the chair was aflame, and the edges of the carpet were smoldering. A moment later Jasper ran to the door and began scratching at it furiously.

His fear drove Jane to action. Turning her back on the shrieking Charlotte, she opened the door and followed Jasper into the hall. He ran toward the kitchen with Jane right behind him. The hallway was already filling with smoke. Jasper ran through the kitchen and hit the back door with his nose. It swung open, and he ran out into the night. Jane was about to follow him when she noticed the kitchen table and the three figures still seated around it.

She went up to the closest one and looked at its face. Skin, or what was left of it, was stretched across the skull. The eyes were gone. The mouth was a bit of shriveled flesh. She looked at the other two bodies. They were equally mummified.

She didn't, Jane thought, looking into the faces of Charlotte's famous siblings and shivering. *Well, that's just wrong.* Then she heard a crash as part of the roof caved in. She ran to the door and pushed it open, following Jasper to safety.

Chapter 27

Jonathan's appearance, although not completely
unexpected, was nevertheless a shock. After so
many months without a word, she had gradually
allowed herself to believe that perhaps he had
moved on to another amusement. Now she realized
that she ought to have known better. He would
never let her go. Never. Not until one or the other
of them was dead.

—Jane Austen, *Constance*, manuscript page 399

"I JUST KILLED CHARLOTTE BRONTË."

Jane was in her hotel room, her cell phone in one hand and a box of bandages in the other. She had practically run back to the hotel, and her blisters were killing her.

"You did what?" said Lucy.

"Charlotte Brontë," Jane repeated. "I killed her. Well, I suppose you could say she killed herself. It's not like I *pushed* her into the fireplace or anything. But I do feel slightly responsible."

"You're going to have to back up," said Lucy.

Jane told her the whole story, beginning with the confrontation at the conference and ending with her escape from the kitchen.

"What happened to Jasper?" Lucy asked when Jane was finished.

"I don't know," Jane told her. "He ran off."

"You have to find him!" Lucy insisted. "He's probably scared to death."

"He lived with Charlotte and her three mummified siblings," Jane reminded her. "If that didn't scare him, nothing will."

"At least go back and look for him," said Lucy. "Please?"

Jane sighed. "All right," she agreed. "I'll go back. But not right now. I can barely walk. Anyway, I didn't call you to talk about the dog."

"Why *did* you call?" asked Lucy.

"Did you hear the part about me killing Charlotte Brontë?" Jane said. "What am I going to do about it?"

"Why do you have to do anything?" Lucy replied. "If she's dead, she's dead. It's not as if her family will be looking for her."

Jane hadn't considered that. "You're right," she said, feeling slightly better. "And technically, she was already dead anyway."

"Would fire really kill her?" Lucy asked.

"It would," said Jane. "Actually, pretty much anything that would kill you would kill her. I mean us."

"Anything?" said Lucy.

"Well, not anything," Jane clarified. "We're immune to diseases. I don't know why, but my guess is that this whole thing—what makes us what we are—is some kind of virus and that it attacks anything else it comes in contact with. I knew a scientist once who—"

Lucy made a snoring sound. "I didn't ask for a biology lesson," she said.

"Cheeky," Jane said. "At any rate, disease is out. Also old age, as we stay at the age we were when we turned. But pretty much everything else can do us in."

"Garlic?" Lucy suggested.

"You've seen me eat hummus," Jane reminded her.

"Holy water?"

"Only if we drown in it," said Jane. "I'm talking about the usual misadventures that kill people off. Plane crashes. Being impaled. Losing one's head. That sort of thing."

"What do you know?" Lucy said. "I thought vampires were all magical, like unicorns and leprechauns."

"I wouldn't call it magic," Jane replied. "And we have to be just as careful as you do."

"What if you lose just an arm?" asked Lucy. "Or let's say a toe. Will it grow back?"

"We're not geckos," Jane said curtly. "But yes, we do have some interesting . . . restorative abilities. Nevertheless, it's possible for us to die if the damage is comprehensive enough."

"Then let's assume Charlotte really is extra crispy," Lucy said.

"Must you say things like that?"

"Sorry," Lucy apologized. "It's just that talking about Charlotte Brontë being dead is a little weird. Anyway, let's assume that she really is gone for good. Like I said, I don't see the problem. Except for poor Jasper. You will go look for him, right?"

"I said I would," said Jane. "But what about *me*?"

"Go back to the conference tomorrow," said Lucy. "Pretend nothing unusual has happened. As far as anyone else knows, you were in your room asleep all night."

Jane considered this. Was it really that simple? She tried to find a flaw in Lucy's argument, but could find nothing. No one else had heard her conversation with Violet Grey. No one had seen her follow Violet home. And certainly no one else knew that Violet was really Charlotte Brontë.

"What about the manuscript expert?" Jane said.

"There isn't one," Lucy told her. "Honestly, you'd think you'd never written a book before. Charlotte made that up when she thought you were a normal person. I mean a mortal. I mean not a vampire. God, this is so confusing."

"That's right," Jane agreed. "She wanted me to think she had expert proof." She heard herself laugh. "She didn't know about me," she said. "That's rather extraordinary."

"Why?" said Lucy. "You didn't know about her either."

"Must you take the fun out of everything?" Jane said.

"Yeah," said Lucy. "Setting fire to the woman who wrote *Jane Eyre* is big fun."

"Well, it *is* sort of ironic when you think about it," said Jane. "Bertha Mason and all that."

"I can tell you're feeling better about things," Lucy said. "I'm glad I could help. Now go look for Jasper. I want a progress report tomorrow."

Jane hung up. She stood and started toward the bathroom to take a nice hot bath. Then she thought about Jasper, alone in the dark, nowhere to go. She imagined having to lie to Lucy about checking on him.

"Oh, hell," she cursed as she bent to retrieve her shoes.

This time she took a cab, asking the driver to drop her off a few blocks from Charlotte's house. Or rather, what was left of Charlotte's house. As Jane got closer she saw that the fire had done rather a good job of destroying the home. The only thing still standing was the brick chimney, rising from the blackened bones of the house like a giant finger flipping Jane the bird. Two fire trucks blocked the street, and a handful of firefighters stood on the sidewalk looking at the ruins. It was raining again. The piles of charred wood and ash sent sickly strings of smoke into the night sky, and the air smelled acrid and dirty.

Jane avoided the firemen as she skirted the trucks and went to the other side of the street. She didn't want anyone to see her, lest she somehow be connected to the fire. She wondered if they'd yet found the bodies of Charlotte and her siblings. Judging from the scene, pretty nearly everything in the house had been incinerated.

Now that she was there she realized that she had no idea how to begin going about looking for Jasper. She'd sort of expected to find him sitting on the sidewalk looking forlornly at what used to be his home. But other than the firefighters and a handful of neighbors gawking at the sight, the area around the house was empty. Finding the dog was, she feared, going to be impossible.

"Jasper," she called softly. "Are you here?"

To her surprise, the spaniel came darting out from behind a neighboring house. He came up to Jane, tail wagging, and sat down in front of her. He gave a little woof and cocked his head, ears alert.

"Hello," Jane said. "I'm sorry about your house," she added after a moment.

Jasper woofed again. He and Jane stared at each other for a long moment as Jane thought about what to do with him. She hadn't expected to find him, so her thoughts on the matter had never progressed beyond that point. Now she considered her options. She could take him to a shelter. That would be the easiest. *For me, anyway,* she thought.

The longer she looked into Jasper's brown eyes, the more sure she was that she couldn't possibly abandon him. It wasn't his fault he'd had the misfortune to live with the Brontës. And in a way he had helped Jane during her confrontation with Charlotte.

"Oh, all right," said Jane. "Come on."

She and Jasper walked to the far end of the street, where Jane managed to get a cab to take them back to the hotel. She had the driver stop at a small grocery, where she picked up some dog food and two large plastic bowls. While she was in the store Jasper sat obediently outside, waiting as if he'd always lived with Jane. She found his devotion appealing, and despite everything, she found herself warming to him. He was, she decided, a very amiable dog.

Getting him into the hotel proved not to be a problem, as no one was at the desk. Once in her room, Jane filled one bowl with water from the tap and opened the bag of food, which she poured into the second bowl. Jasper dove in hungrily, devouring the contents of the food bowl within minutes. Then he took a long drink and, his muzzle dripping, jumped onto the bed and curled up at the foot of it.

The poor beast is exhausted, Jane thought. She left him there to sleep and went into the bathroom, where she finally enjoyed the shower she'd been craving for hours. When she was done, she returned to the bedroom, donned her nightgown, and got into bed. Jasper, waking up, came to the top of the bed and lay alongside Jane, his back pressing against her. After hesitating a moment, she stroked his ears.

"Sweet dreams," she whispered in his ear, but he was already asleep.

When she awoke, her face was buried in the fur of Jasper's neck. He himself had not stirred all night, but when Jane sat up he was instantly awake, yawning and stretching his legs.

"What am I going to do with you?" Jane asked him. "I suppose I'm going to have to get you home with me somehow. And where will you stay today while I'm doing this wretched panel?"

Jasper jumped off the bed and shook himself. Then he looked meaningfully at the door. It took Jane a moment to realize what he wanted.

"Right," she said. "You need a walk. Just give me a minute."

She pulled on some jeans and a shirt and located her shoes. Then she opened the door and watched as Jasper trotted down the stairs to the lobby. She hurried after him, afraid of what would happen should anyone see him. But when she found him he was on his back, having his belly rubbed by Luke.

"I'm sorry," Jane apologized. "I know he shouldn't be here. It's just that I found him wandering around last night and he seemed so lost and afraid that I couldn't—"

"It's okay," Luke said. "We allow dogs. Have you named him?"

"Yes—Jasper," Jane answered.

"Are you going to keep him?"

Jane hesitated a moment. "I believe I am," she said. "But there's a slight problem." She explained her situation to the young man.

"No problem," Luke told her. "He can stay with me today. And to take him on the plane, all you need is a dog crate. I can get one sent over from the pet store if you like. I'll just put it on your bill. He should probably have a collar while we're at it," he added.

Jane thanked Luke effusively. Leaving Jasper with him, she returned to her room and got ready to go to the conference. She'd thought not at all about her panel. Now she considered the question. What *did* women want from romance novels? *Romance, clearly,* she thought. *What a stupid question.*

She knew she couldn't say anything of the sort to the audience. After all, they were there precisely because they believed in romance. And apparently they were buying her book because they found it romantic. She bristled at the idea. She'd always hated being referred to as a romantic. "If anything, I'm a pragmatist," she said to her image in the mirror.

She left the hotel ten minutes later. Jasper was lying on the floor in front of the desk as if he'd been there his whole life. Jane stopped to scratch his head, and he wagged his nub of a tail. "I'll see you later," she told him.

Another cab ride took her to the conference hotel. The gathering was in full swing now, and the lobby bustled with action as people rushed around looking for panels or chasing after friends. Jane located the schedule of the day's happenings and looked for her name. She found it listed in two places—once for her panel and another for a signing she was apparently doing at two o'clock. But first she had to find something called the Peacock Room.

She found it on the third floor. It was a very large room, and it was already filled with people. Jane noticed Chiara Carrington, looking stunning in a ruby-colored pantsuit, standing near a raised platform at the front of the room. She was talking to a short, heavyset woman with badly permed hair. The woman, seeing Jane, said something to Chiara, who turned and frowned. Then she said something to the other woman, who laughed and covered her mouth with her hand.

This is going to be just grand, Jane thought as she walked toward the two women. When she reached them, she smiled and held out her hand to the blond woman. "You must be Penelope," she said.

Chiara gave a stifled laugh as the woman replied, "I'm Rebecca Little, the editor in chief of *Romance* magazine. I'm moderating the panel."

"Oh," said Jane, blushing. Not only had she offended Chiara earlier, she had now revealed that she didn't know who either Rebecca Little or Penelope Wentz was. She was making a wonderful first impression, she thought.

"Penelope hasn't arrived yet," Rebecca said. "I'm actually surprised that she's coming at all."

Chiara made a sound of agreement. Jane resisted saying anything, lest she appear even more ignorant, but she couldn't resist. "Why is that?" she asked.

"Well, nobody's ever seen her," Chiara said, as if this was common knowledge and Jane had once again failed a simple test.

"She doesn't put any author photos on her books, she does all of her interviews by email, and she's never come to any of the conferences," Rebecca explained. "I've been trying to get her for years. I have no idea what made her change her mind this year, but I'm so glad she did. Her identity is one of the big mysteries of the genre." She nodded at the audience. "That's why it's so packed." She patted Chiara's arm. "And of course because they want to see you," she added.

Chiara smiled demurely. "And Jane," she said.

"Of course," said Rebecca. "And Jane."

Jane wished Sally Higgins-Smythe were there. *At least she likes me,* she thought. *These two would just as soon push me off a cliff.* For a moment she wondered if perhaps Charlotte had somehow told them about her supposed theft of her own manuscript. Perhaps the panel was even an elaborate setup, and she was going to be exposed.

You're just being paranoid, she told herself. *Everything is going to be fine.*

"Excuse me."

As soon as she heard the deep voice, she knew it was not going to be fine after all. Jane turned to see Byron standing behind her. He was dressed in jeans, a black leather coat, and a white shirt open at the neck to expose a triangle of pale skin. He had grown a goatee, and if she hadn't known him so well, she almost wouldn't have recognized him.

"What are you doing—" she began.

He ignored her, extending his hand to Rebecca. "You must be Rebecca," he said in his most charming voice. He smiled, showing his white teeth. "I'm Penelope Wentz."

Chapter 28

"Can you honestly say you haven't thought of me?"
Jonathan asked, taking her hand. "Have you not
missed our conversations? Have you not missed
my kiss?" She looked into his face, trying to say
that she had not, but the words died in her mouth.

—Jane Austen, *Constance,* manuscript page 403

REBECCA COULD DO LITTLE BUT STARE AT BYRON. CHIARA DID THE same. Jane, although she was more than a little annoyed, could hardly blame them. He *was* handsome, even more so with the addition of the goatee. It hid his chin, which Jane had never found to be his best feature.

"You?" Rebecca said when she finally regained her voice. "You're Penelope Wentz?" She giggled and looked around, as if surely someone must be playing a joke on her. Then she looked at Chiara, who continued to stare at Byron, completely speechless.

"I know this must come as a bit of a surprise," Byron said smoothly. "But I assure you that I am indeed she." He then turned to Jane and pretended to see her for the first time. "I don't believe we've met," he said, extending his hand. "I'm Tavish Osborn."

Jane gave him a look that said she didn't think this latest caper of his was at all funny. "Jane Fairfax," she said.

Byron stepped back. "Jane Fairfax!" he exclaimed. "The author of *Constance*."

"That would be I," said Jane without enthusiasm.

Byron turned to Rebecca and Chiara. "Have you read her book?" he asked. "In my opinion, it's the finest romance to come out in the past century. Er, decade."

"Aren't you kind," said Jane as Rebecca and Chiara exchanged puzzled glances.

Finally Chiara cleared her throat. "Pardon my surprise," she said to Byron. "I—we—" She looked at Rebecca, who nodded. "We assumed you were a woman."

Byron laughed lightly. "I can understand why," he replied. Then he fixed Chiara with one of his most sensual looks. "But I promise you that I'm very much a man."

Chiara blushed as Jane caught Byron's eye. "Oh, please," she mouthed at him. He grinned and winked.

"Well, this is certainly going to be a *huge* revelation!" Rebecca said. "Honestly, I don't know what to think." She looked Byron up and down. "You. Penelope Wentz." She giggled again.

Byron looked at his watch. "I believe it's just about time to begin," he said.

"Of course," Rebecca said, shaking her head as if she'd been dreaming and needed to wake up. "Why don't we take our seats?"

The four of them ascended the platform. Chiara took the first chair, and Jane took the one farthest from her. She was relieved when she saw Rebecca start to take the seat beside her. Then Byron stepped between them.

"Would you mind?" he asked Rebecca.

Rebecca shot Jane a disapproving look. "Not at all," she said flatly. Jane saw Chiara crane her neck around to see what was happening and frown when she saw where Byron had chosen to sit. *She assumed he would sit between her and Rebecca,* she thought. *That way they could both pretend he wanted to be near them.*

"Penelope Wentz?" Jane said in a low voice when Byron was seated. "I suppose you killed the real one."

"Not at all," Byron replied. "I am indeed Penelope Wentz." He raised one eyebrow. "I am, after all, the most romantic man in the world."

Jane snorted. "I can't believe you," she said, shaking her head. "You promised to stay away."

Byron held up one finger. "But I also said that I would be back one day."

"That was three months ago!" Jane said. "I'd hardly call that a suitable intermission."

"Welcome to this morning's panel." Rebecca's announcement prevented any further discussion between Jane and Byron. Jane sat back in her chair and tried very hard not to look at him.

"We're thrilled to have with us today some of the most exciting names in romance fiction," she continued. "You all know Chiara Carrington, author of such novels as *Whichever Way the Wind Blows* and *The Gift of Love.*"

She paused to allow the audience to applaud. "And we're pleased to introduce Jane Fairfax, whose novel *Constance* is making big waves in the book world."

Jane noted with some disappointment that the applause for her was less enthusiastic than the response Chiara had received. Beside her, however, Byron clapped loudly. She resisted an urge to kick him under the table.

Rebecca took an audible breath. "I'm sure that many of you are here because you want to see the face behind the Penelope Wentz novels," she said.

A murmur passed through the crowd, and several people clapped.

"Well, I think you'll be as surprised as I was to meet her for the first time." There was a dramatic pause. "Or I should say to meet *him*," she concluded, indicating Byron with her hand. "May I present Mr. Tavish Osborn, the man behind Penelope Wentz!"

Gasps were heard all over the room, and several cameras went off, their flashes momentarily blinding Jane as she was caught in their glare. She tried to lean away from Byron.

A woman in the front row stood up. Dressed entirely in pink, she was clutching a copy of one of Penelope Wentz's books. She held it to her chest as she looked at Byron accusingly. "I don't believe it," she said. "No man could understand what it's like to be a . . ." She paused for a moment. "Woman of a certain age," she concluded.

"That's an excellent point," said Rebecca quickly. "After all, the theme of our panel is what women want from romance fiction. Perhaps you could answer this reader's question with that in mind," she suggested, looking over at Byron.

"I'm more than happy to, Rebecca," Byron said. He fixed his gaze on the woman who had spoken. Jane watched as she took a step back and sat down as if she'd been pushed. She knew Byron was casting a glamor on the audience. *As if he needs to,* she thought. *Half the people in here are already in love with him.*

"I know it will come as a shock to many of you that I'm a man," said Byron. "After all, you're wondering, how can I know what it's like to be a woman? Well, I'll tell you my secret." He leaned forward, as if inviting them to come closer. And indeed many in the audience did lean toward the table. "I absolutely love women," Byron said. "I love everything about you, and most of all I love listening to you." He leaned back. "And that's my secret," he said. "I listen. When you read my books, it isn't *me* telling the story, it's *you.*" He pointed to the woman who had questioned him, who blushed deeply. "And you," he continued, indicating another woman. "And you." He pointed somewhere in the middle of the audience.

They all think he's talking just to them, Jane thought. *He's glamored each and every one of them.*

"That's cheating," she hissed softly, knowing that Byron could hear her.

"When I write, I'm giving voice to what you feel," Byron continued, ignoring her. His voice was practically a purr.

The room erupted in applause. Half of the audience rose to their feet, their hands slapping together like the flippers of trained seals. Watching them, Jane wanted to tell them all to sit down and shut up. Byron looked over at her and gave a cocky grin. *You horrid, horrid man,* Jane thought at him.

"What an eloquent answer." Rebecca had resumed control over the panel. Jane, looking at her, saw that she was wiping her eyes. Was she actually weeping? She was. Jane felt sick. Byron had them all in the palm of his hand.

"And just what *is* it women want?" Jane heard herself ask.

All eyes turned to her, including Byron's. Jane felt herself flush, but she knew she had to continue. She took a breath and faced Byron. "I would like to hear what Penelope believes women want," she said.

"I don't think we—" Rebecca began.

"But I do," Jane interrupted. "After all, Mr. Osborn has sold a great number of books based on his *deep* understanding of what women want. I'm wondering if he might care to share that secret with us—his readers," she added.

Byron's mouth twitched at the corners, and Jane knew she had landed a blow. But he quickly composed himself. "I'd be happy to," he said.

"Without glamoring them," Jane whispered as she pretended to take a drink of water from the glass set before her on the table.

Byron ignored her. "What women want," he began. There was a long pause, which grew longer as Byron seemed to think. Jane sensed the audience growing restless. Someone coughed.

"What women want is to be accepted for who they are," Byron said finally. "Not what the media tells them they should be, but who they *really* are."

As the audience clapped, Byron turned to Jane with a triumphant look in his eyes.

"I see," Jane said loudly. "Yet your books don't really depict women as they are, do they?"

"Why don't we move on," said Rebecca, glaring openly at Jane.

"In a moment," Jane said. "Mr. Osborn," she addressed Byron. "Do you really mean for us to believe that you aren't just as guilty of presenting women with an idealized version of themselves?" Having never read a Penelope Wentz novel, she hoped she was correct in her assessment of Byron's prose.

"I think we can all agree that fiction, particularly *romantic* fiction, works best when it contains some elements of fantasy," Byron said smoothly. "After all, a world of laundry, carpools, and helping with homework is hardly the setting for romance, do you think?"

"I absolutely do," said Jane. "In fact, some of the most romantic novels in the world feature perfectly ordinary women. Take *Sense and—*"

"I think we should move on," Rebecca interrupted loudly. "Mr. Osborn, perhaps you could tell us more about how you came to write as Penelope Wentz. I'm sure it's a *fascinating* story."

Jane sat back in her chair. She knew she'd been bested. Byron's glamor was too strong, and she was out of practice. He had upstaged her, taking away what should have been a triumphant moment for her and her book.

For the next hour, Byron fielded questions from the audience. Jane and Chiara were barely noticed. Every so often one of them would start to answer a question, only to be cut off by someone who preferred to hear Byron's thoughts on the topic at hand. While Jane was annoyed by the proceedings, Chiara seemed not to mind being eclipsed by Byron. Finally Jane tuned everything out and just sat there pretending to pay attention.

Only when she heard another wave of applause did she listen to what was going on. It seemed the panel was over.

"And now Mr. Osborn will sign copies of his books," Rebecca announced. "Oh, and so will the other authors," she added hastily. "Please form an orderly line."

It seemed to Jane that nearly every person in the room rushed toward the platform simultaneously. For a moment she feared she would be trampled, but they came to a halt a few feet away and somehow managed to organize themselves into a queue stretching off to Jane's right. The first person, a girl of maybe twenty, stepped onto the platform and approached her. Jane smiled, anticipating the first signing of her novel. However, the woman didn't even glance at Jane as she went right to Byron.

"Could you sign it to Brandi?" the girl asked.

"That's Brandi with an *i*, correct?" said Byron.

The girl beamed. "How did you know?"

Byron answered as he wrote in her book. "A girl as unique as you are is certain to have a unique name," he said.

Brandi giggled and bit her lip.

"Thank you so much for coming today," said Byron, eliciting another titter. "I hope you enjoy the book."

"I will," Brandi said as she was encouraged by Rebecca to move along. Jane noted with some small satisfaction that the girl walked by Chiara without so much as a turn of her head.

By then another reader had bypassed Jane and was talking to Byron. As he had with Brandi, he charmed her to the point that all she could do was giggle.

"Who do you think you are?" Jane asked in the interval between one woman leaving and another arriving. "The Beatles?"

With agonizing slowness the line grew shorter. Not a single person asked Jane or Chiara for an autograph. When the last person had received a signature from Byron and walked away glowing, Jane stood up.

"That was fun," she said. "Now I'm afraid I have to be getting along. It was lovely to meet all of you."

She gathered up her things and started to leave, not caring whether or not she insulted Chiara or Rebecca. Her entire trip had, as far as she was concerned, been a waste of time. *Not quite,* she reminded herself. *You did kill Charlotte Brontë. That's something, at least.*

"Jane, wait."

She heard Byron's voice behind her but kept walking. A moment later he grabbed her arm. "Wait," he said.

She shook his hand off and whirled to look at him. "Why would I possibly want to do that?" she asked.

"I know about Charlotte," he told her.

Jane gritted her teeth. *Of course you do,* she thought. "What of it?" she asked, not even trying to deny his implied accusation. "Anyway, maybe I should be asking where she got the manuscript I gave to *you.*"

Byron held up his hands. "I know," he said. "And I'm sorry. But you don't know how obsessive she is. Was. How was I to know she would take it?"

"So you did turn her," Jane said. "Tell me, is there anyone else I should be on the lookout for? Christina Rossetti, maybe? Dorothy Parker? Truman Capote?"

Byron shrugged. "It's difficult to say," he answered.

Jane turned with a huff and started to walk away. Byron caught up to her. "Jane, darling," he said, "I'm so sorry. It's just that I couldn't stay away. You're like a magnet to my heart."

Jane made a retching sound. "And you are like a purgative to my stomach," she said.

"A fine thing to say after what I've done for you," Byron said. He adopted a hurt expression.

"What you did for me?" Jane repeated. "Do you mean threatening to kill Walter and do worse to Lucy? Do you mean allowing my manuscript to fall into the hands of the one person in the world who would wish me harm?"

"To be fair, she's probably not the only person," said Byron. "But no, I wasn't speaking of those things. I mean in Chicago."

Jane inhaled sharply. "You *were* the one who bit that girl!" she accused him.

Byron shook his head. "No," he said. "Charlotte did that. I was the one who saved the girl. And saved you," he added.

"And just how did you save her?"

"Charlotte was not the most . . . adept of our kind," he said.

"She was never quite able to finish a job, so to speak. She thought she had killed the girl, but she had only weakened her."

"What was she doing there, anyway?" Jane asked.

"Attempting to frame you, I would imagine," said Byron.

It was a plausible enough explanation, although Jane had her doubts. "And what were *you* doing there?" she asked Byron.

"Watching out for you," he said. "I was worried."

"Mmm," said Jane. "Always the gentleman."

Byron lowered his eyes. "Jane, I've kept my promise," he said. "I haven't bothered you, or Walter, or Lucy. I've just been protecting you."

Jane had nothing to say to that. If he really *had* taken care of Farrah in Chicago, she did have something to thank him for. And perhaps Charlotte really *had* simply stolen the manuscript from him years ago. She supposed he could be telling the truth.

"Have dinner with me," Byron said. "It's your last night in New Orleans."

"No," said Jane firmly. "That's out of the question. I might possibly be able to forgive you for—"

"Just dinner," Byron said. "And then I promise I'll disappear forever."

"Your definition of forever is sorely lacking in specificity," said Jane. He was looking at her with his dark brown eyes. "All right," she said. "Dinner. Then you'll go away. Promise me."

Byron smiled. "Promise," he said. "I'll come for you at seven."

"No," Jane said quickly. "I'll meet you there." She didn't want him knowing where she was staying.

"La Maison des Trois Soeurs," said Byron. "I know."

"You're impossible," Jane said as she turned and left him standing in the lobby.

When she arrived back at the hotel she found Jasper lying in a pool of sun outside the front door. When he saw her he jumped up and ran to her, his stub of a tail wagging furiously. As Jane bent to pet him she saw that he was wearing a new red collar. "Aren't you the handsome boy," she told him.

"I thought it was a good color for him," Luke called through the door.

"It most definitely is," Jane agreed. "Thank you for getting it."

"No problem," Luke said. "His new crate is up in your room. All you need to do is check him in at the airport."

Jane looked down at Jasper. "Do you hear that?" she said. "You're going for a plane ride tomorrow."

Jasper woofed at her, and both Jane and Luke laughed. "Thank you for taking care of him today," Jane told the young man.

She headed upstairs with Jasper at her heels. Once there, she took off her shoes and lay on the bed for a while, thinking about the events of the day. It was a little too much. *But it's almost over,* she told herself. *You just have to make it through dinner.*

Chapter 29

Constance drew away from him. His kiss stung her
as much as if it had been his hand slapping her
cheek. More painful even than that was the
realization that she wanted him to kiss her again.

—Jane Austen, *Constance,* manuscript page 411

At a quarter past six she got up, fed Jasper, and changed her clothes for dinner. She purposely put on something casual so that Byron would know she wasn't trying to impress him. *He's not getting to me this time,* she promised herself.

She took Jasper for a quick walk around the block using the new leash she'd found coiled on the dresser, and returned him to the room, where he immediately jumped up on the bed. "Tom's not going to like that at all," Jane told him. She wondered how she could introduce the two of them with the least amount of fuss and bother.

At five minutes to seven she went down to the lobby to wait for Byron. He might know where she was staying, but she wasn't going to let him anywhere near her room. *Absolutely not,* she promised herself.

He arrived promptly at seven. Jane noted that he too was dressed rather casually, and she was surprised to find that she was slightly disappointed. *Apparently he doesn't think it's a date either,* she thought as she stood to greet him.

"Where are we going?" she asked as they walked down the street. They were moving away from the restaurants, toward a slightly more run-down part of the Marigny, and Jane was a little unnerved by it. Was Byron trying to trick her?

"Relax," he said, taking her arm. "I'm taking you to an *authentic* New Orleans eatery, not one of those places designed to part tourists from their money."

"So you live here, then?" asked Jane.

"Lived," said Byron. "Then again, I've lived nearly everywhere, haven't I?"

"And Charlotte?" Jane asked. "How long has she lived—how long did she live here?"

"Let's not talk about Charlotte, shall we?" Byron suggested. "She was merely an . . . inconvenience. Now she isn't."

"That's very easy for you to say," said Jane. "You're not the one who set her on fire."

Byron laughed. "No one will hold it against you," he said. "She was rather a dreary creature. Those mummies," he added, and Jane felt him shiver.

"They *were* a bit ghastly," Jane agreed.

Byron stopped at a doorway over which flickered a red neon sign that said THE PLACE. "This is the place," he said.

"I see that," Jane said. She peered through the small window set into the door. The interior was dark. "You're sure?" she asked.

Byron pulled the door open. "I'm sure," he said.

Jane's opinion of the restaurant was not improved by going inside. The small room contained half a dozen small tables, each one surrounded by mismatched chairs and covered with an oily checkered cloth. The walls were bare, painted a color that probably had originally been white but had taken on a yellowish tinge. A fan hung from the ceiling, spinning slowly in the heat. A length of flypaper hung from it, coated with the bodies of its victims.

Five of the tables were occupied, mostly by men drinking from bottles of Abita beer. Byron led Jane to the lone empty table and pulled her chair out for her. She inspected the seat with her fingertips before sitting. There didn't appear to be anything on it that would stain her pants.

"You're in for a real treat," said Byron. "Outsiders don't normally get to come here."

"Outsiders?" Jane said. "You mean tourists?"

"Of a sort," said Byron.

Before he could explain further, they were approached by a weary-looking woman of indeterminate age. Tall and thin, her long blond hair showed more than a few inches of dark roots, and her face was unusually red.

"Byron *cher*," she said. "Where you been?" Her voice was thick with a Cajun accent.

"Here and there," said Byron. He nodded at Jane. "Emmeline, Jane. Jane, Emmeline."

The woman nodded at Jane. "She one of yours?" she asked Byron.

Byron grinned. "Ask her that," he replied.

Emmeline turned her gaze to Jane. Her eyes were almost black, and something about her seemed impossibly old. Then Jane realized what it was. She looked at Byron, who laughed. "Yes," he said, "she's one of us." He gestured around the room. "They all are. Well, most of them."

Jane was dumbstruck. She'd never in her life been in an establishment that was solely for vampires. "But how—" she said.

"Times have changed, Jane," said Byron. "We don't have to hide all the time, especially not in a town like this one. Why do you think Charlotte stayed?"

"Hear she got herself burnt up last night," Emmeline said. "Can't say she'll be missed round here."

"See?" Byron mouthed to Jane.

"You're wanting the crawfish," Emmeline said. Without waiting for an answer she disappeared into the back of the restaurant.

"This is all very peculiar," Jane said to Byron.

"You've been away from your own kind for too long," said Byron. "You see through human eyes."

Jane began to object, but Byron cut her off. "It's not an insult," he said. "Well, perhaps it's a little bit of an insult," he admitted.

"I don't see what's wrong with trying to retain some humanity," Jane said tartly. "After all, it's what we were."

"Were," Byron repeated. "But not now. Aren't you tired of hiding? Wouldn't you like to live in a world where you don't have to worry about being exposed?"

"I don't really worry about it," said Jane. "Besides, I have Lucy now. And Walter," she added quickly.

"Yes, Walter," Byron said. Jane couldn't tell from his tone whether he was mocking her or just agreeing.

Emmeline reappeared, carrying an enormous metal bowl, which she dumped on the table. A mound of potatoes, sausage, corn, and crawfish spilled out, threatening to slide off the sides. Jane looked at it as Emmeline put down two bottles of beer, an empty bowl, and a thick stack of napkins. "Teach her how to suck heads," she said to Byron.

Jane picked up a crawfish. Its shell was a dark red, and its little black eyes stared unseeing back at her. "What do I do with it?" she asked.

"Like this," said Byron. He held up a crawfish, gripped the head between his thumb and forefinger, and twisted it off. He set the head aside and peeled the shell away from the body, then pinched the tiny fan at the bottom of the tail, pushing the meat up and popping the exposed flesh into his mouth. "And now for the best part," he said, picking up the head he'd set aside. Putting it to his mouth, he sucked loudly on it for a moment before tossing it into the empty bowl.

"And that's how you suck the head," he said. "Go on. Try it."

"I think not," said Jane. "It's very rude."

"It's rude not to," Byron corrected her. "If you don't suck the head, then everyone will know you're an outsider."

Jane contemplated the crawfish in her hand. Although no one in the restaurant was looking directly at her, she had the distinct impression that she was being watched. *Here goes nothing,* she thought as she attempted to copy Byron's movements. The tail and head separated readily enough, and getting the tail meat out was fairly easy. It was also incredibly delicious.

The head was another matter altogether. She placed it in her mouth and sucked. Instantly her mouth was filled with a spicy blast of butter and a lump of something squishy. She choked, just managing to swallow it down. She reached for a bottle of beer and drank deeply.

"What *is* that?" she asked, looking at the now empty crawfish head with distaste.

"Head fat," Byron explained. "It's the best part." He twisted another crawfish apart and ate it. "Pinch the tail, suck the head," he intoned. "Try another one. You'll come to love them, I promise."

"I've been on the wrong end of your promises before," said Jane. She picked up one of the half ears of corn and bit into it. "I'll stick with something safe."

They ate for a while in silence. Jane decided to try another crawfish, and this time she found it much better. She ate several more, then saw that Byron was looking at her.

"I think that first one was off," she said defensively.

"It's nice still being able to eat, isn't it?" said Byron. "It's one of the few human things I still treasure. That and making love," he added.

"I prefer *being* in love, thank you," Jane retorted as she stabbed a piece of sausage with her fork.

"You seemed to enjoy it with me that night I paid you a visit," said Byron. He sucked meaningfully on a crawfish head, licking his lips afterward.

"That was only to keep you away from Walter and Lucy," Jane reminded him.

"So you didn't enjoy it?" asked Byron.

Jane peered closely at the crawfish she was about to behead. "I didn't say that," she said.

"Then you did enjoy it?" Byron tried.

"Is there meat in the claws?" Jane asked him, looking at the crawfish's pincers.

"I'll take that for a yes," said Byron. "I enjoyed it as well."

"Of course you did," Jane said. "You'd enjoy it with . . . with . . ." She tried to think of someone suitably unpleasant. "Oscar Wilde," she concluded.

"Don't know," said Byron. "I never tried. But I don't think it would be all that nice."

"What if I did enjoy it?" Jane said. "What of it?"

Byron licked his fingers. "Perhaps you should ask yourself that question," he suggested.

"Perhaps I have," said Jane. "And perhaps what I've decided is that it means nothing. *You* mean nothing."

"I'm hurt," Byron said, putting his hand over his heart. "I thought we meant something to each other."

Jane ignored him and concentrated on her dinner. Byron was once again getting her all riled up. Why was it so easy for him to do this? *Why are you letting him do this?* a voice in her head asked.

"I don't know!" Jane said loudly. Realizing she'd spoken aloud, she felt her cheeks flush. "When did you start writing romances?" she asked quickly.

"Several years ago," Byron replied. "It's just something to do. And it brings in a little money."

"Now that everyone knows you're Penelope Wentz, what will you do?"

"I haven't decided," Byron answered. "Perhaps Penelope will write a few more novels. Perhaps she'll disappear."

"She won't disappear," said Jane. "You crave the attention. If you didn't, you wouldn't have revealed yourself today."

"Yes, well, there are certain *advantages* to being who I am," Byron said. "My fans are *very* faithful."

"Have one for lunch, did you?" Jane asked.

"You're being petty," said Byron. "It's unbecoming."

Jane ate the last of the crawfish and wiped her hands on a napkin. "Why am I here?" she asked. She was ready to be done with the evening.

"I want to apologize," Byron said.

Jane looked at him suspiciously. "For what?"

"For how I behaved toward you," said Byron. "All those years ago. It was wrong of me."

Jane cleared her throat. "It was," she agreed.

"I took your virginity and I made you what you are," Byron continued.

Jane looked around to see if the other customers were listening. She feared they would think poorly of her if they overheard.

"I took advantage of you," Byron said, apparently not caring if anyone heard him. "A sad, lonely old woman who—"

"I was not *old*," Jane objected.

"For the time," said Byron. "But that doesn't matter. What matters is that I behaved badly. For that I'm deeply sorry. Can you ever forgive me?"

Jane picked a bit of crawfish shell from under a fingernail. "I don't know," she said. "You really were horrible. And after all of the nice things you said in your letters too. It was fairly shocking to me, you know."

"I was young," Byron said.

"You were twenty-eight," said Jane. "That's old enough to know better."

"I meant in *our* years," Byron said. "It hadn't been that long. Besides, I was ill, and there was the divorce from Anne, the nastiness over the child, the business with Claire." He waved his hand around his head. "It was all too much. You seemed to be the one bright light in a storm of misery."

Jane wished she had a toothpick, as there was a bit of corn stuck in her fang. She only half listened to Byron. She'd fallen for his flowery speeches before. "All right," she said.

Byron, who was still talking, stopped. "All right?" he said.

"All right, I forgive you," said Jane. "Anyway, what's done is done. It's not like you can unmake me."

"You're sure?" Byron asked.

"If you keep asking, I won't be," said Jane. "Let's just move on. One thing I've always wondered—who turned you?"

Byron leaned his chair back, resting his back against the grimy wall. "Now that is a story," he said. "You know that I traveled widely in the years before 1816."

Jane nodded. "I do."

"Much of that time was in Greece," Byron continued. "While I was there I met a young man called Ambrose. He was a soldier." He paused, and a sad smile crossed his face for a moment. "You should have seen him," he said. "He was beautiful. I fell in love instantly."

"Shocking," Jane remarked, although not unkindly. She was seeing another side of Byron, and it was rather touching.

"The only thing that troubled me was that Ambrose would never spend the night with me," said Byron. "Every night, after we ate and made love, he would leave my house. He wouldn't tell me where he was going. I assumed there was a woman, perhaps a wife and child. At first I didn't care, but as the summer went on I became jealous." He looked at Jane. "I know that's difficult to believe."

Jane said nothing, sipping her beer. Given how many women Byron had stolen away from their husbands on a whim and then just as carelessly discarded, the idea that he could love someone enough to care in who else's bed he slept was intriguing. *This Ambrose must have been something special,* she thought.

"One night I could take it no longer. I followed him. He roamed the city, finally ending up at the harbor. There, under the docks, I saw him kiss another man. At least that's what I thought he was doing."

"He was feeding," Jane said.

Byron nodded. "I watched, horrified, as he killed the man. Then he turned and saw me. I wanted to run, but even more than that I wanted him to love me."

Byron grew quiet. He seemed lost in thought, rocking his chair back and forth slowly. "You let him turn you, didn't you?" Jane asked.

Byron looked up. His eyes were filled with tears. "Yes," he said. "It was the only way we could be together. And for a while we were."

"But you left him?" Jane suggested.

Byron shook his head. "He was killed," he said. "After I was turned, Ambrose taught me to hunt. One night, I seduced a local girl, beautiful but foolish. It was my first time attempting a glamor, and I was overconfident. The girl woke up while I was draining her, and she managed to get away. She'd seen my face. I ran back to the house and told Ambrose what had happened. When the girl returned with help, Ambrose glamored her into believing that he was the one whose face she'd seen. He'd already told me to leave through the back and escape into the hills."

Jane felt her skin grow cold. She feared what Byron would say next. The story would end badly, she knew, and she didn't want to hear it. But she listened nonetheless, anxious for it to be over.

Byron took a deep breath. "They dragged him to the center of town, drove a stake through his heart, and threw him from the cliffs into the sea," he said. "There was nothing I could do. No one could have survived such a thing. Afterward, I did as he'd told me to. I went into the hills and made my way back to Italy, where I began my new life."

Jane wasn't sure what to say, so she reached out and took Byron's hand. He remained still. "Do you know what the name Ambrose means?" he asked after a moment. " 'Immortal.' Ironic, isn't it?"

"I never knew," said Jane.

"Nobody did," Byron said. "Until now I've never spoken of it. But I owed you. Perhaps now I've repaid that debt a bit."

"You don't owe me," Jane told him, taking her hand back. "I came to you that summer looking for an adventure, and that's what you gave me."

"Yes," Byron said. "But I should have asked whether or not you wanted to be taken on it."

Jane started to say something but was interrupted by the arrival of Emmeline. She had with her a young man, muscular and glassy-eyed. He wore an AC/DC T-shirt and his neck was covered in bruises.

"Did you save room for dessert?" Emmeline asked.

Chapter 30

That night she read to Charles for the first time,
stumbling over the words, then finding her footing
and continuing on, anxious yet elated. All the
while she secretly watched his face for any reaction.
When finally she saw him smile, she felt that her
heart might burst with joy.

—Jane Austen, *Constance*, manuscript page 374

JANE WAS RELIEVED WHEN THE PLANE TOUCHED DOWN. SHE WAS even more relieved when she saw Lucy waiting for her at the baggage claim.

"If it isn't Jane the vampire killer," Lucy said, hugging her.

"That's not funny," said Jane.

She looked around for the oversize baggage area and saw Jasper's kennel. "I was convinced he would freeze in the hold," she told Lucy as she dragged her over to where the dog waited. When he saw Jane, Jasper pawed at the cage door and whined. Jane let him out, and he jumped up on Lucy.

"Hello, handsome," said Lucy. Jasper licked her nose. "I think I'm in love," Lucy said to Jane.

"It's your fault he's here," Jane replied. "If you hadn't insisted I go back for him—"

"If *you* hadn't—you know—then you wouldn't have had to go look for him," Lucy interrupted.

Jane ignored her. "I wonder where my bags are," she said, scanning the conveyor belt filled with arriving luggage.

"I already got them," said Lucy. "See?" She pointed to two bags that had Jane's name tags tied to the handles. "I noticed them in the unclaimed luggage area, and assumed they'd come on an earlier flight."

Jane growled. "Those are the original bags I checked in on my way to Chicago," she said angrily. "They must never have put them on the plane in the first place."

Lucy laughed. "Well, now you have more clothes," she said.

Jane left Lucy with the two bags and went in search of her other ones. She felt a sense of déjà vu as she watched the belt circling and all of the other bags were picked up. Once again she heard the grinding of gears as the belt stopped.

"You've got to be kidding," she said to Lucy. "What did I do to anger the luggage gods?"

"Vampire slayer," Lucy whispered.

"Stop that!" Jane insisted.

"Sorry," said Lucy. "Let's go get in line."

Jane shook her head. "I'm calling it a wash," she said, taking her two original bags in hand. "Besides, there was nothing in there I want."

As they headed toward the exit, Lucy walking Jasper and rolling his kennel behind her, Lucy said thoughtfully, "Just think. Some baggage handler could be fingering Jane Austen's panties right about now."

"Keep it up," Jane said, "and I *will* bite you."

They made their way to the parking garage, where they loaded everything into Lucy's car. Jasper, sitting in the back, whined until Lucy rolled down the window for him. He immediately stuck his head out.

"I wonder what it was like being Charlotte Brontë's dog," Lucy said as she pulled out.

"Can we not mention that name again?" Jane asked.

"You're in a foul temper," said Lucy. "What happened at that conference, anyway? Besides setting Char—"

"Byron is what happened," Jane told her.

"Byron?"

"It's a long story," said Jane. "Suffice it to say we made up."

Lucy looked at her, eyes wide. "You didn't sleep with him?" she said.

"No!" Jane said. "We just had dinner. Then he walked me home. I hate to admit it, but he was a perfect gentleman. It makes me think he's up to something."

"But why was he there at all?" Lucy asked.

Jane told her the whole story.

"Penelope Wentz?" Lucy said when Jane was finished. "Her books are awful."

Hearing it gave Jane some satisfaction, for which she immediately felt guilty. "She's apparently very popular," she said by way of apology to Byron.

"Sure she is," Lucy said. "We sell a ton of her books. His books," she corrected. "Haven't you noticed?"

"I confess I don't always pay attention to what people are buying," said Jane. "And since you've been doing most of the ordering for the past year or so, I'm not entirely up on what people are reading. Frankly, I'm a little tired of the whole thing."

"I never get tired of books," Lucy said as they exited the airport and drove onto the Thruway. "Anyway, tell me more about Byron."

"I feel sorry for him," said Jane. "I know how that sounds, but you should have seen his face when he talked about his friend."

"His *friend*?" said Lucy. "You sound like my mother when she talks about my brother's boyfriend."

"All right, his *lover*," Jane said. "In my day we didn't talk about it at all."

"You also rode around in dogcarts," Lucy reminded her. "But go on."

"He was really in love with Ambrose," said Jane. "To be honest, I never thought he was capable of it."

"Sounds like Ambrose's death killed something in him," Lucy remarked.

"I think you're right," Jane agreed. She fell into silence, watching the dreary landscape of upstate New York pass by.

"It made you think about you and Walter, didn't it?" Lucy said after a few minutes.

"Yes," Jane admitted. "I wonder if I haven't been foolish in that regard."

"Maybe it's time to take a chance," said Lucy.

Jane sighed. She had been thinking the same thing. But still part of her was terribly afraid. After all, her change of heart didn't change any of the realities of the situation. She was still a vampire, and Walter was still human. He was still going to age and die. While she could die at some point, she wouldn't age, at least not in the same way. It was a situation destined to make one or both of them miserable.

"You know, my father died when he was thirty-two," Lucy said.

Jane turned to her. "But I've met him," she said. "When they visited last year."

"Jim is my stepfather," Lucy said. "I call him Dad, but he isn't, at least not biologically. He and my mother have been married since I was eleven. My father died from brain cancer. It was horrible, especially for my mother."

"I can't even imagine," Jane said.

"She loved him more than anything in the world," Lucy continued. "When he died, she could have just fallen apart. But she didn't. She held on to all of the good memories and threw the rest away."

Jane understood what Lucy was getting at. Life never offered any guarantees. Anything could happen at any time, and people could be taken from one another without warning. She thought of Walter and Evelyn. *But look what that did to him,* she reminded herself. *He can barely speak about her.*

"I don't know," she said. "I just don't know."

"Suit yourself," said Lucy. "Spend the next thousand years being lonely."

"You're really an impudent young lady, do you know that?" Jane said.

"I'll tell you another story," said Lucy, ignoring the reprimand. "When I was on the road with the band, one night in Milwaukee I came out after a gig and saw this dog scrounging through the trash outside the club we were playing at. The bouncer was kicking him to get him to go away. He ran down an alley, and I followed him. He hid under our van and wouldn't come out. He was terrified. So I got a hamburger from the club and sat there for two hours, coaxing him out. I guess his hunger won out over his fear, because eventually he crawled out and ate."

"This is a horrible story," Jane told her.

"It gets worse," said Lucy. "Well, sort of. The short version is that I talked the other girls into letting him stay. He was an ugly little guy, a mutt. He limped, and his fur was all patchy. I named him Spike. Anyway, when we got to Des Moines I took him to the vet to make sure he was okay. And he wasn't. It turned out he had a bad heart. The vet said he'd likely been starved as a pup and treated badly. His leg had been broken, which is why he limped."

Jane glanced back at Jasper, who was still looking out the window, his ears flapping in the breeze. "I don't think I want to hear the rest of this story," Jane told Lucy.

"Well, you're going to," Lucy said. "Because there's a point to it. After what happened with my dad, I didn't think I could handle watching someone I loved die. The other girls wanted me to have Spike put down, or at least leave him at a shelter. And I almost did. But then I looked at his funny little face, and I knew I couldn't do it. He'd come into my life for a reason. So I kept him."

She got quiet, and Jane thought perhaps she'd come to the end of the story. *That wasn't so bad after all,* she thought, relieved.

"He died three months later," Lucy said suddenly. There was a hitch in her voice. "We were in Albuquerque. He hadn't been right for a couple of days, panting a lot, and he didn't want to eat. I knew something was wrong, so I stayed up one night just holding him and rubbing his ears, telling him what a good boy he was. At some point I looked down and he was gone."

Jane felt a catch in her throat. She looked over at Lucy, expecting to see her crying. Instead, she was smiling.

"I don't understand."

Lucy looked at her. Again Jane was surprised to see that on

her face was a look of happiness. "He died knowing that I loved him," Lucy said. "Dogs live in the moment. However they're feeling is how they believe they've always felt. For those three months Spike thought he was the happiest dog in the world. He forgot all about being abused and scared and alone. And when he had to go, I was there for him." She paused a moment. "If you ask me, that's about as good as it gets."

"But what about you?" Jane said. "You had to lose him."

"But I got to know him for three whole months," said Lucy. "I got to love him and care for him. If I hadn't taken that chance, I never would have gotten to experience what I did. And now when I think about him, I only think about all of the good things he brought me."

"That's why you wanted me to go back for Jasper," said Jane. "You think he's my Spike."

"No," Lucy said. "I wanted you to go back for Jasper because I knew he was afraid. *Walter* is your Spike."

"That was a horrible trick," Jane said, sniffling.

"It's not a trick," said Lucy. "It's the truth."

Jane spent the next two hours talking about anything but Walter. When Lucy dropped her off at her house, Jane was relieved to be getting away from her. She took Jasper inside, where the first thing he saw was Tom. They stared at each other for a few seconds, and then Tom tore up the stairs with Jasper behind him, barking like crazy.

So much for peace and quiet, Jane thought as she left them to work things out and went into the kitchen to go through the mail that had piled up in her absence. As usual, it was nothing but bills, catalogs, and uninteresting junk addressed to Occupant. Nothing personal. No letters or cards. Nothing from anyone who cared about her.

"You've let Lucy get to you," she told herself as Jasper came trotting into the kitchen. He had a fresh scratch on his nose, and Jane assumed he and Tom had come to some kind of understanding. Jane filled his water bowl and set it on the floor. Jasper drank happily, slopping half of the water onto the floor and dipping his ears in the bowl. Jane made a mental note to pick up some more paper towels.

"You're not going to die on me, are you?" she asked Jasper. He looked up at her and wagged his little stub.

"Good," Jane said.

She was leaving the kitchen to take her bags upstairs when she noticed that the message light on her machine was blinking. *It's probably Kelly,* she thought as she hit the play button.

"Jane, it's Walter," said the familiar voice. "I'm just calling to see how your trip was. I saw you on Comfort and Joy. It was . . . interesting." He paused. "You looked nice," he continued. "Anyway, that's all I wanted to say. Give me a call when you get back. If you want to. Bye."

Jane erased the message, but the words stuck in her head. Walter *did* care about her. She knew that. But . . .

But what? asked a voice that sounded unnervingly like Lucy's.

"But everything," said Jane with irritation. "Everything, that's all. It just wouldn't work."

She continued upstairs, where she threw her bags on the bed and began to unpack them. "It's impossible," she said, tossing some underthings into the hamper. Even though she hadn't worn them, Lucy's comment about the baggage handler had made her suspicious. "For one thing, once he found out about me he wouldn't want anything to do with me."

Jasper came into the bedroom and lay down. A moment later Tom poked his head out from under the bed and crept out, cutting a wide berth as he walked around Jasper and pretended not to be looking at him. He jumped onto the bed and settled down on top of Jane's red silk blouse, which she had just removed from her bag.

"You know I'm right," Jane said to Tom and Jasper. "Stop looking at me that way."

She took a pair of shoes from the bag and dropped them on the floor. "I mean, who would want to be with someone like me?" she asked. " 'Sorry, dear,' " she said in a mocking imitation of her own voice. " 'I can't watch television with you tonight. I have to go find someone to bite.' " She shooed Tom off her blouse and shook the hair from it. "I don't think so," she said firmly.

"Not that it wouldn't be nice," she remarked as she unpacked the pants she'd intended to wear on television. "It has been a long time. And I do miss some things, like having someone hold my hand, and coming home to someone other than a cat." She looked at Tom. "Sorry," she apologized. Then she looked at Jasper. "Not that you aren't lovely," she told him. "But it's not the same."

She finished with the first bag and started on the second. It contained mainly toiletries, which she carried to the bathroom in several trips. "Men are so difficult, though," she said to herself. "One never knows what they're thinking." She deposited her makeup bag on the bathroom counter. "Although Walter always says just what he means," she argued.

When she'd finished, she put the suitcases back in her closet. Tom and Jasper were still watching her, Tom with a decided air of boredom and Jasper as if at any moment she might announce that it was dinnertime.

"What are you looking at me for?" Jane demanded of them. "That's not going to work." She sighed. "Fine. You win."

Going into her office, she picked up the phone and dialed before she could stop herself. Walter picked up on the second ring. Jane forced herself to not hang up.

"It's Jane," she said. "I'm wondering, would you be free for dinner tonight? There's something I'd like to talk to you about."

Chapter 31

When she finished telling him what she had so long
kept hidden, she looked up, her eyes wet with tears.
"Can you ever forgive me?" she asked. He knelt
and took her hand. "Forgive you?" he replied.
"For what? For having a foolish heart? Who
among us doesn't?"

—Jane Austen, *Constance*, manuscript page 431

"IT WENT REALLY WELL," JANE TOLD LUCY. IT WAS THE NEXT morning, and she was filling Lucy in on her dinner and conversation with Walter the night before. "He was particularly pleased to hear that I'm not really celibate. At least not by choice."

"So you told him about the whole, you know . . . situation?" Lucy asked.

Jane, who was alphabetizing the mystery section, suddenly became very interested in the cover of an Ellis Peters novel. "It didn't come up," she mumbled.

"Excuse me?" said Lucy. "It sounded like you said you chickened out. Is that right?"

"I'm going to tell him," Jane said. "Just not right now."

Lucy made a clucking sound with her tongue.

"Don't tut-tut me," Jane warned. "I'll get to that part eventually. It was difficult enough telling him that I have abandonment issues. When he said he would never leave me, it was all I could do not to have a breakdown on the spot."

"Well, you have ten years or so to tell him," Lucy said. "That's about when he'll start wondering why you never gain weight and your hair doesn't turn gray."

"I can always tell him that I'm *very* well preserved," Jane suggested.

Lucy laughed. "At least the two of you are finally an item."

"An item," said Jane. "You make us sound like celebrities."

"Well, one of you is," Lucy reminded her.

Before Jane could answer her, the phone rang. Jane went into the office and picked it up.

"Jane, it's Kelly." His voice sounded odd—shaky and sniffly.

"What's the matter?" Jane asked, worried.

"Bryce is having an affair," Kelly sobbed. Jane could hear him hiccuping as he burst into tears.

"Are you sure?" she asked.

"I'm sure," Kelly said. "Besides, I confronted him and he told me."

"Oh, Kelly," said Jane. "I'm so sorry."

"The worst part is, he met the guy when we were in Chicago."

"How did he have time?" Jane asked, realizing as soon as the words were out that it was probably not the right thing to say.

"They met in the gym at the hotel," Kelly explained. "In the sauna, of course. I *knew* I should have gone with him instead of watching pay-per-view."

"If they just met that one time, it can't be much of an affair," Jane said.

"That's the best part," said Kelly. "The guy was a *guest* at the hotel. He actually lives here in New York, at least part of the time. Bryce has already seen him once. He lied and told me he was at his bowling league."

"I'm truly sorry," Jane said. She'd run out of things to say that wouldn't sound forced.

"He says he doesn't know what he wants," said Kelly, ignoring her. "He says he needs to sort things out. Well, let him sort them out at *Grayson's* place."

"Grayson?" Jane said.

"That's his name," said Kelly. "Grayson? How am I supposed to compete with that?" Jane heard a muted trumpeting sound as Kelly apparently blew his nose. Then he was back on the line. "Oh, and your book is going to be number one on the *Times* list on Sunday."

"That's too—" Jane started to say. "Excuse me?"

"Your book. The *Times* list. Number one. Congratulations. I'm sorry, I should be more up. Congratulations!"

"Number one," Jane repeated, letting the news sink in. "My book. Number one."

"You debuted ahead of the new Rebecca Ingstrom," Kelly said. "I hear she's *furious*. It's the first time she hasn't had the number one spot her first week out."

Jane wasn't listening. Her book—*her* book—was number one on the most important bestseller list in the world. She could barely breathe.

"Do you think Bryce loves him?" Kelly asked.

"Loves who?" Jane asked, confused by the question.

"Grayson," said Kelly.

"Oh," Jane replied. "I don't know. That sort of thing is difficult to tell." *They really do all think only of themselves, don't they?* she thought. *It doesn't matter which sex they favor.*

"I need to get away," Kelly announced. "Take a break from all this drama. I wonder if I have enough frequent flyer points to get to Paris."

"Why not come here?" Jane heard herself say.

"There?" Kelly said, his tone suggesting that he couldn't imagine any possible reason for doing such a thing.

"Yes, here," said Jane. "If you get on the train, you can be here in time for supper. You can stay with me. It's lovely here, and there's absolutely nothing to do. We can talk all night long and figure out what to do about your situation."

Kelly was silent for a long moment. "You know what? I think I will," he said. "A few days in the country is exactly what I need."

"Well, it's not exactly the country," said Jane. "We do have electricity and running water."

Kelly ignored her joke. She heard him typing. "I'm looking at the schedule online now," he said. "If I hurry, I can catch the eleven o'clock," he said. "It gets in at five. Can you pick me up at the station?"

"Absolutely," Jane answered. "Assuming I can get the team harnessed to the wagon by then. You know how mules are."

Again Kelly ignored her jest. "I'll see you then," he said. "And thank you, Jane. I knew you'd make me feel better."

Kelly rang off, and Jane left the office. "Anything exciting?" Lucy asked her.

"I'm having a visitor," said Jane. "And my book seems to be number one."

Lucy's shrieking startled her. She was further disarranged

when Lucy picked her up and spun her around, continuing to squeal joyfully. "You're number one!" she shouted as she set Jane down. "Number freaking *one*!"

Jane looked at Lucy's face. "Oh, my God," she said. "I'm number freaking *one*!"

Their combined shrieking was deafening.

At seventeen minutes past five, Amtrak train number 281 pulled into the Brakeston station. Approximately two dozen passengers emerged onto the platform, among them the unmistakable figure of Kelly Littlejohn. Jane waved to him, and he greeted her with a kiss on the cheek.

"This is charming," Kelly announced as he looked around the station. "I was expecting barns and cows and barefoot children rolling hoops."

"Contrary to what you may have heard, there *is* civilization outside the island of Manhattan," Jane said.

"I thought those were all old wives' tales," Kelly teased.

On the drive back to her house, Jane refrained from asking about Bryce, and Kelly didn't mention him. But he seemed to be in better spirits, for which Jane was glad. She would have had a difficult time enjoying her newly blossomed romance with Walter if she felt Kelly would be saddened by her happiness.

"I thought tonight we would have dinner out," she told Kelly. "With Walter and Lucy."

"Lucy's your assistant at the store, right?" Kelly said. "I think she's answered the phone once or twice."

"That's right," Jane confirmed.

"And is Walter her boyfriend?"

Jane hesitated. *He's going to find out anyway*, she told herself.

You might as well be done with it. "No, Walter is *my* boyfriend," she said.

Kelly looked surprised. "Really?" he said.

"You sound shocked," Jane said.

"No," Kelly said quickly. "It's just that I never thought of you in that way."

"In what way?" asked Jane. "As a human? As a woman?"

"Don't take it the wrong way," Kelly said. "It's just that you seem so . . . I don't know. Proper, I guess."

"Proper," Jane said. "And that precludes my having a romantic life?"

"I suppose not," said Kelly. "Anyway, I can't wait to meet him," he added hastily.

Jane made a vague noise. *Proper,* she thought. *I'll show him proper.*

Once at her house, Jane installed Kelly in the guest bedroom, which had never before been used for an actual guest. She made sure that he had enough towels, then left him to rest and get ready for dinner. She'd made a reservation for seven-thirty at a sushi restaurant she hoped would get Kelly to see the more sophisticated side of Brakeston. Walter and Kelly were to meet them there.

"Come Up and Sashimi Some Time?" Kelly said ninety minutes later, seeing the restaurant's name. "They didn't."

Jane had been hoping he wouldn't notice. "I think it's rather clever," she said as she opened the door to the restaurant and they walked inside. She scanned the room for Walter and Lucy and found them seated at one of the restaurant's low tables where diners sat on the floor. She'd forgotten Walter's fondness for authenticity, and wished she'd been a bit more specific about the table arrangements.

"Hello!" Walter said, standing up. Like Lucy, he'd removed his shoes. Jane noticed that he was wearing white athletic socks. She also saw Kelly glance down at them.

"You must be Kelly," Walter said, gripping the editor's hand in both of his and pumping his arm. "Jane has told me so much about you."

"Has she?" Kelly replied as he bent to untie his shoes. "That puts you at an advantage, then."

Walter, busy greeting Jane with a kiss, didn't hear him, much to Jane's relief. Removing her shoes, she sat beside Walter while Kelly took a seat on a cushion opposite Lucy.

"Hi," Lucy said. "She's told me a lot about you as well. But don't worry, she's not trying to fix us up or anything."

Jane shot her a look, which Lucy pretended not to see. But Kelly just laughed. "I'm afraid you'd be disappointed if she were," he said. "I'm a lousy first date."

"I took the liberty of ordering something to start us off," Walter told them. "I hope you like sake," he said to Kelly.

"That depends," Kelly said. "What kind is it?"

"My favorite is Juyondai," Walter told him. "I almost went with Tentaka, but I think it's a little dry for most people."

Kelly looked at Jane. "He knows his sake," he said. "You can keep him."

"I had no idea," Jane admitted. She looked at Walter. "You're just full of surprises," she said admiringly.

"I've never had sake," Lucy announced.

"Then you're in for a treat," Kelly told her. He addressed Walter. "I don't suppose they have *ankimo* here?"

"Not only that, they have excellent *hotate*."

"Do you have any idea what they're talking about?" Lucy asked Jane.

"None whatsoever," she answered. "I have a feeling they're going to do all the ordering tonight. You and I will be subjected to their every culinary whim."

"As long as nothing is moving," Lucy said. "Raw I can handle, but not alive." She glanced at Jane and grimaced.

The sake arrived and Walter poured some for each of them. Kelly showed Lucy how to drink it, and Walter did the same for Jane. "Make sure you smell it," he said. "The aroma is half the experience."

Jane liked having him show her how to drink the sake. It was intimate in a way she hadn't experienced in a long time. She thought about Byron teaching her how to eat crawfish. It hadn't been nearly the same. Walter made her feel special, as if he was sharing an experience with her rather than telling her how to have one.

The waiter came and, as Jane had predicted, Walter and Kelly ordered for the table. Again Jane found herself enjoying being taken care of in that way. *I suppose it's old-fashioned of me*, she thought as she listened to Walter rattle off the names of the different kinds of sushi. *Then again, I am an eighteenth-century girl.*

She laughed at this thought, and realized that she was getting a tiny bit tipsy. This too she enjoyed, and she didn't object as Walter refilled her sake cup. *It's rather pleasant having a boyfriend*, she thought. *I don't know why I waited so long.*

When the food came, Kelly and Walter refused to tell Jane and Lucy what everything was. "Just try it," Kelly insisted, placing various multicolored pieces on Lucy's plate. "I'll tell you afterward."

"This one is my favorite," Walter said to Jane as he selected a piece of something dark pink for her. "It's—"

He was interrupted by the ringing of Jane's cell phone. It took her a moment to find it in her purse, but she finally located it. *Who could possibly be calling me?* she wondered. Only Lucy, Walter, and Kelly even had the number, and they were all sitting right there with her.

"Hello?"

"Ms. Fairfax, this is Sal Maldonado with the fire department." His voice was scratchy and difficult to hear clearly.

"Fire department?" Jane repeated.

"I'm afraid there's a problem at your store," the man said.

"Is it a fire?" Jane said, struggling to get to her feet. The others stopped talking and stared at her as she waited for the reply.

"No, not a fire. But we did get a false alarm. I think something's wrong with your detector. I just need you to come over and open the store for me."

"Of course," Jane said, relieved that it was nothing more serious. "I'll be there in five minutes." She hung up the phone. "It's nothing to worry about," she told Walter, Lucy, and Kelly. "Just a faulty smoke alarm at the store. They need to get in to check it. I'll be back in no time."

"I'll go with you," Walter said as he stood up.

"No, you stay here," said Jane. "But thank you." She gave Walter's arm a squeeze. "I appreciate you offering, but I don't dare leave these two alone," she added, indicating with a nod of her head Kelly and Lucy. "I think they need a chaperone."

Walter sat down again and Jane slipped on her shoes. Promising once again to return as quickly as possible, she left and got into her car. She was at the store within minutes. When she got out, however, she saw no sign of a firefighter or any emergency vehicles.

She went to the door and found it already open. *I guess he didn't need me after all,* she thought as she went inside.

"Mr. Maldonado?" she called out. "It's Jane Fairfax. Are you here?"

There was no answer, but Jane heard noises coming from the office area. She flipped the light switch beside the door, but the room remained dark. *They must have turned the electricity off,* she thought as she made her way to the back.

"Mr. Maldonado?" she called again. "Are you there?"

She reached the office and stepped inside. Someone was moving around in the dim light.

"Mr. Maldonado?" said Jane.

The figure turned. Jane gasped. Then something struck her in the forehead and everything went black.

Chapter 32

*Jonathan, lying on the ground with his lip
bloodied, glared up at Charles, who towered over
him, hands knotted in fists. The look in Charles's
eyes was murderous, and for a moment Constance
feared that he would kill Jonathan. Instead, he spat
into the dirt near Jonathan's head. "Go," he said.
"Don't trouble us again."*

—Jane Austen, *Constance*, manuscript page 431

THE SLAP WOKE HER UP. *WHERE AM I?* JANE WONDERED. *WHAT
happened?* Her head hurt, and she saw stars before her eyes.

"Welcome to the party," a voice said.

Jane shook her head and blinked to clear her vision. Her
hands were tied behind her, and someone was standing over her,
smiling triumphantly.

"Charlotte!" she gasped.

"Surprised?" Charlotte asked her.

"But you're dead," said Jane.

"That's true," Charlotte agreed. "But not *dead* dead."

"The fire," said Jane. Charlotte looked completely healthy, not a burn in sight.

"Yes, the fire," said Charlotte. "That was a good try. Fortunately for me, our kind heals very quickly as long as nothing *vital* has been destroyed."

"Jane, who is this?"

Jane gave a start at the sound of another voice. She looked to her left and was horrified to see Walter, Kelly, and Lucy all seated on the floor, their hands tied as Jane's were. All three were staring at Charlotte.

Charlotte laughed. "Wasn't it kind of them to come to your rescue?" she said to Jane. "All I had to do was wait."

"Leave them alone!" Jane said angrily. "They have nothing to do with this."

Charlotte cocked her head. "Really?" she said. "You see, I think they do. I think they have a great deal to do with this." She knelt down so that her face was right in front of Jane's. "Do you know why?" she asked.

Jane could feel Charlotte's breath on her face. She refrained from suggesting that Charlotte might consider the use of a mint. "No," she said. "I don't know why."

Charlotte leaned even closer, so that she was whispering in Jane's ear. "I'll tell you why," she said. "It's because *they* will be my revenge. I'm going to drain each of them while you watch. Then I'm going to set fire to this place and watch it burn to the ground, just like you watched my house burn with my family in it." She stood up and straightened her dress. "Oh, and I want my dog back," she said.

"You can't do this," Jane said.

"Why not?" Charlotte shouted. Her voice was filled with rage. "Tell me why I cannot have satisfaction!"

"You're the one who was going to steal *my* book," Jane yelled back. "You're the one in the wrong here."

"Details," Charlotte said snippily.

"Who are you?" asked Kelly.

"Who am I?" Charlotte replied. "Who *am* I?" Her voice grew in both volume and indignation as she walked over to her captives.

"Violet Grey," Jane said. "She's Violet Grey."

"The blogger?" said Kelly. "The one who didn't like your book?"

Jane nodded as Charlotte's face reddened. Kelly stared at her. "All this because you don't like a novel?" he said. "Don't you think you're overreacting just a bit?"

Charlotte clenched her fists and stepped back. She closed her eyes and began to recite: "Women are supposed to be very calm generally," she began. Then her eyes flew open and she pointed a finger at Kelly. "But women feel just as men feel; they need exercise for their faculties, and a field for their efforts, as much as their brothers do; they suffer from too rigid a restraint, too absolute a stagnation, precisely as men would suffer; and it is narrow-minded in their more privileged fellow-creatures to say that they ought to confine themselves to making puddings and knitting stockings, to playing on the piano and embroidering bags. It is thoughtless to condemn them, or laugh at them, if they seek to do more or learn more than custom has pronounced necessary for their sex."

"What does *Jane Eyre* have to do with anything?" Kelly asked her when she finished.

"It has *everything* to do with it!" Charlotte bellowed. She began to pace, striking her fists against her legs as she walked. "When *The Journal of Words* compiled its list of the one hundred best novels written in English, do you know that *Pride and Prejudice* was number twelve?" She stopped pacing and glared at Jane. "And do you know where *Jane Eyre* was?" she asked. She looked at the four of them in turn, but nobody answered her. "Number fifty-two!" she shrieked. "Fifty-two! Below that pornographic travesty *Lolita*!" She spat the title as if it were poison. "Below *Huckleberry Finn*! Below *Ulysses*. Have you ever tried to read *Ulysses*? Have you ever finished it? No, you haven't. No one has. They just carry it around and lie about having read it."

Lucy cleared her throat. "As I recall, *Wuthering Heights* was number twenty-nine."

"That's *Emily*!" Charlotte raged.

"I'm just saying," said Lucy defensively. "If this is an Austen-versus-Brontë thing, at least Emily and Charlotte are on the same team."

"I think I'll start with you," Charlotte told her.

Walter, who had been silent, suddenly spoke. "We all need to calm down."

Charlotte shifted her focus to him. "And who exactly *are* you?" she asked.

"I'm her boyfriend," Walter replied, nodding at Jane.

A smile crept across Charlotte's face. "Her boyfriend," she repeated. Then she laughed. "This has turned out better than I ever hoped. Revenge will indeed be sweet."

Jane felt herself tremble with rage. "It is not violence that best overcomes hate," she said. "Nor vengeance that most certainly heals injury."

Charlotte sneered at her. "So you've read my book," she said. "I'm touched."

"Your book?" said Lucy. "But that's from—" She stopped speaking and looked at Charlotte. Her eyes grew wide. Then she looked at Jane, who nodded weakly. Lucy's mouth snapped shut and she continued to stare at Charlotte.

"Are you all so stupid?" Charlotte said.

"You're insane," said Walter. "You can pretend to be whoever you want to be, but what reason do you have to hate Jane?"

Charlotte stepped back. She looked at Walter for a long time, then looked at Jane. "He doesn't know, does he?" she said. "He really doesn't know."

"Know what?" Walter asked.

Charlotte clapped her hands and held them to her face, covering her mouth. Her eyes glittered with happiness. "Oh, this is turning out to be such fun," she said, clapping her hands like a child. "All right then, let me tell you a story." She took a deep breath. "Once upon a time—"

Suddenly the door to the storeroom burst open. Jane looked up to see Byron striding into the room. "You!" she said. Her voice sounded peculiar, as if she'd spoken through a megaphone. Then she realized that it was because everyone in the room had said exactly the same thing at exactly the same time. She looked at the others, all of whom were glaring at Byron with the same look of consternation.

"How dare you come back here?" said Walter. "Jane told you, she wants nothing to do with you."

"Jane?" said Kelly. He looked over at her with a puzzled expression. "This is the guy Bryce has been sleeping with."

"Bryce?" Jane said, equally puzzled. She looked at Byron. "*You're* Grayson?" she repeated.

Byron shrugged. "I know this is a bit awkward," he said.

Before he could continue, Charlotte lunged at him, her fangs bared. "You left me!" she screeched.

Byron stepped aside, pushing her as she went by. Charlotte

crashed headfirst into a pile of cookbooks, which toppled over, sending her to the floor. She turned herself over and renewed her attack. This time Byron was able to grab her arm. He swung her violently, sending her twirling toward one of the tall shelving units. She hit it hard, and it fell over, burying her in an avalanche of self-help books. Moments later she leapt up, sending copies of *Surviving Menopause* flying in every direction. She picked one up and chucked it at Byron's head, missing him by an inch.

"Untie me!" Jane said to Byron. "I can help."

"There's no time," Byron told her as he looked for a way to stop Charlotte.

Charlotte was throwing books furiously now, picking them up and hurling them at Byron as quickly as she could. A firestorm of young adult novels, pop-up books, and how-to guides bore down on him. Jane saw a copy of *The Lovely Bones* fly by, pages flapping, and cut Byron's cheek.

Ducking and weaving, Byron ran at Charlotte, batting the missiles out of the way. Then the two of them were entwined, Charlotte clawing at Byron as she roared in rage and Byron trying to subdue her. Then, to her surprise, Jane saw Walter stand up. The ropes that had bound his wrists fell to the floor. He bent and helped Kelly and Lucy up.

"Go!" he said. "Get out of here."

As the two of them left the room, Walter came to Jane. Kneeling, he reached behind her and cut her ropes.

"How did you get free?" she asked as she stood.

"Pocketknife," said Walter as he took her arm and ran for the door. "It just took me a while to get it open."

Behind them Jane could hear crashes and screams as Byron and Charlotte continued to fight. In the main room of the bookstore Kelly and Lucy waited anxiously.

"Who's winning?" Lucy asked.

Jane shook her head. "It's hard to say," she replied.

"We should call the police," Walter suggested.

"No!" Lucy and Jane said simultaneously.

Walter looked at them both. "But—" he began.

"Trust me on this," said Jane, interrupting.

"We should at least try to help him," said Walter.

"I say let her have him," Kelly said. "Home wrecker."

"In case you've forgotten, he saved your life," said Lucy sharply.

"For the moment," Jane said. "We need to get out of here."

They ran for the front door and into the parking lot. There they huddled in a group, watching the store for signs. A moment later they saw shadowy figures moving inside the store.

"They're still at it," said Jane.

Loud thumps came from inside, and something fell over with a crash. "That sounds like the audiobooks display," Lucy remarked.

"That's it," said Walter. "I'm going in."

Before Jane could stop him he had run back inside. More crashes filled the air, and then a figure ran toward the large glass window that spanned the front of the shop. The shadow grew larger and larger. Then it hit the window with a sickening thud and the glass shattered. Tiny pieces of glass fell to the sidewalk, clattering like hail, and Charlotte followed them. She landed face-first on the pavement and lay still.

Walter and Byron emerged from the store, panting heavily. They looked at the prone body of Charlotte. Byron clapped Walter on the back. "Good work," he said.

Walter shook his head. "You're the one who clocked her with the Stephen King hardcover. That took some of the wind out of her."

"Thank heavens he's a wordy man," said Byron.

The two of them came over to where the others were standing. Jane gave Walter a hug, holding him close. "I'm so glad you're all right," she said.

"Me too," said Walter. "For a while there I thought that lunatic was going to slit all our throats. I still don't get it. All of that over a book?"

"It's a good thing you came along," Lucy said to Byron.

Before Byron could respond, Kelly hauled off and punched him in the face. Byron reeled back, holding his nose, while Kelly shook his hand in obvious pain. "That hurt!" he yelped.

"Bloody hell!" Byron said.

"Boys!" Jane said, getting between them. "You can work it out later. Right now we need to do something with Charlotte. I mean Violet."

"That could be a problem," Lucy said.

Jane turned to her. "Why?"

Lucy nodded toward the store. Where Charlotte had been lying there was now nothing but broken glass.

Chapter 33

She pressed her head against Charles's chest. His heart lay beneath her cheek, every beat a reminder of his presence. She matched her breathing with his until they became one body, sharing blood and breath.

—Jane Austen, *Constance,* manuscript page 433

"Tell me again why we aren't calling the police," Walter said to Jane. They'd just returned to Jane's house after straightening up the bookstore. It was two in the morning, and Jane was exhausted. She was sitting on the couch, her feet tucked up under her, drinking a cup of tea.

"It would only be a lot of bother," Jane answered.

"Bother?" said Walter. "The woman was going to *kill* us."

"I don't think she would really have done it," Jane said. "I think she was just upset."

Walter gave her a disbelieving look. "You saw the inside of the store," he reminded her. "You saw what she did to the window. That was a little more than just being upset. It was completely psychotic."

"Trust me," Jane said. "We know her name. We can easily track her down if need be. I think you and Byron scared her well enough."

"That's another thing," said Walter. "Why did he come back? And what's this about him and Kelly's boyfriend? I'm so confused."

As if he'd been called, Kelly came into the living room. He had a towel wrapped around his hand.

"Is the ice helping?" Jane asked him.

"A little," he answered. "I can't believe how much it hurts."

"Yes, well, Byron—Brian—has a very hard head," Jane told him.

Kelly leaned his head back and groaned. "I feel like such an idiot," he said. "I behaved like a five-year-old who was mad because someone stole his milk money."

"It sounds like he stole a little more than that," said Walter. "I'd have decked him too." He looked at Jane and grinned. "In fact, I believe I threatened to do exactly that."

"Boys," Jane said. "You're all impossible." Despite what she said, she reached out and took Walter's hand.

"Who *is* that guy?" Kelly asked. "Some kind of bisexual writer kung-fu expert, or what? And how weird is it that right after you had a run-in with him he came on to Bryce?"

"Not as weird as you might think," Jane said. "Speaking of which, how are you feeling about things with Bryce?"

Kelly waved a hand in the air. "I don't know," he replied. "I've been with the man for almost ten years. And I guess if I was willing to fight for him, I must still love him. He's going to owe me big time, though. We're talking a trip to Europe, or maybe a country house." He bit his lip, then raised an eyebrow. "Besides, I have to admit, there really is something about Brian."

"Don't you even think about it," Jane said quickly.

Kelly laughed. "Don't worry. I'll be a good boy." He stood up. "And now it's off to bed for me. This has been more than enough excitement for this city boy. I had no idea you country folk were so wild."

"Wait until tomorrow," Walter told him. "We're planning a barn raising."

Kelly went upstairs, leaving Jane and Walter alone. Jane still hadn't let go of Walter's hand. Holding it was reassuring. He was something solid to cling to, something real and warm and safe. *I could sit like this forever*, she thought.

"I like him," Walter said.

"Like who?" Jane asked.

"Kelly," said Walter. "To tell you the truth, I was sort of hoping he'd say things are over with this Bryce guy. I was going to set him up with Hank."

"Hank?" said Jane. "You mean your electrician Hank?" She got a mental picture of Walter's longtime friend and sometime co-worker. He was a big man, with a thick beard and hands that reminded Jane of bear paws.

Walter nodded. "Big Hank," he confirmed.

"I had no idea," said Jane. "Anyway, I don't think they'd have much in common."

"There you go, making assumptions again," said Walter. "Isn't that what you thought about us?"

"Not at all," Jane said. "Well, perhaps a little," she admitted.

"Hank might surprise you too," Walter told her. "And look at Kelly there. He threw a pretty mean punch. I wouldn't be surprised if pretty boy's nose is a little bit crooked after this."

I wouldn't count on that, Jane thought. More likely, Byron had already healed from the encounter, as well as from the minor wounds Charlotte had inflicted. As for Charlotte, Jane really wasn't terribly worried about her. Now that she'd revealed herself, she likely would be afraid to try anything more. Still, Jane would be on the lookout.

Walter squeezed her hand, and Jane looked at him. He had a somewhat worried expression on his face. "There's something I've been meaning to ask you," he said. "It's a bit difficult for me to say."

Here it comes, Jane thought. Her heart sank. Walter had figured out that there was something not quite right about her. He was going to tell her that they couldn't be together after all.

"Things have been moving very quickly, and I feel that—" Walter began. But before he could continue he was interrupted by Jasper, who ran into the living room. He woofed and looked meaningfully toward the kitchen.

"You already had dinner," Jane reminded him.

Jasper woofed again.

"I think he wants to go out," said Walter.

"Of course," Jane said. "I'll take him. You just hold that thought."

She jumped up and hurried into the kitchen. She was relieved to get away from Walter. She knew what he was going to say, and she wasn't ready for it. *Just when I decided that maybe things can work*, she thought sadly as she opened the back door and watched Jasper run into the yard. She stepped outside and shut the door behind her.

"I suppose it was inevitable," she said.

"What was?" Byron stepped out of the shadows, startling her.

"Why must you do things like that?" Jane asked him. "Can't you just ring the bell like other people?"

Byron looked up at the moon, which was full and round.

"First, I'm not like other people," he said. "Second, I don't think Walter would be very keen to see me right now."

"I don't think it will matter after tonight," said Jane. "I think he's about to end things."

Byron laughed.

"Why is that funny?" Jane asked him. "Don't think it means I'll come running to you."

"Oh, I think I know better now," said Byron. "Besides, I have a new distraction."

"That's another thing," Jane said. "Why did you have to go and seduce Bryce?"

Byron held his hands up in protest. "That was entirely accidental," he said. "I had no idea he was connected to you. It was a happy coincidence."

"Not so happy for Kelly," Jane snapped. "He's very hurt. Oh, and don't think I don't know that the only way you could get Bryce was by glamoring him."

Byron looked hurt. "Are you saying I'm losing my looks?"

"Unfortunately, no," said Jane. "But I know those two are very much in love."

"Yes, well, then it might amuse you to know that Bryce phoned me earlier today and told me in no uncertain terms that things are over."

"See!" Jane said. "Serves you right." Then something occurred to her. "What are you doing here, anyway?"

"It's a beautiful night," said Byron.

"You're hunting!" Jane accused.

"Not hunting," said Byron. "Watching. For Charlotte."

"You don't think she'll come back?" Jane said.

"No," Byron said. "At least not for some time. But I don't want to take any chances."

"I think I can handle her myself if need be," said Jane.

"Actually," Byron said, "I don't think you can." His voice suddenly took on a serious tone. "Charlotte isn't the only one we have to worry about."

Jane looked at him. "What do you mean?"

"You know that throughout the years there have been vigilantes who have sought to eradicate our kind."

Jane shuddered. She knew all too well the people to whom Byron was referring—well-known personages whose special skills had led them to be recruited as vampire hunters. One name in particular came to her, and instinctively her fangs descended as she recalled their last meeting—and the taste of the woman's infamous coq au vin. "Of course I do," she said.

"There has been renewed activity," Byron told her, his voice taking on a worried tone. "Rumblings of a resurgence. This incident with Charlotte may have . . . repercussions. Particularly now that you've raised your profile."

"Wonderful," Jane sighed.

"It would be wise to be prepared for any eventuality," Byron continued. "There are things we can do, Jane—things *you* can do—that you aren't even aware of. You've barely tapped the possibilities."

"I don't know what you mean," Jane said.

"You've never been taught," said Byron. "You've spent so many years apart from your own kind that you don't even know what you are."

Jane looked into his face. *He's telling the truth,* she thought.

"I can teach you," Byron told her. "If you'll let me."

"I knew it," Jane said. "For the last time, I am *not* going away with you."

"I'm not asking you to," Byron replied. "I can stay here."

"Here?" Jane repeated.

"Not *here*," Byron said, nodding at the house. "But here in Brakeston."

"Are you mad?" said Jane.

"Probably," Byron said. "But it's time I made things up to you, and I can start by showing you what you really are. Besides, I already have the house."

Jasper, who had marked every bush in the yard, ran over to where they were standing. Byron bent to pet him, but Jasper growled. "He never did like me," Byron said.

"He's a good judge of character," said Jane.

"I'll go if you tell me to go," said Byron. "I swear I will. But please consider my offer."

Jane started to tell him to leave. Getting rid of him once and for all would make things much easier for her. But then she thought about what he was offering her. *What kinds of things can I do?* she wondered. Was there really more to being undead than just being undead?

"I'll think about it," she said quickly, before she could change her mind. "In the meantime, stay away from Lucy. I suppose you've figured out she isn't really one of us."

"I have," said Byron. "But it was a good ploy."

"Thank you," Jane said. "But I mean it—stay away from her."

"What if I promise not to turn her?" Byron asked. "I have to say, I'm rather fond of her. She has quite a spirit."

"Don't make me change my mind," Jane threatened. "Now go. We'll talk more tomorrow."

Byron nodded good night and disappeared into the shadows. Jane herded Jasper back into the kitchen, where he stopped to get a drink. Jane continued on to the living room. Only when she saw Walter sitting there did she remember that she'd run away from what was certain to be bad news.

"That was a long pee," Walter remarked.

"Wasn't it?" said Jane. Her mind had gone fuzzy, and she couldn't think straight. *He's going to dump me,* she thought. She sat down and kept her hands in her lap, afraid to reach for Walter's hand lest he pull away from her.

"As I was saying," Walter said. He cleared his throat. "This is harder than I expected."

"You don't have to—" said Jane.

"Yes, I do," Walter said. "It's something I should have said a long time ago."

Jane's heart fluttered wildly. All of a sudden she felt not like a woman of 234 but like a girl of 18. All of her years of experience disappeared in an instant. Lifetimes no longer mattered. Walter was about to break her heart as if it were the very first time.

"I love you," Walter said.

Jane stared at him. *What did he just say?* she asked herself.

"I know you don't want to hear that," said Walter. He was speaking quickly, stumbling over his words in an uncharacteristically anxious way. "I know I'm probably going to scare you off. But it's true, Jane. I do love you. And if that frightens you, then I can accept—"

"I love you too," said Jane, stopping him.

He looked at her for a long time. "You do?"

Jane nodded. "I do," she repeated.

Walter opened his mouth, then closed it again. He repeated this several times.

"You're looking a bit like a fish," Jane teased.

"I'm afraid if I talk I'll wake up," said Walter.

Jane took his hand in hers. "You won't wake up," she said. "Unless, of course, you mean in my bed in the morning."

Walter stood up, pulling Jane to her feet. He took her in his arms and kissed her for a long time. When he broke away he continued to hold her against him. She looked into his eyes, seeing in them everything she'd been longing for.

"Jane Fairfax," Walter said, "are you propositioning me?"

"Yes, Walter Fletcher," said Jane. "That's exactly what I'm doing."

Walter kissed her again. "It's about time," he said, taking her by the hand and leading her toward the stairs.

Acknowledgments

Many thanks to Liz Scheier (for starting it), Caitlin Alexander (for finishing it), Mitchell Waters (for championing it), John Scognamiglio (for loaning me out), and Patrick Crowe and the Fur People (for everything else).

About the Author

MICHAEL THOMAS FORD is the author of numerous books, including the novels *What We Remember*, *Suicide Notes*, *Changing Tides*, *Full Circle*, *Looking for It*, and *Last Summer*. Visit him at www.michaelthomasford.com.

Our favorite heroine returns in
Michael Thomas Ford's

Jane Goes Batty

Hollywood VIPs have descended on Jane's sleepy town in upstate New York to film the movie version of *Constance*. As if that's not bad enough, a terribly intrusive team of cameramen has been following Jane around, filming her every move for a reality TV show. Of course, the Janeites have decided to hold their annual convention in Brakeston at the same time, and there are never fewer than ten women in period costumes trailing behind Jane or peering in her windows. Dear Walter has been asked to restore a house for the movie set, so he's off in his own world of special plasters and varnished wood. Meanwhile, Byron insists on teaching Jane a few new vampire tricks. And something is really *off* about those twins who've been hired to work at the bookstore . . .

Keep those fangs in check, Jane!

Coming soon from Ballantine Books